# THE

# END

# OF

# OUR

# STORY

## MEG HASTON

**HARPER TEEN**
*An Imprint of HarperCollinsPublishers*

HarperTeen is an imprint of HarperCollins Publishers.

The End of Our Story
Copyright © 2017 by Alloy Entertainment and Meg Haston
All rights reserved. Printed in the United States of America.
No part of this book may be used or reproduced in any manner whatsoever without written permission except in the case of brief quotations embodied in critical articles and reviews. For information address HarperCollins Children's Books, a division of HarperCollins Publishers, 195 Broadway, New York, NY 10007.

www.epicreads.com

alloyentertainment
Produced by Alloy Entertainment
1325 Avenue of the Americas
New York, NY 10019
www.alloyentertainment.com

Library of Congress Control Number: 2016949894

ISBN 978-0-06-233577-7

Typography by Elizabeth Dresner

17  18  19  20  21   LSCH/PC   10  9  8  7  6  5  4  3  2  1

First Edition

*for David*

# BRIDGE

*Spring, Senior Year*

NOW that Atlantic Beach and I are about to part ways, something strange has started to happen. With just two months left in senior year, suddenly I'm noticing every little detail: the way the salt-screened classroom windows smudge the sun. How the beach rats' feet are permanently plastered with sand. The color of Wil Hines's skin, perpetually an end-of-August bronze from hours spent between the ocean and the sun. Now that it's all about to disappear, everything around me is sharper, brighter. My brain is trying to convince me that I'll miss this place once I leave for Miami and The Rest of My Life, but that's impossible. I've been plotting my escape for almost a year now.

At the desk next to me, Leigh props up her sketchpad. On it is a drawing of a concrete wall with *What time should I pick you up tonight, biotch?* graffitied in blazing hot-pink flames. Weeds crawl through the cracks in the wall, and a girl leans against it, smoking a joint. Leigh is incapable of texting like a normal person.

She flips to the next page, where she's written *First bonfire of senior year!!!* When I shake my head no, she rolls her eyes and flips again. The third page says *Dude. Bridge. Come on.* The girl is slumped against the wall in defeat. She looks like Leigh: shoulder-length dreadlocks, warm mahogany skin, and dark brown eyes. Even the cartoon-version of my best friend finds me lame these days. I shrug and mouth *Sorry*, even though we both knew the answer before she asked the question.

At the front of the room, a substitute stares blank-faced at her computer screen. We're supposed to be doing trig practice problems, but the thirty-four of us seem to have an unspoken agreement: We'll do nothing, leaving the sub free to analyze her sort-of-boyfriend's Instagram posts.

As Leigh sighs and goes back to her sketchpad, Ana Acevedo leans across the gray linoleum aisle and puts her lips close to Wil's ear: "We should go to the bonfire, babe. You never go out anymore."

*Babe.* I can't believe they're still a thing.

I can't believe we're not anymore.

I stare at the back of Wil's neck, taut from Ana's whisper. I remember the first time I sat behind him. It was the beginning of fourth grade at my new school, and my entire body was raw with sunburn. I was on fire. Breathing hurt. Even holding a pencil hurt. So I sat as still as I could on the edge of my seat and counted the sun-bleached hairs on the head in front of me. On hair number eighty-six, the boy turned around.

He said, "Your skin matches your hair, almost."

I blinked.

"You have sun poisoning. Like, bad," he told me.

"Duh," I replied, but secretly, I was relieved by his diagnosis. I had been considering something in the flesh-eating disease category.

"Didn't your mom put sunscreen on you?"

"She had to work." I didn't tell him that yesterday had been the first beach afternoon in the history of Bridget Hawking. That I didn't understand the Florida sun. I lay on the sand, feet and palms pressed into the fine grains, the fireball searing me slowly and without my knowledge. The water looked exactly the way I thought it would, like a beach diorama I'd designed in first grade. Crinkled aluminum foil scribbled cerulean.

"What about your dad?" he asked.

"My dad is dead," I lied. Or maybe I didn't. Mom told me once she had no idea.

"Oh," he said. He poked his tongue in the space between his two front teeth. "Do you want to come over after school? My dad has a workshop and you should probably stay inside."

"I don't even know your name," I said.

"Wil. Short for Wilson, which is my dad's name, too."

That afternoon, Wil's dad picked us up in a truck that had been patched and repainted too many times to tell its true color.

"This is Bridge," Wil told his dad.

"As in, Brooklyn?" Wilson Hines smiled. "Or maybe Golden Gate?" When he turned to wink at Wil, I noticed that he had longish hair. The dads I knew back in Alabama had buzz cuts, mostly.

3

"As in Bridget," I said. "From Alabama?"

"Bridget from Alabama," he said. "Of course." He had us ride in the cab so my burn didn't get worse. He fished around in a bag at Wil's feet and found a trucker's hat that said MAMA P'S SEAFOOD SHANTY. He put it on my head to keep the sun off my face. In the truck, there was a tiny fake pine tree on the dash, which made everything smell like Christmas.

He buckled my seat belt and was quiet most of the way but every now and then he'd ask me a question, like what Alabama was like this time of year or whether Wil had caused the teacher any trouble in class today.

"Just between us," he said, as though Wil wasn't there. He winked.

Wil's family lived in a white ranch-style house that was low and long, ten blocks east of the water. The house was situated on a double lot, and behind the main house was a large workshop. It looked like a barn, which reminded me of home. Over the front door of the workshop was a neatly hand-lettered sign: HINES BOAT BUILDING AND REPAIR. Inside, the light was watery, and it smelled like varnish and sawdust. In the center of the workshop, the upside-down skeleton of a small wooden boat balanced on a large worktable. The walls were all pegboards and wood shelving and straight lines.

Wil's dad went to get us some snacks and told us that when he got back, he wanted to see that everything was as he'd left it.

"Got it," we said. We sat with our legs outstretched on the stained concrete floor and compared things, like mothers (his was an office manager at a dentist's office in downtown Jacksonville; mine was a *hospitality expert*), and least-favorite things about our fourth-grade teacher (his: how she had only picked girl line leaders so far; mine: how when she read to the class, she licked her finger each time she turned a page, which meant that every book in our classroom was covered in her spit), and favorite holidays (his: Halloween, because you can't buy packets of fake blood any other time of year without looking crazy and also because of the candy; mine: my birthday because my mom made Funfetti waffles).

"Also, sick days in quotes," I announced as Wil's dad returned with a paper plate full of celery and apple wedges smeared with peanut butter. A *sick day in quotes* was something special Mom did for my brother, Micah, and me once or twice each school year. We'd get up at the regular time, get dressed for school and eat breakfast, and just as Mom was rushing us out the door, she'd yell, *"Sick day in quotes!"* and pull us back inside. She'd call the school and tell them we were "sick" and make a big show of the air quotes while she was on the phone. Then we'd pile in her bed together and eat sugar cereal straight out of the box and watch cartoons until we all fell asleep.

"What about sick days?" Wilson crouched on the floor and placed a single napkin in front of each of us. One celery stick for me; one celery stick for Wil. One apple chunk for me; one apple chunk for Wil.

Wil rolled his eyes at me. "Don't get him started about sick days."

"No such thing." Wil's dad shook his head. "No matter what, every day—"

Wil finished the sentence for him: "You show up to play."

When Wilson dropped me off at home that night, he told me

I was welcome anytime. So I showed up the next afternoon. And the next. I spent nearly every day in that workshop, until Wil and I morphed into friends. Best friends. More. We were solid: made of layers of afternoon snacks and middle-school dances and first kisses. We took years to get that way. And I undid it all in a blink.

Somehow, I've survived our senior year without Wil. But now it's April, and with Miami only a couple of months away, Wil's absence seems sharper, just like every other detail of my Florida life. If I had to get all Intro to Psych about it, I guess I'd say that before I make the biggest change I've ever made in my very small life, I need something familiar. I want to find Wil in his dad's workshop. I would talk through the cloudy life questions that have been hovering over me since August: *What if I don't get a good work-study job?* and *Mom can't set Micah straight all by herself* and *But I don't want to stay here, I most definitely do not want to stay in Atlantic Beach for the rest of my life. Not anymore.*

The bell rings, and I watch Wil slide out of his seat and rest his hand on the small of Ana's back. He steers her toward the door, leaving the smell of varnish in his wake.

He must be working on a new boat. He always smells like sawdust and varnish when he's finishing a skiff. Varnish is his favorite smell—he used to sniff the can as a kid. I bet I'm the only person in the universe who knows that. I know all his real secrets, like how he can't sleep without the National Geographic channel on low in the background. How he knows his dad loves him and his mom tries but doesn't know him. How he can only cry underwater.

It's such a waste, knowing those kinds of things about a stranger.

# BRIDGE

*Spring, Senior Year*

"LAST chance," Leigh singsongs in the parking lot, searching for Iz, the spray-painted VW bus she named after a famous dead graffiti artist from New York. "You can always come and not drink, you know."

"There he is." I point to the far end of the lot where Iz sags, fat-bellied, in the sun. "And it's not that."

It is that, and Leigh knows it. I can't risk getting busted. After Wil broke up with me, there was no one there to pull the red Solo cup from my hand, no one to whisper that I'd had enough, that maybe I should go home. Junior year spring and summer spun by in a haze of beer and bonfires and house parties until reality slammed into me hard and fast, in the form of a minor-in-possession citation from the Atlantic Beach PD.

My MIP has earned me mandatory community service and a

letter from Florida International University, informing me that one more run-in with the cops will jeopardize my acceptance and my shot at a future.

I don't mind the community service. I finished my hours months ago, but I still spend a couple of afternoons every week hanging out with Minna Asher, the elderly woman I was paired with as my court-ordered atonement.

"I couldn't go if I wanted to. Mom's working late, and I need to make a Publix run and check on Micah," I tell Leigh.

She laughs. "This is, like, the third time you've lost in a row."

"Fourth." My mother and I have this game called Culinary Chicken. We take turns cooking dinner and try to make the most of whatever we have in the refrigerator and pantry. Whoever chickens out and goes to the grocery store first loses. Last night's meal (mine) was oatmeal-crusted pork chops with a strawberry jam sauce. I called chicken on my own dinner, threw it out, and ordered Chinese. I lose most weeks, because Mom cheats and brings leftovers home from blu, the gourmet restaurant at the resort where she works. The place is so pretentious they can get away with leaving off the *e*.

"The bonfire won't get started till eight," Leigh tells me. "If you change your mind—"

"I'll call you," I promise.

"You'd better." She bumps her hip into mine. She smells like coconut oil, which she uses now for everything from shampoo to surf wax. She has a free ride to Savannah College of Art and Design, and she's preparing for the life and budget of a legit artist, she says. She can say things like that, because her dad is an orthodontist and her mom stays home and I've never heard either one of them use the word *money*, which is how I know they have enough of it.

I hook my thumbs under my backpack straps and cut across the parking lot, maneuvering around old pickups and hatchbacks and a dented rack of beach cruisers. I find my pickup truck at the edge of the lot and toss my backpack through the half-open window. Soon I'm cruising north and the ocean is a jeweled navy band glinting to my right. Tile roofs and kidney-shaped swimming pools and a couple of dive bars painted dingy pastels swim past my window. *The poorest post-card of itself*, I think, which is a line from this poem about Florida that we read in English last year.

The grocery store is only a few miles down Atlantic. I wind my cart through the aisles, stocking up on pasta, frozen veggies, and Micah's favorite bread from the bakery, the kind with cheese baked into the middle, even though he doesn't deserve it at the moment. Not after the school counselor called my mother to inform her that my brother is showing—and this is a direct quote—*pre-delinquent behaviors*, skipping class and mouthing off to teachers.

The salmon looks good, so I splurge. I cross everything off my mental list and make one more stop: the refrigerator next to the balloon station. It's crammed with sagging bouquets of gladiolas and glass vases of tulips and roses. I reach for the last handful of sunflowers.

"Well, if it isn't Golden Gate."

I drag the sunflowers out of the bucket and turn around slowly.

"Hey, Wilson," I say. Wil's dad is a hulking guy, with shoulders broad enough to rescue a girl from the ocean, like he did when I was nine and Wil dared me to swim past the breakers. For as long as I've known him, he's worn the same uniform every day: jeans, work boots, and a HINES BOAT BUILDING AND REPAIR T-shirt, threadbare and stained. I have one just like it, shoved at the back of my dresser drawer. His hair is pulled into a half bun.

"Sunflowers," Wilson observes.

"My mom's studying to get her real estate license," I say. "She's kind of stressed, so—" I hold up the flowers. I want to tell Wilson that the sunflowers remind my mom of summers at her grandmother's house, and ask if he knows about the link between smell and memory in the brain. He'll call me "smarty-pants" like he did when I was a kid.

"I'm here for tulips," he says with a smile. His eyes are the same color as Wil's: turquoise with flecks of gold. His beard has reached epic, inscrutable proportions, and his hair has gone silver at the temples.

"It's our anniversary. Henney and me," he says. "Twenty-five years. I brought her tulips on our first date. And doughnuts from Anastasia's."

"Oh, wow," I say. "That's—congratulations. Tell her—congratulations."

"I will." He nods. We're quiet for a moment, and I imagine what it'd be like to have a dad that'd stuck with my mom for twenty-five years. What Wil doesn't realize is that when he cut me out of his life, I didn't just lose him. I lost apple wedges and peanut butter served on a paper plate and bodysurfing contests and forts made of old sails and couch pillows. Dad things.

"I should get home," I say, taking a small step backward.

"You two gonna fix whatever happened between you?" Wilson asks, pressing pause on my heart. It's one of the things I admire about Wilson—the words in his head are the words on his tongue.

I try to swallow, but my throat is tight. "He's with Ana now—"

"My son has a lot of my good qualities," Wilson interrupts, "but he's got some of the bad, too. He's stubborn. Can't let things go."

"We've both changed a lot over the last year," I mumble. The words are greeting-card generic. They don't belong to Wil and me. "We drifted apart."

Wilson shakes his head.

I study the floor. "It's up to Wil. He's the one who's pissed at me. So."

"Fix it, Brooklyn," Wilson says sternly. "Whatever happened, happened. It's never too late to fix your screwups. Trust me." He reaches into the fridge for a bouquet of tulips. Yellow. Then he claps me on the back with his free hand.

"But Ana—"

"Ana, what?" he says roughly. "I'm talking about the friendship. I'm not talking about dating or whatever. You don't think about painting the boat if the hull is rotted, do you?"

"No," I whisper.

"I think we got everything." Wil emerges from the produce section, his arm looped around Ana's waist. I want to hate her, but she's not the kind of girl that elicits emotions of that magnitude. She's pretty, even under grocery store lights, and somehow isn't a jerk about it. She's our senior class president, and I heard she tutors kids downtown twice a week and didn't quit once she got into college. She makes good grades. She probably flosses. She's good. Wil deserves a good girl.

"Oh," Wil says when he sees me. "Hey." He studies my ear. He hasn't looked directly at me in a year.

"Hey, guys." I accidentally snap a sunflower neck.

"Bridge." Ana smiles a little too big and reaches for Wil's free hand. Her hair is dark and shiny. Her eyes are the color of a ring Wil bought me at a museum gift shop during a fifth-grade school trip—an amber oval with a scorpion frozen inside.

"Anniversary party?" I ask. Someone has to say something.

"Oh. Yeah." Wil holds out his basket. I pretend to be interested in the three different brands of crackers and four hunks of cheese. "We're doing a family thing, the four of us."

"Fun." I don't mean to sound hurt, but I can see my pain register in Wil's pursed lips.

"It's not a big deal," Wil murmurs. He doesn't like to hurt people. Even people who deserve it.

"Speak for yourself," Wilson says gruffly. "Twenty-five years of marriage feels like a pretty big deal to me."

"So!" Ana chirps. "We're going to the bonfire after. Are you going, Bridge?"

I shake my head. "I don't really go to those things anymore."

She claps her hand over her mouth. "Oh my God," she says.

"It's okay," I say, feeling suddenly exhausted.

"No. I think it's, like, really mature, how you've turned things around."

"Ana." Wil rubs the back of his neck.

"I should get home," I say.

"Hey. Think about what I said, missy." Wilson shakes his tulips at me.

"Yeah." Face burning, I wave good-bye and push my cart

12

down the aisle with entirely too much speed and purpose for the balloon aisle. I can feel Wil and his dad and Ana watching me, and I wish I were oceans away from all of them. Wilson was wrong: There is no way to fix what I did to Wil and me. I didn't damage us. I incinerated us. Whatever I felt earlier—that sudden, strange burst of nostalgia—has evaporated. I want to be gone again, more than ever.

# WIL

*Winter, Junior Year*

BRIDGE has been gone too long. She's not coming back tonight. I can feel it.

I'm standing in the workshop doorway, staring into the December dusk, waiting for the rattle of her pickup. The longer the silence stretches, the more charged I get. By the time it's too dark to tell the sky from the ground, I'm pacing.

I've only felt this way once before, when we were little kids at the beach and still brand-new to each other. Without warning, Bridge leaned her pink salt lips close to my ear and said, *Do you ever think about swimming toward the horizon and not stopping till you get there? Just to see?* Then she jumped up and ran into the surf, and the panic turned my veins to live wires. She didn't understand the ocean yet. I yelled after her to *Wait, hold up*, but she didn't stop until I screamed, *I can swim out farther than you!*

*Bet you! Twenty bucks!* Bridge has always had a way of shaking me up. Most of the time, it's a damn good thing.

Not tonight.

I knew it the second she left for the party: I should have swallowed my pride and gone with her. It didn't matter that I had something else planned for us. I should have gone. But not for her reasons (*Leigh's parents never go out of town! We have to celebrate the end of midterms! Blow off some steam!*). For mine. Even though I kind of hate high-school parties, which I know amounts to teenage sacrilege, I should've gone just because she wanted me to and the clock is ticking on our time together.

Junior year will be gone before we know it, and soon after that, she'll pick a college. She hasn't said it, but I know it won't be here. Bridge is not the kind of girl who stays in one place. She belongs everywhere.

I head back into the shop and flip the switch near the door. The white Christmas lights I wound around the rafters last night light up for a second before one of the bulbs pops and the middle strand goes dark.

"Ah. Shit." I launch myself onto the long wood worktable and unplug the dead strand. The remaining strands are too dim, and make the walls and shelves look yellowed and frayed, like old newspaper. This was supposed to be a romantic way to congratulate her on finishing her exams. If I've learned anything from the movies Bridge secretly loves, it's that girls freaking melt over white Christmas lights. Christmas lights and candles. It's girl science: The more tiny lights there are in a room, the more likely a girl is to take off her clothes in that room.

I unwind the bad strand and drop to the table, almost

15

knocking the bottle of sparkling cider and the box of Anastasia's doughnuts to the floor. Suddenly, I see the shop the way she'll see it when she walks in: the weak lights hanging limp from the rafters; the fake booze and the dented doughnut box. Pathetic.

I should know better. Every time I plan a big romantic moment between Bridge and me, the moment disappears before she even knows it was supposed to exist. Somehow things work out for us anyway. It's like the night I was supposed to tell Bridge I loved her, for the first time out loud. Freshman year, our first high-school party. I went because Bridge was excited and because for some reason, my mom wanted me to go. She has always had a very specific picture of what she hopes I am. I honestly think she pictures me at parties fist-bumping other guys and saying things like *Nah, bruh.*

The party was being thrown by a junior girl named Isabella, a girl whose parents were the kind of people who said things like *If you're going to drink, I'd rather you do it here.* That night, I knew things were going to change for Bridge and me. No longer *Bridge and Wil, platonic childhood buddies.* We'd see each other across a crowded lawn or kitchen and we'd be magically transformed into *Bridge and Wil, smooth ninth-grade love machines.* Or something. I practiced in the mirror; studied how my mouth looked saying unfamiliar things like *You're the coolest girl I've ever known—we, like, make sense.*

I showed up to the party in khaki shorts and a new T-shirt my mother had ironed, my hair frozen with some gel I found in my parents' bathroom. Standard uniform for love machines everywhere. I had my speech ready. Bridge was already there

16

when I made it to Isabella's back porch. I'd specifically told her to go without me. You can't notice someone across a crowded porch if you show up together.

She looked maybe the prettiest I'd ever seen her that night, in shorts and this white tank top, and her hair was braided but wild around the face. Buck Travers was handing her a beer. I stuffed my hands in my pockets and I tried to catch her eye, but her eyes were everywhere else, so I gave up on my big romantic moment and headed their way.

"Hey," I said. "Buck." I wedged myself halfway between them.

"Hines, man. How's it going?" Buck dipped the brim of his trucker hat.

"Wil!" Bridge looked up from her drink and grinned like she was surprised to see me. She threw her arms around my neck. She smelled like Bridge and a little too much like beer. "So glad you've popped in for a spell, bloke. Care for a pint?"

"Uh, what?"

She listed toward me. "We're speaking in Bri-ish, love."

"Blimey, darlin'," Buck said halfheartedly, which Bridge found hilarious.

"Oh." I tried it out. "Hines. Wil Hines," I said, and it didn't sound Bond-ish at all, but Bridge laughed harder than she'd laughed for Buck.

"You look sharp, mate," she observed with a grin.

"That's Australian, I think," I said. "But, like, good Australian."

She shrugged and sipped her drink. "Master Travers, dost thou think thou could get Master Hines a pint of ale?"

"Huh?" Buck sounded thick.

"Get him a beer," Bridge said.

Buck licked his lips. "Oh. Yeah. I guess."

"Great, man. Thanks," I said. I didn't want a beer, but I wanted Buck gone.

"Um," I said once he'd left. "Hey. So do you think we could talk about something?"

"He's been flirting with me all night," Bridge said, putting her hand on my chest.

"Oh—" I didn't know what to say after that.

"But you know what?" Bridge leaned in close, and her hair enveloped us. "I. Fancy. You."

I breathed her in. "I—" Were we still pretending? My body hovered in the space between nirvana and devastation. "Are you—"

"I fancy you," she said again in her normal Bridge voice, and her eyes got clear and sharp. And then she kissed me.

I always thought girls were supposed to taste sweet, like cotton candy. But Bridge tasted like floating in the ocean and getting a slow even burn. She tasted like grass and salt air and mangoes, like good sore muscles after a day in the shop and the sound of the waves at three A.M. She was everything good in my life. And she wanted me. Even without a big romantic moment.

Back in the shop, I peel myself off the table and yank the green cord from its outlet. I tug the lights gently, until the strand worms its way from around the beam and collapses in a heap at my feet. Then I wind the cord from my elbow to my palm and around again. Again and again until it's a perfect oval. I twist one of Dad's garbage bag ties around the loop at the north end and the south end. Dad won't forgive a half-assed job, even for

18

the sake of romance. I store the lights in the bottom drawer of his toolbox.

"All right," I tell the walls. "I'm going."

I leave the windows down as I gun over the Intracoastal. At the top of the span, I close my eyes for just a second, imagine Bridge and the way her eyes go from faded blue to aqua when she's surprised or embarrassed. She'll be surprised, that's for sure.

I recognize Leigh's street a second too late and make the turn too fast, almost sideswiping a brand-new beamer. Cars are parked on either side of the street for the entire length of the block. No wonder Bridge was mad when I refused to go. Every kid in the junior class must be here. I park behind a Jeep with a SALT LIFE bumper sticker and walk the few blocks back toward the party.

The dull roar of the party swells behind three stories of stucco. I start down the drive, which is lined with tiny spotlights on either side, like a mini airport runway.

"Wil? That you?"

I squint at the house. There's a girl, not Bridge, sitting on the front steps. A red Solo cup hovers just above her knee.

"Yeah?"

"It's Ana. Acevedo?" She says the last part like she's not sure.

"Oh. Hey." I don't know Ana well, just that she's part of Emilie Simpson's crew. One of the tame ones, I think. She raises her hand in class a lot, and if you get put in her group for a class project, you're pretty much guaranteed an A. "What're you, ah, doing out here?"

"Emilie." She shrugs. "She dragged me out, but now she's wasted. Nothing's that hilarious when all you're drinking is Coke

Zero." She lifts her cup over her head and sloshes it from side to side, miming Drunk Girl. *"Wooo!"*

I laugh. The tiny spotlights show her in parts: jean shorts, long hair that looks wet, a neon-pink bra strap that I try to un-notice.

"I didn't think you were much of a party guy, either," she says.

"Not really." Why a guy would want to spend his free time standing around with people he sits with Monday through Friday is a mystery to me. The only difference between high school and high-school parties is beer, and I don't drink. "I'm here for Bridge."

"Right." Her lips turn down. "Sorry."

My heart rate picks up. "For . . ."

"Oh. I don't know." Her plastic cup cracks like gunfire under her grip.

"Have you seen her? My girlfriend?" I don't know why I said it like that.

"She was out back earlier, in the yard. You could text her."

"I kind of want to surprise her." My neck gets hot all of a sudden, as if I've just told Ana a secret I should have kept between Bridge and me. "It's—"

"That's really sweet." She jerks her thumb at the door behind her. There's a red wreath on the door knocker that looks like it's made out of snow-covered cranberries, even though it's been in the seventies all week. "Good luck in there, soldier."

I give her a little salute and she angles her knees so I can pass. Behind the door is a pack of girls whose voices bounce off the elevated popcorn ceiling. I pass a game of beer pong on an expensive pool table and a guy I know from trig spilling Easy Mac powder all over the granite countertops in the kitchen. I make it to the other side of the house as fast as I can, and pump the handle on one of the doors leading to the water.

I find Leigh outside, curled up on a cushioned lounge chair next to Wesley Lilliford, Atlantic Beach High School's most enthusiastic and purple-haired thespian. They're both laughing at the sky. High, drunk, probably both, which is why I'm not a huge Leigh fan to begin with. With a house like this and parents like hers, she can probably afford to fuck around for a while without consequences. That's not true for Bridge. Leigh should know that.

"Hey, Leigh." I crouch next to the lounge chair.

"*Wiiillllll! You caaaame!*" She reaches for my hand and slips her fingers through mine.

"Yeah. Great party." I pull away. "Have you seen Bridge?"

"On the dock, maybe? Sitting on the dock of the bay?" She bursts out laughing and starts singing the song, and Wesley Lilliford jumps right in with the harmony. Sweet Jesus.

"Great. Thanks." Thick, dry grass hisses under my flip-flops as I cross the yard. I stop at the bulkhead, where the yard meets a long, winding dock, and find her sitting at the very end. She leans against one of the rails, her long, pale legs crossed one over the other. There are a few other shadows clustered along the length of the dock, but she's alone, watching the shattered moon on the water.

Her head tilts to the side a little, the way it does when she's had one too many. Her body looks loose and happy, exactly the way it did the night everything changed between us back in ninth grade.

I think about yelling, *Hey! I fancy you,* but that's not exactly the kind of thing you yell when there are other guys around. I open my mouth to say something else, but I close it again when I realize she's not alone. There's a shadow next to Bridge lying on the dock. It's a dude. Buck Travers, I think, because he's wearing the same stupid trucker hat he's worn since birth. He sits up and slides his hand around her waist, and I think I see her shrug him off but my brain is going to explode, so maybe I'm hallucinating.

He moves closer to her, murmurs something I can't hear. The vibrations of his voice register somewhere deep, like shock waves. She starts to push away again (*I could put this guy's head through these planks in two seconds flat*) but then she leans into him, just like she leaned into me two years ago, and their shadows merge.

Everything stops. My heart. My breath. The tides. After a while she ends the kiss. She pushes herself to standing and he reaches for her, but this time, she keeps walking. She stumbles down the length of the dock, winding toward me, and with every step, she is farther and farther away. There are only a few feet between us when she sees me standing there.

I hear the *whoosh* of Bridge's breath, her soft, terrible "Oh my God."

"Don't," I bleat. The yard is still. Everyone is watching.

"Wil," she says. Her tongue is thick. She reaches for me.

"Fucking *don't*." I step back.

"*Ohhhh,*" some dude yells behind me.

A million different versions of me fight it out beneath my skin. Raging Me could fly down the dock to beat the shit out of Buck Travers. Devastated Me might puddle in front of Bridge, sob like a baby for days. Fourth-Grade Me doesn't believe that the Girl from Alabama could *ever*.

"I'm drunk," she says. Her eyes are bleary, like watercolor mistakes.

"That's worse," I whisper.

"How?" she moans.

"I don't know." I want to explode out of my skin.

"Just—can we talk?"

My chin drops. She's barefoot, the black glitter polish flaking on her big toe. We laughed about that yesterday. Pretended her toe was an inkblot and took turns analyzing what the chipped part looked like. *The top of a palm tree! Maine! Donald Trump's toupee!*

"Have you guys—are you . . ." My voice crumples like tinfoil.

Her lips are moving—*No, no, oh my God, of course not*— but the sight of her, her fire-red hair and drunk-girl mouth and blazing aqua eyes are too much. I turn and I walk and I'm moving fast, stumbling through the wall of whispers and laughs.

I run. Back through the yard, through Leigh's cloud of weed, through the too-big house, out the front door, down the street, past the truck, and back again. I run all the way back to the fourth grade, to the trailer with the even rows of desks and the erasers that smelled like pineapple and the markers that made you dizzy if you sniffed them and the beautiful, burned new girl.

*Don't*, I tell the boy in the second-to-last row. *Don't you dare turn around. That girl is going to end you.*

# BRIDGE

*Spring, Senior Year*

I watch the digits on my bedside table clock tick toward the end of the day. It's too late for me to be alone in this house. Micah should be here. My mother should be here. But I haven't seen Micah all night. He's been staying out later and later with his friends. I'm tired of wishing he'd care enough to come home for dinner. Mom is working a double shift at the resort.

I listen hard, hoping for the *ding* of Micah's cell or the sound of shoes being kicked off and flung across the tiled floor. But the house is quiet, except for the labored churn of the window unit and the whir of the ceiling fan.

As I get ready for bed, I lift my gaze to the glittering ocean. A tiny square is visible from a very particular angle in my room. The tiny two-story we've rented since Mom moved us here from Literally Nowhere, Alabama, eight years ago is only a block off the water. Atlantic Beach locals call it the Pepto Pad, because it's painted the brightest, ugliest shade of pink in the color spectrum. Swim out far past the breakers and I swear you can still see it, glaring like a stucco zit from behind a row of spectacular beachfront homes.

I turn away from the water, which will always remind me of Wil. I sit cross-legged in sweats and a tank top on the floor of my room, sifting through the only Wil pieces I have left. My bottom drawer is filled with tiny mementos from the boats I worked on with him and Wilson. Wilson would slip small treasures into my palm at the end of every project: a piece of polished teak from an old deck, a sail scrap with the boat's name scribbled in the corner, and once, a brass-rimmed compass.

I nudge the drawer shut with my foot and lean against the foot of my bed. I threw everything in that drawer away the night I let beer-soaked Buck Travers kiss me on that dock. Maybe if I'd had a reason, I could put Wil behind me. But I've looked for a good explanation for why I betrayed my best friend, the boy I'd loved since I was eight, combed my memory for it, and all I can come up with are broken half excuses. Buck had been trying to drunk kiss me for years. I was pissed at Wil for refusing to come with me to Leigh's. I was exhausted and stressed at the end of the hardest semester of my life, and I just wanted to have *fun*, do something stupid. I was drunk.

But what really happened had nothing to do with Buck or booze or junior year. What really happened is this: For those few moments on the dock, I stopped showing Wil I loved him. I didn't stop loving him. I still haven't. But Wil Hines is not the kind of guy who appreciates that difference.

Since that night last year, there have been a million times I've wished that Wil wasn't the type of person who lived his life by such absolutes. That he could understand a moment of weakness and forgive it. But he's not. He doesn't see the grays.

Maybe if he had the kind of dad who bailed without a word, like mine; if he had the kind of dad who cheated, bailed, came back, and bailed again, like Micah's . . . maybe then he'd understand that life is never black-and-white. That most of us have learned to tread in the gray.

A footfall jerks me awake. I flop onto my back and open my eyes. The shadows in my room are all wrong. I check the clock by my bedside table. 4:43 A.M.

"Bridget."

I sit up. My mother is a foggy ghost at the edge of my bed, repeating my name. "Bridget. Bridget. Wake up. Bridget."

"God. Mom. Are you okay?" I fumble for my lamp and twist the switch. Mom never uses my full name. *Kid* or *Offspring*. *B* or *Honeybee*. *Bridge*. Never Bridget. "I thought you were working a double shift."

The lamplight shows her in contrasts: messy auburn bob and crescent shadows beneath tired eyes. "Oh, honey."

I sit up. "Where's Micah? Are you okay?"

"No. I'm—we're fine." She kicks off her work pumps. Tears polka-dot her blouse. "I have something to tell you. Something bad, baby."

"Whatever it is, say it, Mom. It's okay." My mother is the kind of mom who let Micah and me believe in the tooth fairy for so long that once we found out, it was a million times worse than if she'd just told the truth. "I can take it."

She reaches for me. She presses one of my hands between hers.

"Wilson Hines is dead," she says. The words are frantic and dry: hundreds of moths escaping the black cave of her throat.

"What?" I almost laugh. It seems too absurd to be real. "No. Mom. I just saw him."

"Honeybee," she whispers, and then I know it's true.

I shake my head. I close my eyes and see yellow tulips. My mouth tastes like rust.

"It was a break-in. They think it's related to that string of burglaries that's been on the news."

I blink for a minute. The words sound strange, like gibberish.

"When?" I breathe.

"Couple of hours ago."

I bend over and stare at the spinning floor. I'm going to be sick.

"Wil," I croak. "Henney."

"Wil and his mom are both fine. Not fine." Mom's features collapse. "I think they were there, but . . . they didn't get hurt or anything. I can't—" Her face twists like crumpled paper and she slides into bed with me. I stroke her hair while she cries. I'm cold, like Wilson and I are standing in front of the flower refrigerator again.

*Fix it, Brooklyn.*

Wil had a dad this morning and now he doesn't, and in some small way, I know what that's like.

"I have to go," I tell Mom, kicking off the covers. "I have to see Wil."

* * *

27

The drive to Wil's house passes in a blur. Someone has ripped the black sky open with bare hands, releasing the rain. I barely register the streetlamps bleeding gold on the rain-slicked pavement or the garish neon of the car dealerships that line Atlantic, and then I am tearing down his street. At the end of Wil's block, red and blue lights flash between the raindrops.

There are cruisers and news vans barricading the street. I go as far as I can and throw the truck into park. Wil's house is three down, at the corner, and all the lights are on. Yellow crime tape spans the perimeter of the yard, taut around the palm trees.

It is too loud. Neighbors are inching close, yelling questions to the cops. Their voices are high and thin. They press their children against their bodies. The cops hold an unwavering line at the crime tape, murmuring into their radios. At least three reporters are testing opening lines ("—a horrific scene tonight, Bill, on this quiet residential street." "Neighbors say Wilson Hines was a local boat builder who cared deeply for his wife and teenage son." "—shattered the glass door and entered the house." "—latest victim in a recent string of break-ins that have been escalating in violence."). I recognize the one closest to me, the brunette from Channel 12.

"We'll be back with more on this developing tragedy, tonight at eleven. Back to you in the studio." She stares wide-eyed and solemn at the camera, until the light goes down. I worm my way through the crowd. Before long, I am pressed against the police tape at the edge of Wil's yard.

A lanky blond cop hooks his thumbs through his belt loops and says: "I'm gonna need you to stay back, ma'am." He can't be much older than I am.

"But—he's my—" There is no way to explain us to a stranger. The police tape warns me: DO NOT CROSS.

I step back on wobbly legs and let myself cry, hard, because it's raining and everyone here has a wet face.

I find Wil's bedroom window, fix my gaze until Wil's shadow appears, just for a second. I want to sprint across the lawn and dive into the house. I want to hold him so tightly neither one of us can breathe.

But I do none of those things, because I don't get to be that person for Wil anymore. We aren't us. So I stand in the crowd with everyone else, alone under the grieving sky.

# BRIDGE

*Spring, Senior Year*

I lose count of how many days have passed since Wilson was murdered.

*Since Wilson was murdered.* The words are cold salt water filling my lungs. I haven't even said them out loud. I turn off the news every time it comes on. I can't stand to hear the story again: how Henney went downstairs for a drink of water and interrupted the burglar. How Wilson saved her, but couldn't save himself. How Wil woke to his mother's screams after the killer had vanished through the shattered glass door.

I tell Mom I don't want to talk about it. I shrug Micah off when he leans against me on the couch and hands me the remote. The only person in the world I want to talk to about this is Wil, and I feel guilty for even having the thought. If I can't sleep for more than a few hours at a time, if it's hard to catch a breath when I open my eyes and remember, if I feel blank, I can't imagine how Wil must feel. I lost the man who felt like a dad to me. Wil lost the real thing.

I've almost called him a million times. I've driven by his block every day after school, and every time there is one less cop car, one less officer, one less gawking neighbor. The crime scene tape is still wrapped around the yard, but it sags and the yellow has faded. On the news, they talk about the "hunt for a killer," but the segments don't last long. New, terrible things happen every day, and there's only so much time between commercials.

On the morning of the funeral, I am full of hot sadness that boils up to the top, threatening to spill over. Mom is short-staffed at work, so she stands on the front stoop with Micah and me and gives us too-long hugs when Leigh pulls up to the curb.

At the church, I sit between Micah and Leigh in a middle pew. The benches are a worn-down wood and the high ceiling looks exactly like an upside-down boat, which I think Wilson would like. We don't talk about the police cruisers parked out front or the two detectives standing in the back, guns and badges clipped to their belts.

Leigh slips her fingers through mine. I can feel her heartbeat through her palm, and I try not to think about how fragile we are.

"You okay?" Leigh murmurs. "Sorry. Stupid question."

"Yeah." My heart is racing and I'm clammy, sweating in a black wool dress that I dug out of Mom's closet, along with a pair of hand-me-down pumps that gap on the sides. The dress is wrong—the fit, the itchy winter fabric, the occasion—but it's all I could find. Micah's shirt and tie are a little too big. They belonged to his dad, maybe. His hair is slicked back. He's been quiet this morning. Sweet.

Micah leans into me. "I've never been to a funeral before."

"Me neither." I loop my arm through his and rest my head on his shoulder. He tolerates my affection for about a minute before he inches down the pew.

The church fills quickly, and it feels like the entire senior class is here. Ana shows up in a gauzy black dress. The tip of her nose is red and her eyes are glassy. *She's beautiful*, I think without meaning to. By the time the organ music starts, there are people standing around the perimeter of the church, spilling down the steps and into the street. The entire congregation turns around at the same time to watch Wil and Henney enter the church and stand in front of the arched doorway. Hundreds of people trying not to see the purplish marks creeping around Henney's collar on either side of her neck. Someone's hands made those marks. Someone who is watching television right now, or drinking coffee. My stomach surges.

Wil is holding his mother so tightly there is no room for air between them. It's a strange sight. I can't remember Henney ever reaching for Wil's hand or stroking his hair or kissing him good night. Henney has always felt like the exact opposite of my own mother. Where my mom is constantly hugging Micah and me, letting her thoughts and feelings roll off her tongue, Henney is quiet. Full of unsaid things. In all the years I've spent in the workshop, Henney never joined us. Every once in a while, she'd stand outside with a tray of gritty lemonade. But she never came inside. She never grabbed a piece of sandpaper.

But I think tragedy can change people chemically. It can

soften them or harden them, and maybe Henney has become a different version of herself.

Wil guides his mom down the aisle. He's an echo of his dad: tall and broad with nut-brown hair that curls a little around the temples. When he passes the detectives, his gaze stays fixed straight ahead, but the color leaks from his face and neck. He tucks Henney into the front pew and settles in next to her.

The priest begins the service. When Leigh squeezes my hand, tears pop from the corners of my eyes. I hear the sermon, ebbing and flowing like a steady wave, as I break Wil down into familiar pieces: the slope where his neck meets his shoulder; the long twiggy scar on his finger from freshman year. His dad really chewed him out for that one, even with me thinking, *He's bleeding, though; we should do something*. This is what happens when you've been looking at—no, *seeing*—someone for as long as I've been seeing Wil Hines. You don't see them as some seamless whole person, the way the rest of the world does. You see them broken down into the millions of essential atoms that make them Not Everyone Else.

After a final *amen*, Wil gets up and goes to the lectern at the front. He pulls a piece of paper from his pocket and blinks several times.

"I wanted to read part of this poem for my dad and say some words." Wil clears his throat. His voice is dry and brittle, like dead leaves. "Under the wide and starry sky / Dig the grave and let me lie."

I hold my breath. Watch Wil lean over the lectern, watch him grip the edges so hard his knuckles turn white. His jagged breath echoes through the church. Henney bleats a low, awful sound

33

that knots my insides. Wil looks up, his eyes staring blankly at the back of the room and rakes his hands through his hair, like he's trying to claw the sadness from his brain.

In the quiet, every little noise is amplified. All the uncomfortable noises we emit because silence itself is terrifying: the coughs and sniffs and the creak of wood under shifting live bodies.

"I'm sorry," Wil whispers into the microphone. "I can't—"

The priest gets up and guides Wil back to his seat, murmuring soft words. Then the priest says to us, "At this time, prayers for or recollections of the departed are welcome, either silently or aloud."

Somebody stands up and starts talking about how Wilson once built him a beautiful dinghy out of eastern red cedar so that he could spread his wife's ashes on the Intracoastal. When the man returned, Wilson refused payment.

I gather story after story. They are precious now.

When the service ends, the church aisle fills. Everyone acknowledges one another with weird, tight smiles. Death is too close here and we jostle past one another, trying to outrun it in heels and dress shoes that pinch.

"Are you—" Leigh starts.

"I don't know." I search the crowd for Wil.

"I'll take Micah home. Call you later." Leigh kisses me on the cheek and steers my brother into the current of mourners and out the door.

On the church steps, Wil and Henney greet the flood with vacant stares. The same two detectives stand on the curb near a police cruiser: a tall black woman with cropped hair, and a pudgy white guy in a wrinkled shirt and jacket that doesn't quite fit. They are granite-faced. Every so often, Wil glances over at them, then at his mom.

*Leave them alone.* I glare at the cops. *Just for a few hours.*

The adults leaving the church stop to hug Henney or give Wil a pat on the shoulder. The kids from school leave a wide berth. They pretend to be in deep, sober conversations with friends. Only Ana stops to give Wil a hug. She stands on tiptoe and sobs into his suit. After a moment, he nudges her back to her best friend, Thea Tritt, who is wearing a dress that's too short for church.

I wait until the steps are almost empty. I force one heel in front of the other until we're standing toe to toe. Wil's dress shoes are so shiny I can see my hazy reflection.

"You had to buy new shoes for this," I whisper.

"They're his. He only ever wore them once." Wil tugs at a piece of hair curling against his ear. I remember the softness of his hair. My fingertips burn with the memory of it.

"I loved him, you know," I say quietly.

"Yeah." When I look up, Wil's eyes are wet and rimmed red. "He would be really glad you came, Golden Gate." When he hugs me, he smells like varnish and sawdust.

After the service, I sit in my truck, taking in the heat with the windows rolled up, like I might be able to sweat these ugly feelings out of me. I don't want to go home. I don't want to hear the sympathetic slide of Mom's voice on the phone or watch Micah ditch me for his loser friends. What I really want is a drink, but I'll settle for the next best thing. I jam my keys in the ignition and head for Minna's.

I pull through the front gate of her assisted-living community and stop at the guard's cottage. The usual security guard is there, balanced on the back legs of a metal folding chair. She's watching a miniature television and eating granola straight out of the bag.

"Hey, Rita." I pull up to the open door.

Rita bolts upright and the chair hits the floor. When she sees that it's just me, she gives me a sheepish grin.

"Oops. Hey, Bridge." She wrestles with the chair until it pops into place.

I smile. "Hey. Is Minna home?"

Rita rolls her eyes. Her bright red lipstick weeps beyond the borders of her mouth. "Three complaint calls about how the landscaping guy is 'giving her the eye' say she's here. You look nice today. Big date or something?"

"Something." I pull through the gate.

The housing complex is arranged in concentric circles. The outer few rungs are comprised of small homes, carbon-copied and dip-dyed in Florida colors, shrimp and aloe. Beyond the homes are the duplexes. They are slightly smaller, with garden patios in the back or a view of the man-made lake. All have staff weaving in and out—nurses to help with medication or cleaning ladies with chemical-loaded carts. In the center of the grounds is the hospital. The game works like this: The players start in the houses, then move their game piece closer to the center of the property as they get older. It's like the worst possible game of Monopoly. Minna calls the hospital the Epicenter of Death.

I park in front of one of the duplexes. Minna's door opens a crack before I even knock. A thin gold chain stretches between the door and the wall. She peers through the crack with her strikingly green eye.

"Good. I thought you were the yard guy," she says. "Guy's a pervert." The door slams and I hear the slide of metal on metal before it opens again. Minna looks like a seventy-five-year-old Mother Earth, with papery skin that's folded into itself and long white hair that falls in rolling waves to her elbows.

"Sorry I didn't call," I say.

"The funeral," she says, and pulls me inside. "I saw it on the news this morning. They had a reporter outside the damn church in the middle of the thing, if you can believe it. Girl was dressed like a stripper. Now sit," she commands, guiding me to her velvet eggplant settee.

I lean into the cushions while Minna makes mint tea. Her apartment is small, with vaulted ceilings and sliding glass doors that look over what she calls "the fake lake." The furniture is so old that it's stylish again—dark wood, rich fabrics, curved lines. There are picture frames everywhere, all holding stock images of anonymous smiling couples. The walls used to be white, but before school started this year, she had me paint them a deep, almost-red pink. I don't think the staff was too happy about it, but no one said anything. *Don't fuck with Miss Minna* is practically the national anthem around here.

Minna sets two mugs next to the Scrabble board that has a permanent place on the coffee table, then settles into the tufted armchair across from me.

"Want to talk about it?" she asks.

"Not really."

"Want to play Dirty Scrabble?"

I shrug.

"I'll take that as a yes." She watches me while she divides the tiles. "How's Wil?"

After our third week together, Minna knew everything there was to know about Wil Hines. She says small talk is for small people.

"I ran into Wil's dad. At Publix, just a few hours before." A shiver worms down my spine. "He told me to work it out with Wil. To fix it before we graduated."

"And?" Minna raises her eyebrows, two silvery crescents, and nods toward the board. "If you're not going to take your turn, I'll take it for you."

I nudge my tiles around the board. "And I want to. But I just don't want to be one of the hundreds of kids who decide to be there for him now that his dad is dead."

She shakes her head. "Tragedy is a powerful magnetic force. It either draws people in or pushes people away. After a while, the drama will die down, and Wil will see who's left beside him."

"It doesn't feel real," I tell her.

She tsks. "You've got a case of the *things like this don't happen around heres*."

"Things like this *don't* happen around here."

"False," she says firmly. "Violence happens everywhere, Bridget. It happens behind closed doors and sometimes it happens to people we don't care about, so we pretend it hasn't happened at all."

Minna is the human version of Florida. She is harsh, intense—extreme heat or torrential rains. The lines that map her face, travel her hands, and snake down her neck are packed earth that has been baked under harsh conditions for so long that she has no choice but to crack. But she is strange and lush, too, rich with understanding about the world and how it works or how it doesn't.

"I should feel sad, like, all the time. But sometimes I feel blank. Like nothing's happened at all," I confess.

"Shock," she says, and she leans across the coffee table, and she rests her hand over mine. "It will fade. And when it does, you'll know." She squeezes my hand. Then she slides a few tiles into place. "You lost your turn."

I glance at the board. BAZOOMS. I roll my eyes.

"You know! Breasts!" she says impatiently. "Twenty points."

"Minna. *Bazooms* hasn't been a word since, like, 1920."

"I'll use it in a sentence," she argues. "Just because Bridget doesn't have *bazooms* doesn't mean they don't exist."

I close my eyes and lean into the couch. Just last week Wilson Hines existed, a random collection of atoms blown into life. The calloused hands that rested on Wil's shoulder. The silvering temples and stern mouth; the jaw muscles that tensed while he examined his newest boat for imperfections.

It is strange and awful to think that Wilson Hines just . . . *isn't*, anymore. All because someone else decided to erase him, for no reason at all.

# BRIDGE

*Spring, Senior Year*

WIL still isn't at school on the following Monday, but the day ticks by as usual: PE and Spanish and Econ and lunch. When teachers call roll, they trip at Wil's name. And then they say that if we want to talk to a counselor, ours has an office on the third floor—the third floor? They're pretty sure—and we move on. There are equations to contend with, essays to write.

The halls are bubbling with talk of the murder, only nobody says that word. Everyone uses language that dances around the truth: *the accident, the thing with Wil's dad. It. It's so sad, it's so awful, they were nice, a nice family.*

People whisper about the cops' theory: that this man has killed before. According to the paper, Henney's police statement matches the description of a guy who broke into a house in Neptune Beach, just a few miles away. The woman he attacked was a teacher. Dana York. She worked with a sketch artist at the hospital, describing in excruciating detail the man who had knocked her unconscious before he fled with her mother's jewelry. Three days later, her injuries killed her. The kids at school pass phones back and forth, zooming in on the sketch of the guy. White, buzz cut, a nose that's bent a little like it's been broken. The sketch chills me every time. He looks ordinary. He looks like anyone and no one.

After the last bell, Leigh and I head to the senior courtyard, where Ana has called an emergency class meeting. *Senior courtyard* is a generous term for a concrete slab that extends outward from the left side of the school. There are a couple of stone benches pushed up against the concrete wall. Since it's almost summer, somebody's busted out a Dora the Explorer blow-up pool and a couple of lounge chairs.

As Leigh and I squeeze in, I watch Emilie Simpson hug Ana while Thea Tritt hovers. Buck Travers wanders over to Emilie and flashes a smile whiter than bleached sand. She tosses her hair with unnecessary violence.

My stomach wrings itself out. I still can't look at Buck— the green mirrored sunglasses wedged on the back of his neck, the SURF LIFE shirt when I know for a fact he's never touched a surfboard—without feeling generic.

Ana disentangles herself from Emilie and heads to the front of the courtyard. She clears her throat. "Um, hey, guys. I feel like we should talk about what we can do for Wil as a class," she says, her voice rippling. "I want him to know that we're thinking about him while he's gone, and I'm wondering if anybody has any ideas."

41

"When is Wil coming back?" asks a girl I recognize from English class.

"Ah—" Ana clasps her hands together. Her voice wavers. "I'm not sure. He's not ready yet?" Her eyes fill, and Thea rests her hand on Ana's shoulder.

Everyone is silent, baking under the sun. I shift on my feet. Wil would hate that we're talking about him when he's not here, and I wish Ana knew that. I wish she knew what to do without asking: an informal gathering on the beach, maybe, or an afternoon on Wilson's latest boat. *If she'd ask me*—I think, and erase the thought before it's fully formed. Ana would never ask me about Wil. Neither would anybody else in our class. After Ana and Wil started dating, the entire school forgot about Wil and me. It was as if the seven years before had never even happened.

"Maybe we could have a sign-up sheet to bring him dinner. A casserole or something. Or we could send flowers as a class," Ana says.

"I have to get out of here," I mutter to Leigh. I don't want to be here, with these people, talking about casseroles. I need to do something that will actually make a difference. "Call you later."

I decide to walk. I slip off my shoes and follow the bricked sidewalk, which is rough and just hot enough to feel good. I pass Nina's Diner and the seafood restaurant with the good tartar sauce Micah eats with a spoon. I move slowly, reading the bricks as I go. They are etched with people's names or dates or sometimes a quote. Wil and I used to alternate making up stories to go with the bricks on our way to the beach.

I pass IN MEMORY OF KYLIE MITCHELL. In seventh grade, Wil decided that Kylie Mitchell departed this world after a tragic spray-tanning accident left her insides filled with toxic orange goo. I told him that was disgusting, and Kylie Mitchell was probably a sweet old lady who fell asleep painting watercolors and never woke up. That was stupid, he said, because if you think about it, how many old-lady Kylies do you know?

The turnoff for Wil's is only a few blocks away. The closer I get, the slower I walk. I don't know what I'm doing. I don't know what to say or how to say it or whether Wil will want to hear it. I just want to see him. I want to be someone who doesn't gossip about what happened, someone who knows better. I want to be someone who doesn't say the word *casserole*.

When I get to Wil's street, its blankness surprises me. There are no cop cars or news vans. The crime scene tape is gone.

I cut across the side yard and stand just outside the workshop doors, listening to familiar sounds: the buzz of the circular saw and the electric sander. It sounds like Wilson is in there and for a second I think maybe he could be, until Wil calls, "Come on, Bridge. Everybody knows what happens when you stand in the sun too long."

I smile a little.

"How'd you know I was here?" I ask, ducking into the shop. Wil is wearing an old HINES T-shirt and shorts, and he's sanding a flat piece of wood by hand. I try not to notice his lines beneath the T-shirt; the way they deepen around his chest and arms with every stroke. "Saw you coming through the window." His voice is quiet. Sad. There's an old stereo on the floor in the corner of the shop, playing a Beach Boys tune. At the back of the shop, sheets are draped over the long, thin form of a boat.

I stand there, wishing I had flowers or a casserole after all.

*Fix it, Brooklyn.*

"Is this okay?" I pick at a sore hangnail.

He looks up at me, and I see him taking me in. His face softens; then his Wil wall goes back up. "What?" he says.

"I don't know." A thin, dark crescent of blood appears. "Me. Here."

He keeps sanding. "None of this is *okay*."

Fleetwood Mac comes on the radio, a band I know because of Wilson. I take a step toward Wil. I feel him curl inside himself, like he's afraid of me. "Wil. I'm sorry, okay?"

"You're always sorry, Bridge. But what does that really even mean?" He flings the words across the table, and I can't duck in time. "You should"—he sucks the remaining air from the room—"be sorry. It's like—where *were* you?" White dust coats his fingertips as he presses the sandpaper harder.

"What?" I force the word past my lips. "I was there. At the funeral?"

"I'm not talking about the funeral!" His expression is a volcano: molten anger and neon sadness exploding from the deepest part of him. "I'm talking about where you've been for the last year and a half! You can't just show up like this!"

My skin goes cold, then hot again. I thought I felt something at the funeral. An opening of the door between us; just the tiniest crack. I thought I saw the light streaming through. But it's dark again now, and too quiet. The only sounds are Fleetwood Mac and the lullaby of the sandpaper, back and forth. There aren't enough words in the world to make this okay.

"It's just . . . I get how much you loved your dad, Wil. I know how close you were."

"That's the thing, Bridge." He finds a hammer. His hand goes pale when he grips it. "You think you know about my family because you hung out over here." He says the last words slow, waits for them to sink beneath my skin. "You know nothing."

*That's a lie*, I want to say. I know enough to know that Wil has never eaten a casserole in his life. I can imagine the smell of this workshop in three seconds and get it exactly right. I was there when Wilson caught Wil trying his first and last cigarette in eighth grade, and I've seen the way Wil's face goes blank when he's really mad. Like now. I know plenty.

"I'm sad, too, you know," I spit at the floor.

"Yeah, well. Sorry for your loss." Wil drops the hammer and goes back to sanding.

"I just meant that I'm sorry, Wil. Okay? I won't come back. I just wanted to say sorry."

I turn away from him, and I'm slow to leave, even though I should be bolting for the door. But it's the last time we'll be here like this, just the two of us and real music on the stereo, and I miss us so much that the broken version is better than nothing at all.

# WIL

*Spring, Junior Year*

IT'S been almost three months since Bridge wrecked us. Four days since she stopped trying to repair the damage.

I still feel her staring at the back of my neck in class. But she's finally stopped apologizing—no more *I never should have* texts, no more *Please, Wils* sniffed onto my voice mail. No more notes beneath the workshop door. She evaporated from my life, but like salt film on beach glass, she's there, and always will be.

She stopped trying because I asked her to, in a note that I slipped through the vents of her locker like we were middle-school kids. I hated how she lived everywhere: in the halls and on my voice mail and scrawled across pages and pages of yellow legal paper. Everything reminded me of who we weren't anymore. So I asked her to stop, and she did, which was somehow worse.

"Seam needs caulking," my dad announces. We're in the

workshop, just before sundown. We've been working all afternoon and I'm stiff, like my joints are screwed together wrong. Dad is bent over the sweet wooden skiff on the worktable. It's quiet in here, cool and dark, with the sun filtering through the cracks in the shed, striping his face pink.

"Oakum's on the bench over there. Want to try feeding it in?" Dad rakes his varnish-stained hands through his hair. It's pulled back in a ponytail like always. But there's silver around his temples, and his hairline's creeping back.

I'm ready to quit for the day, even though we can't afford that kind of attitude around here. The word *money* has been seeping through the vents into my room lately, a lot more often than usual. Mom usually brings up college and then Dad says *But he doesn't want*—and my mom counters with *But one day he might.* Maybe if we'd gotten more jobs recently. Maybe if I worked faster.

Still, I'm tired tonight. It will take me forever to sweep up and hang the tools just right. And hell if I'm gonna do it before early-morning crew practice tomorrow. I stop for a second, shake the thought from my head. It's a Generic Teenager thought, not a Real Me thought.

Sometimes thoughts fly through my head that don't actually belong to me. Truth is, I don't mind staying late to clean up. I like how every tool has a hook and how Dad keeps the cord to the stereo wound with a yellow trash tie so nobody trips. I like sweeping the wood dust into straight lines and Skynyrd in the background singing "Simple Man."

I think Ronnie Van Zant had it right when he wrote that song. It's a song about how simple is the better way to be. How a guy doesn't need money or things to be happy, and how bad times will come and go like the waves. That's just life. As long as a man can look inside himself and be okay with who he is, that's enough. (Also, it says he should find a woman.)

The idea is right. My dad gets it, but my mom doesn't. She wants college and a desk job for me. She wants me to have a house that's bigger than our perfectly good house. She's told me in millions of little ways since I was a kid. The clothes she buys are name brands from the consignment shop near her work: someone else's preppy clothes meant for someone else's pretty life. And this morning she left a University of Florida Gators sweatshirt on my desk next to the third copy of the common app she's passed my way this month. It's not even senior year.

Here's what she doesn't get: By Skynyrd standards, my life is good. I have a family and a job I'll love once high school is done. The only part that isn't there anymore is the woman part, although Ana has been hanging around my locker lately, and she volunteered to help me study for our next science test.

"Any word from Golden Gate?" Dad tries to say it casually. "She hasn't come around in a while."

"Dad. Come on." I get back to work, lifting the thick coils of oakum I'll use to caulk the seam. I wrap them in a loop from my elbow to my palm and around again. Dad has already set the caulking iron and the mallet on the bench. "I don't want to talk about her."

I'm dying to talk about her. It's the only way to have her here: her name hanging in the air between my dad and me in my favorite place on the planet. But she doesn't get to be here with us anymore.

I wish I could just get over her. But the awful truth is you don't just get over a girl like Bridge. She can piss you off and pull your heart out through the soles of your feet, and when she's gone, there will be this ugly, jagged space in you. You can try to patch it, but you know: You're a different shape than you were before.

"A girl doesn't spend nearly every day over here for seven years and just stop for no reason." Dad keeps his eyes on the boat.

"She's changed, okay? Reason enough?" My heart is flopping around in my chest like a beached fish. I cram the oakum between two wooden planks, pushing it into the seam with the caulking iron. The material will seal the seam once we finish the process. If I do it right, if I take my time, it will make the boat impenetrable. Nothing will be able to touch its insides. I hammer the caulking iron with the mallet. Tiny beads of sweat surface along my hairline.

When I glance up, my dad's looking at me like I've just told him I don't *get* Hendrix.

"People don't change, son." He gives me a look. "She is who she is. Whatever she's done to piss you off doesn't make her a bad person. People aren't the things they do."

I hammer harder. I don't believe him. I think people are exactly the things they do. In sixth grade, I had to do an oral report on Ralph Waldo Emerson. The first thing that came up when I Googled him was this quote: "What you do speaks so loudly that I cannot hear what you say." If that's true, Bridge screamed, *Fuuucckkk yoooouuu!* on the dock that night.

I jump when Dad puts a hand on my shoulder. "Ease up on that mallet," he orders.

I don't for a few strokes.

"Drop it, Wil," Dad says. "Now." He rubs his hands together

and takes a seat in the corner of the shop. He nods at the floor next to him. I sit. He's solid, and if I could, I'd curl into him.

"You know, son, you and I are the same. We take it hard when someone does wrong by us."

"I'm not pissed at Bridge," I say through clenched teeth. "And I don't want to talk about it anymore."

"Then what's the problem?" Dad asks roughly.

"It's Mom, okay?" I bleat at the walls. I didn't mean it. I just can't talk to my dad about Bridge yet. Mom was the very next worry in my head and I didn't shut my mouth quick enough.

Dad rubs the back of his neck. "Mom."

"She put this UF sweatshirt out for me this morning, next to another app." This isn't her fault. But it's out there now, and I can't suck the words back in.

Dad takes a sharp breath.

"It's not a big deal," I backpedal. "I just—I don't know why she cares so much about college."

"She wants you the hell out of this place."

His voice sounds like steel, but just in case I say, "Yeah, but I love it here. You know that, right? I want to stay and run the business with you."

It's quiet for a while. Then he coughs. "Next step?"

"Primer," I say, and we both get up.

He hands me an upside-down Frisbee that holds putty mixed with primer. Carefully, I paint the seam.

"You boys ready for dinner?" My mother's voice sounds from the doorway.

"In a second," Dad grunts.

"It's ready now, Wilson. I made dinner and it's ready now."

50

"We're coming, Mom," I say. "Just give us a second, okay?" The sunlight's streaming in behind her, and she's nothing more than a shadow.

She turns back toward the house. My parents are masters with silence. They can mold it into the sharpest blades, hurl it at each other so it slices deep. They can do much more damage with silence than they can with noise. Bridge always used to talk about how lucky I was, having parents who were married. *It's not that simple*, I'd tell her, and she'd look at me like I was the dumbest asshole on the planet. *At least you know where you came from*, she'd say.

I'd shut up then. I couldn't imagine what it would be like, knowing I had a father in Texas or China or maybe even a few blocks over. Knowing he was out there, part of me or me part of him or however that works. My own dad could be a jerk sometimes, but when you're walking around with another person's DNA in you, that means something. You don't just cut the tie and bail.

Dad inspects the seam for longer than he needs to.

"Dad," I press. "Come on. She's waiting."

He grunts and we wash up and go inside. Mom's standing at the kitchen table in her work uniform: black scrubs and a nametag shaped like a tooth. Her lipstick is a neon pink that creeps past the corners of her mouth in a weird, constant smile.

"Smells good," I say.

"Nothing special," she says, hovering over a tray of lasagna. She's lined an old plastic bowl with a paper napkin, the corners pointing at the ceiling. She empties a log of garlic bread into the bowl. There's already a sweating pitcher of tea on the table.

Mom and Dad sit around the pine table my dad made my mom

as a wedding present. Underneath one of the leaves, he carved their names and wedding date and the words *We will go together, over the waters of time*, which is from a poem. I never thought of my dad as a poetic guy, but those words are proof that my parents were real once. I used to hide under the table as a kid, usually when they fought, and close my eyes and run my fingers over the words again and again.

"This is really good, Mom," I say over a mouthful, to make up for the sweatshirt remark.

"Good," she says absently. "Oh. I almost forgot. You got something in the mail today, Wil." Her knuckles whiten against her glass.

I raise my eyebrows at her. "What is it?"

"Something about a college fair in downtown Jacksonville. Lots of southern schools. The flyer said there would be representatives there to talk about scholarship opportunities and financial aid."

"We don't need financial aid," Dad mutters into his tea.

Mom's face doesn't even register Dad's voice.

"Now," she says, "before you say anything, Wil, I know you think you're not interested in college. But college will open doors for you. You'll have options."

"Thing is, I don't really need options." I should say *Okay, great, thank you.* I should end this. "I have the shop."

"The shop." Mom runs her tongue over her teeth and lets out this half laugh, half sigh that brings my dad's fist down on the table.

The plates jump. Mom jumps. I jump.

"Where'd the UF sweatshirt come from, Henney?" Dad asks.

My mother doesn't answer—swallows her tea and sharpens her Silence Weapon.

"Dad. It's okay," I say. I don't want my lasagna, but I take a huge bite anyway, because everything's fine and when everything's fine, a person eats his lasagna.

"My boss is on the Board of Regents," Mom says. She has gray in the same places my dad does, around her temples and streaked through her hair. They've made each other old. "He brought it back from a meeting. For God's sake, Wilson, it's a *sweatshirt*."

Again, she looks at me with her tight smile. "They have club rowing there, you know." She slides out of her chair. "Who needs a napkin?"

I hate it when they do this—fill the air up with so much anger and hate that it's like breathing through a straw. "It's fine, Mom. Tell Dr. Larkin I said thanks."

"Bullshit, Wil." Dad shoves his chair back and stands up. His voice is getting softer, but his energy almost blows me back.

"I don't want to talk about this right now. Please," I say.

"Wil doesn't want to go to Florida, Henney. He doesn't want to go to Florida State or University of Miami or Central Florida. He doesn't. Want to go. To college." He follows Mom around the counter and into the kitchen. "Would you look at me, goddamnit? *Look* at me." He grabs Mom's shoulders and whips her around.

"You guys!" I yell.

"How does he know if he wants to go to college?" She's shouting now, so loudly my ears are buzzing. "We don't always know what we want at seventeen, do we, Wilson? We don't know that we could go to college, that we don't have to get married right away! We're too young and stupid to know!"

53

"Mom." I taste bile. *"Mom."*

She keeps going. "Sometimes we make choices at seventeen that we regret for the rest of our—"

My dad lunges. The *crack* sends an earthquake through me.

Everyone is still, and the house is filled up with silence.

My stomach heaves and heaves again. No one moves. The whole damn world can hear my heart. I get up, and my glass tumbles toward the floor. I watch it shatter. I leave it there. I walk through the kitchen, calm and slow.

"Wil," my dad says. "Son."

"It's okay," my mom says with a bloodied lip. "It's okay."

I open the door. I slam the door. I heave my lead body across the yard, and I duck into the workshop and he better not follow me. He better not.

I circle the sawhorse, my breath coming in ragged gasps. I scream at the weathered walls and the perfect floor. I scream until my throat is pinched and my temples throb.

I stop and bend over the boat. My hand slides over the mallet and the electricity flows through me. I lift it over my head and bring the mallet down again and again, destroying perfect wood. I watch the seams pull apart; watch the wood splinter like I'm watching time in reverse.

I don't stop swinging the mallet until the boat is a pile of splinters on the floor, and I slide down to the concrete and, fuck, my hands. I stare at them, the dark blood running down, and they don't look like my hands. They are someone else's hands, hands that are capable of destruction. His hands.

*You and I are the same*, he said.

He was right.

# BRIDGE

*Spring, Senior Year*

*WIL was wrong,* I think as I twist the shower nozzle. It screeches, and I hold my breath. I'm up extra early, while the moon is still suspended in midair outside the bathroom window. I duck under the spray and twist the nozzle again, making the water as hot as I can stand it. I haven't cried since Wil kicked me out of the shop last night. I can feel the tears trapped beneath the surface, waiting.

*You think you know about my family,* he said. *You know nothing.*

The backs of my calves and thighs are bright pink, my knees and shins dead white. I turn and face the spray until every inch of me is humming with heat. It's useless. The tears and the knots in my neck and shoulders and back don't budge. I repeat all the truths I already know: Wil is grieving. Angry. Irrational. A dead father gets him those things.

*But still*. There are plenty of things I don't know. I don't know what Wil saw that night when he woke up and stumbled into the kitchen. I don't know the sound Henney made when the killer pressed his hands around her neck. But I know Wil Hines, and I know his family. I know that Ana will never understand him better than I do.

I turn off the water and reach for the waffled resort robe Mom gave me as a stocking stuffer last Christmas. I twist a towel around my head. In the hallway, the smell of burnt coffee hangs over the top step. I stop for a second and listen for the thick hum of early-morning quiet. Instead, I hear the clang of pots tumbling.

"Nonstick piece of—" Mom hisses.

"Morning, Mother," I call out. I find her downstairs in the kitchen.

"Did I wake you?" Mom's in a robe that matches mine, her hair sticking out of her head at strange angles. She fell asleep in her eyeliner again. She's pretty still, in an undone way. Books and papers and the used laptop Leigh let me have when she got a new Mac litter the kitchen table.

"Why are you up so early?" I ask, capping a pink highlighter.

"No reason," she says in the voice she uses when she's lying. She drags a spoon through a mixing bowl on the counter. "I was just up studying, and decided to make some breakfast." She hands me a mug of coffee.

"Thanks," I say.

"Pancakes will be ready in a sec." She turns back to the stove. "And then I thought we could talk."

I put down my coffee and slide my arms around her waist, hugging her from behind. "I wish I could," I say. "But I have

to get to school. Trig test. Haven't had much time to study."
The lie slides off my tongue. *Talking* means my mother asking a
million questions I don't know the answers to. And I don't want
to explain: I'll never know the answers. Wil wants nothing more
to do with me.

"Oh. God, you'd think they'd cancel all the tests after
something like this." Mom turns around and scrunches her nose.
She yawns and switches off the stove. "All right, then. I'm going
back to bed. Be careful out there," she says.

"Got it." I kiss her cheek and head upstairs again, her words
ringing in my skull. *Be careful out there*. It's been her sign-off for as
long as I can remember. I think it's supposed to make me feel safe
or empowered or something. Grown men are being killed in their
homes for no reason at all. But as long as I know to *be careful out there*.

At school, Wil is so close. If I wanted to, I could reach out and
touch the back of his neck, the place where his curls meet his
collar. I could lean into him as he unearths his Spanish book from
his locker. But I can't ask him what I really need to know. What
he meant when he said those things to me yesterday afternoon.
Whether he meant them.

Leigh is quieter than usual, watching me watch Wil, doodling
little hearts on her sketchpad; a drawing of me in a Superwoman
cape with generous *bazooms*, as Minna would call them. But after
third period, Leigh explodes.

"That's it." She slings her bag over her shoulder and points
at the door with both hands, like a pissed-off flight attendant
pointing out the emergency exits. "You need to get away from
here for a period. Lunch at Nina's. On me. Let's go."

Leigh is a respectable human being in most cases, and so she waits until we're wedged into the window booth at Nina's Diner with a platter of sweet potato fries and coffee before she says it: "Want to talk?"

"Nope." I blink out the window. "I just—I can't stop thinking about what happened in that house. What Wil saw, you know?"

"Channel 12 says he didn't see anything." Leigh tries to reassure me. "Says the guy had hit Wil's dad in the back of the head and gotten the hell out of there by the time Wil made it to the kitchen—"

Tears fill my eyes. I feel sick. "I can't. Can we talk about something else?"

Leigh jumps in without missing a beat. "So, I have three days to submit the final proposal for my senior art project, and I have no idea what I'm doing." She arranges her fries in a greasy bouquet before cramming them in her mouth. "It's, like, twenty-five percent of my grade."

"You girls doing all right?" Leonard, the owner of the place, stops by our table and fills our coffee mugs. Leonard is in his mid-sixties, bald, with a potbelly that looks like it might topple over the rest of him any second now. There is no Nina, not anymore. Leonard told me that once, a million lives ago, he was engaged to a lady named Nina. When she left, she took almost all the money he'd saved up for his restaurant. He was forty-two by the time he'd resaved enough to open the 50s-style diner, and he was pissed. He named the place after her. A reminder that women were dangerous, he said.

"All good. Thanks, Leonard," I manage.

"How's Wil?" Leonard wipes his hands on his apron.

"Hanging in there," I say, like I know. Wil and I came on our first real date here. We were freshmen, so we had to ride our bikes. We chatted with Leonard and played songs on the jukebox in the corner. It was just like every other afternoon we'd spent at Nina's, except I was sweatier than usual. Before we left, Wil etched our initials into the table, next to the initials of other couples that probably didn't exist anymore, either.

"Nice kid. Shame. People are animals." Leonard goes back behind the counter and turns on the mini black-and-white television next to the waffle iron.

"As I was saying," Leigh starts. "Senior project. I've narrowed it down to two options: spray-painting the underpass next to the Target, or going mainstream and actually asking permission to paint the exterior of the school. The wall facing the courtyard."

"I like that idea. Giving back. Plus, a substantially lower chance that you'll get arrested."

"I don't know." She grins. "I kind of think showing up to art school with a record would be a badass move." Her eyes snap to the door. "Uh-oh. Incoming."

I follow her gaze to the street. Micah and his buddies are shoving one another through the door. They are laughing loud enough that everyone in the place turns. My chest caves. He's flown under the radar for the last few days since the funeral. For me. I was stupid to think it could last.

When he sees us, he makes a dramatic show of meandering over to our booth. "Bridge! Hey, guys, you remember my big sister? The one who keeps me in line." He slumps into the booth and throws his arm around my shoulder.

"You're supposed to be in class, Micah." I try to elbow him

out of the booth. A low chorus of *Ooooohs* oozes from his crew. His eyes go wide for a second, and I catch a glimpse of the real Micah, before he goes back to being a Jerkwad Who Doesn't Give a Shit.

"I'm a lifelong learner, Bridge," he says. "My learning cannot be confined within classroom walls. Right, Lenny?" he calls.

Leonard glares at the boys from behind the counter and I want to evaporate.

Micah's friends crowd around the table by the bathrooms.

"So, is this what you do now?" Leigh says under her breath. I stare out the window. "You sneak out of the house to go to bonfires? You sneak out of school to come here?"

"What?" I cry. "You snuck out?"

"Leigh. Not cool. I thought we had something special." Micah slumps.

"We don't. Which frees me up to inform your sister that you were drunk and hanging all over Emilie Simpson the night of the senior bonfire."

I don't scream, *You went to the senior bonfire* and *hooked up with a girl in MY CLASS?* But trust me, I want to.

"Emilie Simpson and me are none of your business," Micah tells Leigh.

"*Emilie Simpson and I*, dumbass." I glare at him.

"She's cool," Micah says lamely. He runs his fingers through his hair, which is every teenage boy's insecurity tell. "She surfs and stuff."

I roll my eyes at Leigh. "She's not cool. She's too old for you. And she almost failed junior year for skipping too much."

"Don't be a bitch, Bridge." He says it loud enough for his boy gang to hear. "Besides, are you seriously pissed at me for drinking when you got busted for the same thing last year?"

"Back to Emilie Simpson," Leigh continues. "Just make sure you wear a life jacket. Hers are not uncharted waters, my friend."

"Oh my *God. Leigh*," I moan. "He's fifteen."

"You can both die." Micah shoves out of the booth. I watch him march back to his boys in a huff, the back of his neck flaming red. We redheads can't hide it when we're embarrassed or upset. It's in our DNA—it's the only way I know that he's still in there.

"Go back to class," Leigh yells after him. She pulls a twenty from her bag and tucks it under the napkin dispenser.

We walk back to campus and she doesn't say a word about Micah, just like she doesn't force me to talk about Wil. I'm glad. I love her for being pissed on my behalf, but I hate the little spark of defensiveness that flames when anyone rags on Micah. I know he deserves it.

We talk about nothing: how hot it is already and what we're wearing to graduation, which Leigh already knows even though it's still months away. Some kind of white caftan, but her mother is lobbying hard for a sundress, just this once. I can wear the sundress, she says. (I don't even have to ask.)

I want to talk forever about white dresses and hot air—frothy, foamy things, things that tug my mind away from dead fathers and mistakes I can't seem to undo and brothers I don't know what to do with. I want to escape.

# WIL

*Spring, Junior Year*

NO matter where I go, I can't escape what my father has done. When I yank open the refrigerator door, the tired sucking sound is replaced with the *crack* of my dad's hand. When I turn the hot water faucet to shave, the shriek of metal on metal is my mother's sharp breath. Violence is coiled up tight in everything, I realize. The world is a fighting place.

My mother doesn't leave the house for three days. She says she doesn't want to talk about it. *It!* Too small a word for what's happened here.

"It's private, Wil," she says one night before dinner. "A private matter between me and your dad. We don't want you to worry." She stares out the window and scrubs the lunch dishes for the third time today. Her hands are withered and red under the faucet.

"Seeing your mother get hit makes a person worry." I dry the dishes as she hands them over. She's moving too slowly. I shouldn't be annoyed with her, but I am.

"*Hit.*" The word whooshes out like the last bit of air from a dead balloon. "God, Wil. You make me sound so—" Her face gets as pinched and red as her hands. "Pathetic."

"Not you, Mom. Him," I snap, and she winces.

I pat her back a little. It's my fault. If I hadn't brought up that stupid sweatshirt, Dad wouldn't have been so angry.

"He didn't mean it," she says. "It was an accident."

"Don't make excuses for him," I tell us both.

When she finishes the last spoon, she fills a juice glass with water and tilts it into the vase on the kitchen table. Dad's put fresh flowers in there every morning: red roses on the first day and pink ones with those tiny white dried buds around them on the second day and today it's flowers that have been dyed neon colors: pink and yellow and orange. She hovers over them and plucks the bad leaves.

"Get the salad out for me?" Mom says, fiddling with the stem of an electric-pink flower. "In the fridge."

"Sure." I tug the fridge open and lean into the cool. "Spaghetti ready?"

"Give it another minute. I set the timer."

"Mom. Has he ever, like, has this ever . . . happened before?" I clench my jaw so tightly, my face could shatter.

"I don't want to talk about it, Wil. I told you. Please." When the oven timer screeches, she jumps behind me, startled.

"I got it, Mom. It's okay," I say. Soft, the way you talk to a scared kid.

"Let me get it." She slides around me and grabs the pot and if I don't ask her now, I'll never ask her.

"Hey. Mom. Do you think I'm like him? Do you think I'll turn out like him?"

She opens her mouth just as my dad comes through the door. He looks like a stranger who's wandered into the wrong kitchen, searching for a family. I want to tell him to move along. We don't need him here.

"Supper ready?" He claps me on the back. I cringe.

"Just about," Mom says. I wait for her to answer me with her eyes, but she doesn't. She just flips the pot into the colander in the sink. Dad slides up behind her and wraps his arms around her waist.

"Something smells good," he says.

*Screw you*, I think.

Mom says, *"Wilson,"* like a high-school girl. She never says his name like that.

*God*, I think. *She's pathetic. I could just—*

It happens that fast.

*I could just. I could just . . . what? Hit her?*

The thought blazes through my brain and then it's gone, and God Almighty, I hope that wasn't a Real Me thought. But it wasn't a Generic Teenager thought, either, because Generic Teenagers think about getting laid and scoring weed and maybe the SATs.

Mom tells Dad and me to have a seat and we stare at the flowers instead of each other. I haven't looked at the whole of him since it happened. If I look at him, he will try to have a talk, try to apologize. So I break him down into pieces, and I sneak a look now and then: his rough hands, his sunburned forehead lines. Looking at him at all makes my body ache. Three days ago, he was one person, and now he's another. And I am half of him, but I don't know which half.

"Here we go." Mom serves us each plates of spaghetti.

*I could just.*

"Let's say grace," Dad says, and if I were looking at him, I'd look at him like he was crazy. We've never said grace in this house. Mom's forehead wrinkles but she bows her head. This is a nightmare. We are playing at Happy Family.

Dad clears his throat. "Gracious Father, we want to thank you for this day and all its blessings. Most of all, we thank you for your grace, and for how you forgive us, even when we don't deserve it. Amen."

"Amen," my mother says.

*What. The hell?*

"Missed you in the shop this afternoon, son," Dad says, twirling a chunk of noodles around his fork.

"Homework," I lie.

"Well, school comes first," he lies back.

The food is too hot, but I force it down.

"It's good, Henney," Dad grunts. He wipes his mouth with the back of his hand, leaving a bloody stain.

"I'm glad, Wilson." I still see Dad's handprint on the side of her face, flashing red like a Mini Mart sign.

When the doorbell rings, I'm up. At the front door, on the other side of the decorative glass, Ana Acevedo is in abstract girl pieces: cutoffs and one hip jutted out to the side and her hair flowing over one shoulder. None of her quite fits together. I think about these Picasso paintings we had to look at on the first day of the art history elective Mom signed me up for last year.

"Hey, Wil Hines," she says before I've opened the door.

"Uh, hey," I say. I'm so glad for an interruption, any interruption, that I don't even care what she's doing here.

We look at each other for a while. She bounces on my front porch with this pretty scrubbed skin and hair that floats in midair and I'm not even sure her bare feet are touching the ground. There is nothing weighing this girl down. I want her lightness.

My dad calls from the table. "Wil? We're in the middle of dinner."

I don't mean to laugh. *Of course! It would be rude for a girl to show up here during dinner! Maybe you should put her in her place, Dad.*

"Oh." Ana's eyes get big. "Not a good time? I just—we said we'd get together to study. Seven-thirty, right? Your house?"

"Study?" My brain isn't working. The last few days I've been swimming through the school day, underwater and against the current. I forgot that Ana had asked if she could come over and study.

"Marine bio? The test tomorrow?"

My dad's footsteps make the whole universe shake. When he gets to the door, he clamps his hand over my shoulder like a vise. My insides crumple. *We can't stay here. She can't watch us pretend.*

"Hey there. Can we help you? Wil's in the middle of supper right now."

"This is Ana, Dad." I mouth *Sorry.* "We have to study for science. And I'm done eating, so—" I duck outside of Dad's force field (it was easier than I thought it would be; I should have tried it sooner). I can feel his eyes on me, but what's he going to do? Hit me right here in front of a pretty girl in the middle of *family time*? "I'll be back later. We're going to her house."

"Are you sure?" Ana's eyes dart from Dad to me and back to Dad again.

"I'm sure," I tell her. "Tell Mom dinner was good," I toss over my shoulder as I head for Ana's Jetta.

"Um, bye, Mr. Hines," Ana says too brightly. She's a nice girl, and she must have nice parents who taught her to use her manners even in the most awkward of social situations.

"Sorry for inviting myself over," I say under my breath with an embarrassed laugh.

"No problem." She presses a button on her keys, and the door clicks open.

"Rough night, huh?" she teases once we're speeding down Atlantic. She's got the sunroof open and the wind sends her hair whipping around.

"I had a fight with my dad. Needed to get out of there."

She studies me. "You look sad, Wil Hines."

"Eyes on the road, Ana Acevedo."

She laughs a little and we're quiet for a second, damp evening wind flowing through the car and me all at once. When we stop at the third streetlight, I look over. Ana's hair is big and twisted around her face, and her cheeks are flushed.

"My parents are out with friends," she says, and this time she does keep her eyes on the road. "They'll be out late, so you can stay as long as you want." Her cheeks flush deeper. Ana is so good. I should save her. Leap out of the car at the last minute and put as much distance between us as possible.

67

Instead, I say, "Okay."

Walking into Ana's condominium in jeans and a T-shirt feels like walking into a fancy restaurant where the guy at the front podium has to pull you aside and offer you some other man's tie because what kind of an animal eats steak tieless? That's never actually happened to me. I saw it in a movie once. But that's exactly how I feel now: tieless in a steakhouse.

"This is really nice," I say. It's the best I can do, because I'm concentrating hard on trying not to knock over the huge oriental vase on the stand next to the door.

"Thanks." Ana tosses her purse on the nearest beige sofa.

The condo is one enormous room with windowed walls that would show me the ocean if it wasn't so dark. It's lit like a museum. There are three or four beige couches, identical, at different angles all over the place. Clustered around them are beige chairs and wooden side tables, and beneath these are woven rugs that are the same color and feel like straw under my feet. There's a hallway at the far end that probably leads to more beige.

I wonder what Ana is doing in public school.

She walks into the kitchen. I sit on a smooth wooden barstool. My phone vibrates in my pocket. I shut it off without looking.

"So, do you need a drink or something?" she asks. She dips below the counter and emerges with a frosted bottle and a couple of short glasses. Vodka, I think. I'm surprised that she can just do that, reach into a cabinet and produce booze. We don't even have any in the house.

"But you don't drink, right?" I say. I stare at the grayish veins in the marble countertop, feeling my face get hot. Maybe I shouldn't have noticed.

"You don't drink, either." Ana fills our glasses to the brim. She's clumsy with the bottle, and the booze sloshes over the side of the glass. It makes me like her, the way she's never done this before. "But you look like you could use one tonight."

I don't argue.

She raises her glass. "To Agnatha."

"Huh?" I lift mine, too, because what the hell? Maybe this is exactly what I need. Maybe it wouldn't hurt to be someone else for a while. Somewhere else. This feels like the kind of house where the worst thing that happens is running out of organic coffee in the morning.

"Agnatha. Jawless fish." She laughs. "Have you even read the chapter?"

"You got me." The vodka is cold and crisp and tastes good, which I didn't expect. We take another shot each and she tells me to grab the bottle. We're going to the balcony.

On the balcony, we stretch out on lounge chairs that probably cost more than the good inside furniture at home and stare into the dark, taking turns sipping from the bottle. The cool air chills my skin and the vodka warms me on the inside. I can hear the waves, and it's not long before my heart beats with them.

"You and your dad gonna be okay?" she asks. She pulls her knees to her chest and rests her chin on them. She looks sweet, like a girl who really wants to know.

"Ah." I take another swig and it gets stuck halfway between my mouth and my heart. For a second I consider telling her everything, because it's too heavy and Bridge isn't here anymore to help me carry my weight. "I don't know. He's just been kind of an asshole lately."

She nods. "My dad can be a jerk, too, sometimes. Especially about college. He's got me lined up for all these college tours I don't really want to go on, when I keep telling him Notre Dame is my number one choice."

I feel the pinch of disappointment, even though it isn't her fault that she doesn't get it. No one on earth should understand what this feels like, this miles-deep blackness.

"Notre Dame sounds good." I lift the bottle again and the night in front of me gets swirly—dark blue spinning just out of my reach. I wonder if this is how Bridge sees things when she's drunk. I stand up and bend over the balcony, dizzy and loose. I'll say it: I'm homesick for Bridge. She would get how confusing this is, how I hate my dad and want him back at the same time, just like she does. She'd get how lost I feel; how I don't really belong on a high-rise balcony with a good girl and a bottle of vodka. *Ana Acevedo, Wil? Really?* she'd say. I wouldn't know what to tell her. I don't know what I'm doing or where I'm going or who I am. That's what she and my father have done to me. Without my dad, without Bridge, I am aimless. Tethered to no one. At the mercy of the currents, and too tired to swim.

# BRIDGE

*Spring, Senior Year*

"DID you know grief can literally kill a person?" I ask Leigh. We're sitting in Iz's front seat in the school parking lot after school. I prop my bare feet on the dash and watch Wil heading for his dad's pickup a few rows over. His shell is the same, but his head is down and his walk is syrupy; nothing like the loping gait that used to make it so easy to find him on the beach.

"Makes sense." Leigh slurps the last of her Big Gulp. "When the heart chakra is blocked—"

"No. I'm talking about the pituitary gland, which is an actual thing." I keep my eyes trained on Wil. He stops at the truck; notices the envelope I slid under his wipers at lunch. I see the moment—the exact moment—that his fingers recognize the scrap of sail tucked inside. One of the countless boat treasures Wilson had passed my way. On the corner of the sail, in Wilson's precise handwriting, is the name of the boat. *Freedom*. Maybe Wil wants nothing more to do with me. But I know what he needs. And right now, he needs this small piece of his dad more than I do.

Wil's face shatters, and he sweeps up the pieces quickly. He stuffs the sail into the back pocket of his jeans and dives into the front seat, deflated.

"Um, rude," Leigh announces. "The heart chakra is absolutely a thing. And a certain person's heart chakra is totally blocked right now." She elbows me, hard.

"Ow. I'm serious," I protest. "The pituitary gland secretes this chemical in your brain that puts you in fight mode." My toes curl against the glove box. "I read this article last night. After you lose someone close to you, your body is in this heightened state of stress all the time. Your cells actually start to die."

"Bridge. My love." Leigh turns in her seat and interlaces her fingers with mine. Her mood ring hurts like hell. "First, he's gonna survive this. But in the meantime, it's just going to suck, you know? You have to let it suck."

"Let it suck. The lesser known follow-up to Paul McCartney's—"

"And *second*, this is too much neuroscience for my brain." She jams her keys in the ignition. "Come on. I'll drive you home."

"Nah. That's okay. I could use the walk." I lean over the console and kiss her on the cheek. When I glance in Wil's direction again, the truck is gone.

I take the beach route home. The air is hot and thick, an August day that has wandered into spring. I slip out of my sneakers and jog barefoot on the soft sand until my lungs aren't big enough, and in minutes I'm slick with sweat and the muscle fibers in my legs are sparking. My skin is flushed the ugly, pale girl kind of pink.

Looking out over the water, I think, *I could take a running dive and I could swim and swim until the beach is gone.* I used to have those kinds of thoughts as a kid, and sometimes I still do. Driving over the Hart Bridge I'll think, *I could veer off this bridge and for a second it would feel like flying,* or I'm sitting in class and it will cross my mind: *I don't have to go to college at all.* These are my secret urges. I won't do any of these things. But I like thinking I could.

*I could run to the workshop. Refuse to leave until Wil speaks to me. Until he explains what's changed since he broke up with me. What's so big, so important, that I don't understand his family anymore.*

By the time I turn down my street, I've decided: He doesn't mean it. He's angry. He wants to hurt me like I hurt him. I kick through my front gate, sweat stinging my eyes and the spot above my ankle where I cut myself shaving this morning. I'm wiping my face with my T-shirt when I hear his voice.

"Took you long enough. What's that? Like, a thirty-minute mile?"

I yank down my shirt. Wil is sitting on my front porch, folded in half. His crumpled backpack sags on the step.

"What are you doing here?" I let the gate snap shut. I want to be pissed. I want to be pissed and I don't know if I can be pissed at a boy whose family is in pieces.

"I don't know," he says. His eyes are foggy, a murky green that won't let me see past the surface. "I was a dick the other day. In the shop." He stands up and sort of sways in place.

My T-shirt melts into my skin and I wish I'd worn shorts. "I probably shouldn't have shown up like that."

"I don't know," he says again. "I really don't. There's no manual for this shit." His hands curl into fists, then relax and curl again, as if they are beating hearts resting outside of his body. I want to hold all his hearts close to mine, but he won't let me. I grit my teeth until my head hurts.

"I know. No manual." I don't want to take a step. I don't want to breathe. We are fragile.

He rubs the back of his neck. "Ana keeps asking what kind of casseroles I like, and it's like, *My dad is dead, so really I don't give a fuck about casseroles.* But you're not allowed to say that, you know?"

"Chicken tetrazzini. Done. She'll never ask again." I don't know whether to smile or not.

His lips curve up, and I relax a little.

"We literally don't have room in the freezer for another casserole," he says. "I want her to know that. I don't want to have to tell her. She just—" He blows out a breath. "Whatever. I can't talk about this with you." He looks past me.

That *whatever* isn't just a *whatever*. If you cut the word open, so much more would spill out.

"This you?" He leans to one side and reaches into his back pocket.

"Yeah," I say before I see the scrap of sail.

"You have anything else like this? Stuff from other boats?" His eyes light up.

"Yeah, definitely. Lots of stuff. Yours, if you want it all." I take a step toward him, and his face hardens.

"Nah," he says. "I have too much of his stuff already. I've been packing it up, and it's, like . . . It's the weirdest thing, trying

74

to pack up another person's life. It makes you think that we're nothing more than the books we always said we'd read and old underwear and spare change."

"No. Wil." I cross my arms over my chest, reminding me to keep the space between us. "Your dad was so much more than those things. Your dad was this—"

"Stop it, Bridge. Stop." He covers his face with his hands.

"Okay. Okay. I'm sorry." Emotion rises up in my throat, fills my eyes, bobs beneath the surface of my skin.

He clears his throat, hard. "I found something. Thought you might want it."

I blink and he's small, like the grief is shrinking his cells right in front of me.

"What?" I ask softly.

"This, ah—this." He tears open his backpack and pulls out a cap. It's worn and dirty and I haven't seen it in years, since Wilson tugged it over my head to shield me from the sun.

"Mama P's Seafood Shanty," I murmur.

He Frisbees the hat in my direction. I catch it.

"Man. My skin gets itchy just looking at this thing." I pull it on and it smells like Wilson and Christmas-tree air freshener. "I don't know if this is a weird thing to offer, but if you need help with the packing . . ."

The words hang in the air. He looks past me. "You want to take a walk? I haven't seen the water all day."

"Yeah."

There's a careful amount of space between us as we head the few blocks to the water. We don't know how to be this version of us. When the water appears, Wil asks about Micah and Mom. He doesn't know to ask about Minna, which feels strange. I tell him almost everything about home, about how Mom's studying for her real estate exam so she doesn't have to work the front desk at the resort anymore, and about how for me, the most exciting part of her career change will be being able to buy shampoo in a regular-sized bottle like a normal human being. I tell him about how Micah's been staying out too late, not doing his homework. I tell him I'm worried.

"He'll get it together," Wil says, his eyes on the ocean. "Besides, college isn't for everybody."

"I know." When we get to the sandy part of the street, we step out of our flip-flops at the same time and scoop them up.

"I'm not going." He squints into the sun. The pinks and oranges make him look like an oil painting of himself. "I want to stick around here. I want to work on boats. I kind of think it's in my DNA."

"Probably," I say, relieved. At least one thing hasn't changed.

He stops. "You ever wonder about that kind of thing? Like, how much of you is new and how much of you is just passed down and you were always going to be that way, no matter what?"

I almost elbow him and say, *"Deeeep,"* but when I look into his eyes, I realize he means it seriously.

I shrug. "I wonder about my dad sometimes."

Occasionally at night, in the minutes before I fall asleep, I think about which parts of me came from my father. Maybe he kept Mom organized, too: made the grocery runs and told her when it was time to go to bed. Maybe he got tired of being the adult. But I doubt it. Responsible isn't Mom's type. It's more likely that he's the part of me that said *screw it* last year after Wil and I broke up, the part that sank into beer and boys.

"It seems kind of fucked up, doesn't it? If we're born a certain way and that's just how we're wired—"

"Yeah, but we have our choices. And those are ours, not our parents'," I say.

He's quiet for a while, and I wonder if the wind swept my words away. But then he says, "Maybe," and that's the end of it.

The beach is crowded for a late-April afternoon. A chocolate lab bounds toward us, tongue flapping, until a tennis ball catches its eye and it doubles back toward the jagged foamy waterline. There are kids building sand castles and screeching at one another in a language that only kids at the beach understand. The water is pink beneath the sun, and people are swimming in fire.

We drop to the sand. I draw hieroglyphics between us and try to think of things to say, things that are right and won't make this worse than it already is.

"You can help," he says quietly. "With the packing. If you want. I fucking hate having to do it by myself."

"Yeah." I pretend to rub sand from my eyes. "Okay. I will. Anything I can do, Wil." My pinky finger is only inches away from his. There are one hundred grains of sand between us, maybe. I am acutely aware of this.

One of the little kids screams, *"Nooo! Doon't!"* Suddenly, Wil's whole body tenses and he jerks toward the sound. Like a magnet, my hand goes to his back. He shrugs me off and cups his face with his hands.

"Sorry," he mutters into his palms. The hairs on the back of his neck are damp. "Sorry."

"We can talk about it, you know," I say softly. "Maybe it would make you feel better to—"

"I don't want to *talk* about it." Before I can tell him that it's okay, of course it's okay, that I'm sorry, he whips off his T-shirt and jogs toward the water. The closer he gets, the faster he runs. He leaps over the soft waves that lick the sand, and then he dives beneath the surface, his toes the last part of him to disappear.

He stays under long enough that I know what's happening. He'd do this as a kid: get really upset, and go out for a swim to calm down, and when he came back, his eyes would be bloodshot and his face would be puffy. *It's from the salt water,* he'd say before I could ask.

*Fix it, Brooklyn.*

I dig my toes in the sand, anchoring myself here. I'll wait for him to surface. I'll stay here for as long as I have to, until we find our way back. Until I fix us. I promised.

# BRIDGE

*Spring, Senior Year*

FOR years, I knew Wil the way I knew my own name; the knowledge was automatic. Involuntary, even. I didn't have to think about his most embarrassing moment of the first day of middle school (Spanish. Picking the name *Manuel* for his Spanish name, only saying it like *Manuel, uhh* . . . and being called *Manuela* by the teacher and the students for the rest of the year). I never asked stupid questions like what kind of cake he wanted for his birthday (pie, always) and where he wanted to live when he grew up (here, always). Because it was instinctual, the way I knew him.

"He feels like a stranger now," I tell Minna later that night. I'm curled up on the settee, pretending to skim my physics textbook, but the words swim in front of me on the page. "I hate it."

"You don't understand him," Minna says. "Of course you

don't. Has anyone ever come into your home in the middle of the night? Killed your family?"

I stare at the text again. "Obviously not, Minna."

She shrugs. "How should I know? Families keep secrets."

"I'd have mentioned that kind of thing." I don't know much about Minna's family before she moved to Florida. I know that Long Ago, she lived in California and was married and had a daughter she named Virginia because that was a state she'd always wanted to visit. And then she wasn't married anymore, and she's never seen Virginia the state. Virginia the person, she hasn't seen in twenty-seven years.

Minna writes and addresses a letter to Virginia every night. Sometimes I bring homework and we sit together on the settee with the news on low. In the background: bombs, floods, open-mouthed, long-faced grief. Minna says that the world has always been like this. She says that people will try to fool you with the phrases like *back in my day* or *people never used to*, and they are lies. People always used to. It's just that the world didn't have as many ways of finding out what humans were capable of. It makes me feel a little better every time she says it. Not that the world has always been a spinning ball of assholes, exactly. Just that things aren't getting any worse.

I go back to my homework. I read and reread a line about gravity and my mind keeps clicking back to Wil. Trying to make sense of what happened on the beach today, what set him off. Remembering the look on his face brings cold beads of sweat to the surface of my skin.

At the commercial break, Minna flicks her pen at my head and says: "Say it."

I duck. The pen narrowly misses my temple. "Minna! What the—"

"Whatever you've been wanting to say since you got here, say it. Sitting here listening to you sigh every two seconds isn't exactly my idea of a good time."

"I'm not sighing. I'm breathing." I stare at my textbook while she stares at me. On the television, a studio audience whispers, *"Wheel! Of! Fortune!"* My eyes are on the book. Minna's eyes are on me. I will not win this.

"I miss Wil. I want the old Wil back. I want us back." I whip the pen back at her. "There. You're welcome."

Minna mutes the television, and then she turns it off. She looks at me. She has this dangerous, beautiful face that can unravel me. One look from her, and everything I've been holding on to since the beginning of time could spill out.

"We talked this afternoon, for the first time in"—I close my eyes—"forever."

"How did it feel?"

"Awkward." I scratch at the velvet couch with my index finger. "But at least he's talking to me again. Or did today, anyway."

"So what's the problem?" Minna asks pointedly.

"There is no problem."

"You said it yourself. Things are *awkward*."

"I meant that things are different. What time is it?" I check the clock on Minna's microwave. *:14*. She's paused the timer after making tea. "I should get home to Micah."

"Different how, Bridget?" Minna has never called me Bridge. *"A bridge is a structure spanning and providing passage over a body of water. Bridget is a girl's name,"* she told me on our first day.

"*Different.*" My skin feels hot and damp against the velvet. "Different because we've spent so much time apart. Different because Wil just isn't the same."

She raises a silvery eyebrow. "Never will be."

"I *know*, Minna. But I don't have to like it."

She reaches for my hand. Hers is mapped in delicate veins, blues, and greens. "Remember what I said about tragedy. Sometimes it pushes people further apart. Sometimes it draws them together. It always intensifies what's there already. It magnifies the good and the bad and the absolutely unspeakable. And you two have a lot of good between you."

"Had."

"So little faith." She sips her tea and wrinkles her nose. "Cold."

"Here." I take the cup. "I'll warm it."

"That's my mother's good china. Keep it out of the microwave."

I escape to the kitchen, gripping the teacup with sweaty hands. Minna's voice reverberates inside me. *It magnifies the good and the bad and the absolutely unspeakable.* There is so much good between Wil and me. He was there for me on my birthday for so many years in a row, made it bearable even though I've always hated my birthday. When we got older, he would plan a million things on the day, back to back, from early-morning waffles at Nina's while it was still dark out to evening beach campouts as the moon rose. I never had to tell him that I dreaded that day because it was the one day of the year that my father should think to call. He never had to tell me what I already knew: that my father never would. There are literally years of good, miles of good between us.

But there is a single night of the bad: my choice on the dock that night. Wil's anger.

There is the unspeakable: Wilson's murder.

And with the weight of those things on our shoulders, in our hearts, I don't know if all the years of good are enough to buoy us.

I catch myself having a silent conversation with Wil on the drive home, and as I unlock the front door and toss my keys on the couch in the dark living room. My lips move, forming the wishes I have for us: *Please forgive me for real; we need each other now more than ever; I can't take this away but I can be there; I will be; I promise.* I wonder if he can hear me. I wonder if it's possible for us to have that kind of connection.

It's one thing to miss Wil. It's another to talk to him like he's here. But even after my lips have stopped moving, there's a sound. It's too far away, too soft for me to grasp. Coming from upstairs. But it's there, and it shouldn't be. Adrenaline floods every inch of me. I try to remember the pencil lines on the wanted poster I've seen on the news. I wonder if Wilson heard the same soft sounds before. I slide my house key between two of my fingers and the spare key to Leigh's between another two and I make a fist.

I listen so hard my ears might bleed. The sound is muffled. Low, urgent. A moan, like someone's hurt. It's not Mom. It's not Micah. Something in me clicks and I sprint up the stairs, stopping long enough to decide that the sound is coming from Micah's room. I throw my shoulder into the door.

"Micah?"

A girl screams, but the girl isn't me at first. By the time Emilie Simpson dismounts my brother and claws her shirt off the floor, all three of us are screaming. I stop screaming long enough to notice my favorite candle, the expensive one Leigh bought me from Anthropologie last Christmas, flaming on Micah's bedside. Hell no.

"Bridge! Get the hell out!" Micah's voice cracks, and his face is all red and splotchy and hormonal, and I look away to avoid the rest of him but I want to scream *That! That voice crack is exactly why a kid your age shouldn't be screwing Emilie Simpson!* but my brain is throbbing with our humiliation. I trip on Micah's backpack on the way out, which pisses me off more than I ever thought possible.

"Get out!" I yell at the closed door. I take the stairs two at a time and throw myself through the front door. Outside, I pace the front walk, from the door to the mailbox and back again. I wish I could rinse my brain free of the last three minutes.

If Wil were here, he'd know how to talk to Micah. He'd know what boy words to use to get through Micah's thick skull. But Wil isn't here. Mom isn't here. It's just me, bracing beneath the weight of my family and my many mistakes. And I'm worried I won't be able to carry this weight forever.

# BRIDGE

*Spring, Senior Year*

I remember the exact moment when I realized that I loved Wil Hines. We were in the eighth grade. Even then, I knew school wasn't important to him the way it was to me. School was something he did out of routine, like brushing his teeth. So when I volunteered to be his partner for a science project, not because he made good grades in science but because I had recently come to understand that his hair was a whole new color under the splintered light of the workshop, I knew. We spent long hours working on the project at his dad's worktable and I tried not to touch Wil's hair while he read out loud about the moon, about how its gravitational pull was so strong that it controlled the tides.

It freaked me out, knowing that something so mysterious and far away could control us. I told Wil that's why I didn't want to believe in God, exactly. He said something stupid, like how he'd been thinking of taking up surfing, and I thought, *Oh my God, I accidentally love you.* I didn't tell him I liked him out loud for several months after that. I wanted Wil to say it to me first. He almost did.

For a few nights in a row now, the idea of sleep drifts out my open bedroom window while I watch that same moon tug shadows across the floor and over my bed. And I can't stop any of them: Micah and Emilie, Wilson's death, the new strangeness between Wil and me. I can try to catch them, but they'll just bleed between my fingers. I'm powerless to stop them.

When the Friday moon turns into the Saturday sun, I stand outside Wil's front door and stare through the familiar decorative glass in an unfamiliar pattern. I thought the gold curlicues were shaped like flowers, but these look more like clouds. I feel sick when I remember: The old door shattered the night Wilson died. This is a new door, a door that shouldn't be here.

I balance a cardboard tray of coffees and a box from Anastasia's in one hand, and I trace the design with another. The glass is cold despite the warm morning, and a sour taste rises in the back of my throat. Wilson fought for his last breath here. His eyes dulled here. His heart stopped here.

I suck in a surprised breath when Henney's fragmented face appears on the other side of the glass. She opens the door just a crack. She's tucked into a cotton-candy robe that overwhelms her frame. Her dark, salt-streaked hair is wild around her face.

"Bridget?"

"Mrs. Hines! You scared me." Then I remember. I'm the one on her stoop. She's the one who will never feel safe in this house again.

Henney opens the door a little wider. The muscles around her mouth twitch, as if she's attempting a smile. "If I'd have known you were coming, I would have changed."

"Oh. It's no big deal. Believe me, when you've seen my mom in the morning—" I force a laugh. "Um, Wil didn't tell you I was coming?" A few drops of coffee slide down one of the cups and I bite my hand. I lean in a little to hug Henney. I haven't seen her up close since the funeral. She stays perfectly still, and I'm left swaying back and forth in her doorway, an odd dance.

She shakes her head. "No. But—please." She opens the door a little wider. Not wide enough for me to move past her.

I hold up the bag. "I brought coffee. And cream and sugar. I don't know how you drink it."

"Isn't that sweet?" Henney mouth-smiles at me. That's the way I described it to my mother when I met Henney for the first time. Henney had chaperoned our fourth-grade trip to the aquarium, and by then I'd spent almost every afternoon for weeks in the shop with Wil. I expected her whole face to warm when she saw me. But she just mouth-smiled, her irises dim, the skin around her eyes smooth. She said, *Nice to finally meet you, honey,* and that was it.

"I just wanted to say that the service was really beautiful," I blurt, instantly making her eyes wet and red.

"You know, a lot of people have said so. Thanks. Thank you." She swallows and pulls the door open the rest of the way, guiding me into the tiled hallway. It's gray inside, and there are boxes stacked in the hallway. The air in here is old and sad.

"Bridge?" Wil appears where the hallway meets the kitchen and the breakfast room, wearing jeans and an old HINES T-shirt.

His hair is still wet from the shower. His eyes are red and glassy. Something twists inside me.

"Hey." I lift the coffee tray in a little wave, and he takes it from me and sets it on the kitchen table. "Is this still—do you still need help?" I choose my words carefully. I don't talk about our walk to the beach the other day or how Wil scrambled for the water faster than I'd ever seen him run. I don't mention our silent walk home or how he's avoided me at school for the last few days.

"Only if you want."

"Of course. Of course," I say stiffly.

Henney slides her arm over Wil's shoulder and squeezes hard. It feels like there are a million things being said between them, all in a foreign language I can't decode. *This is crazy*, I want to tell them. *I've slept in a tent in your backyard. I've puked up Halloween candy in your kitchen sink when Wilson couldn't carry me all the way to the bathroom. It's just me.*

"Anastasia's," Henney observes.

"Actually, Mr. Hines once told me that he brought you these doughnuts on your first date." My cheeks catch fire. Now that I've said it out loud, it seems all wrong, me bringing this box here. It's a personal, intimate detail that belongs only to them. I might as well have started rifling through her underwear drawer.

"We did have Anastasia's on our first date." Henney clears her throat. "Well. I've got to get ready for group. Good to see you, Bridget. Really." She pulls Wil in close, murmurs something I can't hear, something in their private grief code. His head dips and I think I hear, *"I won't,"* but it could be something else entirely.

"It's really good to see you, too." I dig my nails into the doughnut box, wishing I could fast-forward this and us. While I'm wishing, I wish I could rewind.

Henney disappears into her bedroom.

"Thanks for the coffee," Wil says, taking a few steps toward me. The smell of his boy soap tilts me. "Sorry if that was weird. She's still—it's hard."

"Yeah. Sure." I extend the doughnut box, but he motions for me to put the box on the table. "So what kind of group is your mom in?"

"Huh?" Wil pops the plastic top off one of the coffee cups and empties all the sugar packets inside.

"Group. She said she was going to group."

"It's nothing." He chugs half the cup and wipes toffee-colored film from his lips with the back of his hand. "This support group at the church where we had Dad's service."

"Your mom has never really seemed like the therapy type to me," I say carefully.

"Yeah, well. It's not therapy." His eyebrows jump.

"Okay."

"It's just getting together with other people whose family members have died unexpectedly. It helps her to be around people who get what she's going through." Wil turns away, toward the den, leaving me with the accusation.

"I didn't mean anything by it, Wil." I swallow.

He shakes his head like he's trying to erase the last few seconds from his brain. "I know. Sorry," he says, without turning around. "You want to get started?"

I grab a coffee and follow him into the wood-paneled den.

A weak desk lamp is the only light. I drift for a while, around boxes of clothes and boots and tangles of electronic cords that lead to cell phones and a laptop and a defunct GPS. Against the wall, there are columns of taped boxes stacked as high as my chest. There are stacks of books on sailing and woodwork. There's a caddy of soap and shampoo and there's a blue razor with a slightly rusted blade. There is a single box of pictures, some upside down and backward, some with smudged dates and names on the back. There is a whole life here.

"It's weird, right?" Wil's features are pinched. "I never thought he had much stuff until I tried to pack it all."

I nod but don't look at Wil because he won't want me to. I don't say Wilson's name. Instead, I busy my hands with the books piled on the floor, making the piles unnecessarily neat.

"Hey. This is kind of cool." I page through a coffee-table book about Atlantic Beach. There are pictures of the beachfront properties in the fifties and images of the old downtown. Its lines are almost exactly the same, but the font on the signs and the skirt lengths are different. And the bricks in the street aren't imprinted with peoples' names and the dates when their pets died or their kids graduated from high school. I look up. "I meant to tell you, I saw Kylie Mitchell's brick downtown the other day."

"Poor orange Kylie." Wil's voice lightens a little.

"Hey, remember DAN & NATALIA 4EVER?" I turn around and try again.

"Who could forget Atlantic Beach's very own computer software billionaire and his Russian mail-order bride? Although you'd think he'd be rich enough to spell *forever* the right way. Buy another brick, dude." He shoves his hands in his back pockets and cocks his head to one side, and for a second, he is the Wil I have always known.

"Dan, you cheap, wife-ordering bastard." I laugh loud enough that I snort, which makes Wil smile his lopsided grin. Without trying, I remember the way he used to smile in the split second before we would kiss. As if the two of us knew a joke no one in the world knew. The first time we slept together, he laughed as he was slipping my T-shirt over my head. Later he told me he'd laughed at the thought *I can't believe my best friend might actually sleep with me*, which made me feel a little better.

I miss him and it hurts to be this close to him and not closer.

"What would your brick say?" Wil asks.

I tilt my head. "What do you mean?"

"I mean, like, if you had a brick. And it could say whatever you wanted about your life so far and the kind of person you are. What would it say?" His face is suddenly blank, like it is when he's on the water, watching a storm on the horizon line or sawing a teak board; getting it just right.

I cross my ankles and sink to the floor. "My brick?" I ask, sipping my coffee to buy time. It's lukewarm and bitter. *"Bridget Christine Hawking. Florida transplant. Unapologetic redhead. Excellent at mandated community service and pissing off my younger sibling and—"*

"The *real you*, damn it," he snaps.

I suck a few drops of coffee into my lungs and double over, coughing. After I catch my breath, Wil rakes his hands through his hair and says, "Sorry, Bridge. It's just that I've been thinking about this a lot since my dad died."

"Yeah. Okay," I sputter. "Sure."

"You could list the facts about him, all the things people think of when they hear his name, and it wouldn't tell you a damn thing about the real Wilson Hines." His fingers curl around the edge of the couch cushion.

"Okay, not facts." I wish I knew what he meant about the real Wilson Hines. I wish I could ask. "So what would yours say? About the real Wil Hines?"

His head drops back, collides with the couch frame and makes a *thud*. "I'm nothing," he says. His eyes flutter closed, shutting me out. "I'm the guy whose dad is dead."

"That's not true," I protest.

"Hell it isn't," he says to the ceiling. "Tell me who I am now that he's gone."

I want to tell him that he is everything. That he has always been everything to me, and Wilson's death won't change that. "Wil," I say carefully. "You're more than that."

He shakes his head slowly. "You have no idea what that night did to me. Who I am now."

I tilt my head back, blink at the ceiling. It cuts me, every time he says something like that. "Have you talked to anybody about it? It might help, talking about what happened that night." I close my eyes. "You could talk to me. I'm here."

"Hasn't felt like it." Wil's voice cuts from across the room, and my eyes snap open again.

"What do you mean?"

"I mean, it hasn't felt like you've been here." Wil's features swim on the other side of the room. "Felt like you left me. Quit on us."

"I quit trying to get back together because you *asked* me to, Wil. That's not fair." I stand up.

The door to the bedrooms opens, and I swipe my eyes with my T-shirt as Henney comes into the den, her lipstick the brightest shade in the room, her keys jangling. She's wearing skinny jeans and a kind of dressy top and her hair is pulled back into a tight ponytail. She looks pretty, which is a thought I've never had before. She bends down to kiss Wil and then she's gone again, leaving us alone in this sad, angry room.

"You know, I'm here now," I say pointedly, picking up a pile of Wilson's old T-shirts on the floor next to the couch. I take my time smoothing the wrinkles. Making sure the sleeves are even.

He doesn't say anything.

"I'm here now," I say again, louder this time. "You say I haven't been there for you and that's fair, but I'm here now, so you don't have that excuse anymore. And you still won't talk to me, and you won't—God, Wil, would you at least open your eyes?"

He does, and the softness that was there has vanished beneath the surface.

"I'm trying." I slide the pile of T-shirts off the couch and I sit next to him. I reach for his arm. His skin is slick, clammy. "Talk to me. Tell me what's going on. Tell me what happened that night. I swear, once you get it off your chest—"

"Why would I talk to you?" Wil says quietly. He pulls away and scrambles off the couch. Pushes through the maze of Wilsons's things to get to the other side of the room. He leans against the wall, desperate to get as far away from me as possible. "It's too late, Bridge. I needed you then. I needed to talk to you. I needed to tell you some real shit, Bridge, shit I couldn't tell anybody else, and you were too drunk to hear it." His bright green eyes are mirrors.

"Wil," I whisper. "I know. I'm sorry. How many times can I tell you I'm sorry?" I claw at the couch. "Tell me now. Please."

"I can't." In the dim light, I see silvery trails branching down Wil's cheeks. I want to hold him, pull him into me, keep him there next to my heart for as long as it takes for him to forgive me. I'll wait with him forever. I need him, and I know he needs me. "It's too late."

"Stop. Stop saying that. Please."

"It's true, though. It's too late for you to show up and talk about being there for me. You think I need you to be there now more than ever, but you don't get to pick when to show up!"

"I'm not—"

"The fuck you're not! You're here because my dad is dead, right? You're here because of him! Not because of me." His chest is caving, rising. "I wanted you to be there for *me*, Bridge. When *I* needed you. And you bailed and there's nothing you can do to change that." He spins around and slams his fist into the wall. I cringe at the crunch of bone.

"Fuck!" he yells. Adrenaline lights me on fire. "Fuck!"

"Wil!" I scream. "Stop it! Stop!"

"Get out, Bridge. Get out," he tells the wall.

I lift my hands in surrender. "You're right. You're right, okay?" I push myself off the couch and watch him crumple into the wall. "I'm sorry. You're right. I'll go. Just—stop. Please." I take shallow breaths as I back out of the den and run down the hall toward the gold-edged clouds. I can't believe I'm leaving him again. Running, just like I've done before. But everything about him is telling me . . . he wants me gone. And everything in me believes him.

# WIL

*Summer, Junior Year*

I was starting to believe that he had come back. My dad, my real dad, the guy who used to make things with his hands instead of destroying people with them. The original simple kind of man. He bought so many goddamned flowers that I think the Publix flower fridge was running on empty for almost a week. And he touched my mother, but in a good way. In a way that makes a person groan, *"Get a room, guys,"* and look away, even though he's secretly happy. In a way that makes it all right for a person's new possibly girlfriend to come over to the house once in a while.

I was starting to believe things were going back to normal. But six nights ago something happened. It was small, it was nothing, but I knew immediately: It was something. They started arguing, slowly at first. Mom was pissed at Dad for leaving the garbage cans on the curb overnight, saying it made us look like white trash. Dad heard her say words that never left her mouth—that he was white trash and she was sorry she ever married him. Their voices got louder and louder and made my insides shake and the water glasses in the cabinet rattle, so I went to the workshop.

He left.

He didn't hit her. He peeled out of the driveway in his truck.

And I thought, *That's pretty good, actually. At least he didn't do it again.*

He didn't come home for four hours. At the four-hour mark, a guy named Pete from a bar called Big Mike's called Mom to come and get him. He was too drunk to stay and too drunk to leave. I pretended to be asleep when they got home, even though he made the air inside the house smell like a rich kid's high-school party. The next morning at breakfast, the only thing my mother said was, *"If you boys want cereal, you'll have to get it yourself. I'm late for work."*

They didn't fight for a few days in a row after that. But he went to Big Mike's every night anyway, because that was something he did now. The house smelled like stale booze when he got home. It is exhausting to stay awake and listen for violence, and one night I must have fallen asleep because at breakfast the next morning there was another bruise. She tried to cover it with makeup and curly hair and pancakes, but I could see. I could see her and could see that the dad I wanted wasn't coming back.

I want to tell Bridge. I keep hoping she'll try, just one more time, even though I told her to stop. Another note or text or voice mail. All I need is one more. So far, nothing.

Tonight, I'm in the shop cleaning Dad's tools, pretending

there's work to be done. Sometimes, just to get out of the house, I'll bring a magazine out here. Or if I'm really desperate, I'll bring one of the poetry books Ana keeps shoving in my backpack. Apparently, I only *think* I hate poetry.

I'm winding one of the extension cords in a coil that's tighter than it needs to be when I hear her.

"Hey. Your mom said you'd be in here."

Ana is standing in the doorway, leaning against the frame in cutoffs and a white T-shirt and a lacy white bra that looks good against her tanned skin.

"Hey." I smooth my T-shirt and run my hands through my hair like that's going to fix anything.

"Hey. What's going on?" I'm not sure if I'm supposed to hug Ana or kiss her. Ana and I have hung out a bunch of times since the night we got drunk, but I don't know what we are yet.

She shrugs and looks down at the floor and kind of smiles. Ana has this way of making you feel like she's got a secret, and you're dying to know it.

"Just thought I'd come by," she says. "There's a party later. We should go."

"You hate high-school parties." I rest the coiled cord on the table. "Or is this some kind of practice for a blowout senior year?"

"Actually, yeah." She laughs and walks toward me, almost in slow motion. She gets really close, touching me without touching me. I never knew the smell of suntan lotion could turn me on. "Next year, I'm getting crazy. I'm calling senior year the *Year of Woooo!*" She scrunches her nose and cheers with an invisible glass. "I've always been an overachiever, so I figured I'd get started early."

97

"You're kind of cute when you *woooo*," I tell her. I guide her over to the worktable and press her back into it.

"You think so?" she says, draping her arms around my neck.

"I do." My voice is low.

"Take me to this party, then." Her eyelashes brush my neck.

"Where's it at?"

"Okay. Don't freak out, but it's at Buck Travers's place."

It takes all the willpower in the universe not to put a hole through the worktable.

"That's not funny," I snap, and back away.

"Hear me out."

"I'm not going anywhere that asshole's going to be."

"Wil."

"What are you, crazy?"

"Wil!" Her voice bounces from the ceiling beams, louder than I've ever heard it. "Don't you want to show that asshole that you've moved on? Don't you want to show—everybody?"

All of a sudden, I'm woozy, a strange combination of pissed and sad and still a little turned on, and I don't know what to do with any of it.

"I don't really care about . . . other people," I say.

Ana's eyes don't believe me.

"You have to live your life," she says. "We can't decide not to go out just because we might run into Buck or—"

"Here. Come here." I reach for her and pull her into my chest. Breathe her in. "You really want to go?"

"I'm just saying," she murmurs.

I close my eyes and I see Christmas lights hanging from the shop's rafters. I open my eyes, but it doesn't matter. Bridge lives in everything: in this concrete floor, in the bricks downtown, in our booth at Nina's Diner, in the waves. There's no way to erase her. The only thing I can do is let her fade.

"We'll go," I say into Ana's hair. "We'll have fun."

We take Dad's truck and I tell Ana that she looks good in a pickup. She tells me she loves how *retro* the truck is, which makes me smile because my asshole dad bought it new.

"Do you know how to get there?" she asks, propping her bare feet on the dash just like Bridge used to do.

"Not this house. Give me directions?" Growing up, Buck lived down the street from me. One morning, in the summer between eighth and ninth grade, Buck's mom got bitten by a plastic surgeon's German shepherd. Now the Travers family lives in one of the rich gated communities off Atlantic. It's hard to tell the houses apart, so you have to go by the cars in the driveway. Travers drives this year's F-450, probably the most expensive truck a lawsuit can buy.

Ana slides her hand over the console and rests her palm on my thigh. I think about saying *screw it* and taking her to the beach.

"Down this way," she says without hesitation, and I wonder if every girl I know has fooled around with Buck Travers. But when I look over, I see the glow of her iPhone and realize she's just looking up directions.

I turn where she tells me to, and soon we're coasting down a street lined with parked cars and pickup trucks.

"If you want to leave, we'll leave, okay?" Ana fixes her gaze on the house.

"Thanks." I smile and put my hand over hers.

We park as close as we can get to the house and walk. The party is every high-school party: loud music with a bass so deep it rattles you, a couple of guys puking their guts out in the shrubs, too-sweet air. The front door is wide open, so we just walk in. The place is enormous, and everything is white: the walls, the couches—even the painting over the fireplace is white canvas, which is probably supposed to mean something.

"This place is huge," I yell over the music, accidentally kicking a red Solo cup under a round entry table.

"Huh?" Ana shouts.

"Huge!"

Ana smiles and nods back.

"Ohmygod, you guys came!" Emilie Simpson bellows, looking up from a game of flip cup on the coffee table.

"Give me just a second," Ana yells as she waves at her friend. "I'm gonna go say hi."

"Sure."

I push my way through the house by way of the kitchen, waving and nodding when people call my name, grateful for the loud music. If it was quiet, I wouldn't know what to say. There's a patio out back that looks over a lake, and there are a few tiki torches stabbed into the grass. Three or four kegs litter the yard, and a girl is doing a keg stand in a jean miniskirt. I look for Bridge because I can't help it.

She's just across the patio, only a few bodies between us, hanging on Leigh. My eyes adjust to the low light and I watch her. Her body's not her body, and she looks like she's learning to walk for the first time: these jerky, unsure baby-deer movements. I've never seen Bridge this drunk. The sky must be spinning for her.

"I got it, I got it," she slurs. She pushes Leigh away and tries to stand on her own. Her eyes roam the yard, sweeping past me and then returning.

"WilohmygodWil." She takes a step forward and trips, falling to her knees in the grass. I'm on my knees next to her without even thinking about it.

"Don't!" The word bursts out of her. "Don't. I'm okay."

My heart is going to explode. I want to get her out of here: take her home and tuck her in.

"I got her." Leigh kneels next to us and pulls Bridge into her lap. Bridge's skirt sneaks up her thigh. I look away.

"I'll carry her to the car or something," I tell Leigh. "Are you driving her home?"

"Later. She needs to lie down for a while."

"*You* needa lie down for a while." Bridge's eyelids flutter.

"Here." I scoop her up and stand, holding her head against my chest while her knees flop over the cradle of my elbow. *This is why!* I want to scream. *This is why I wanted to hang out in the workshop, with the goddamned lights!*

I carry her back into the house and up the carpeted stairs, Leigh trailing behind me. And I know people are watching us, but I absolutely do not give a fuck.

Bridge fights me the whole way, pushing against my chest, telling me to leave her, leave her, she's fine without me. I clench my jaw so tightly, my skull could shatter at any second. Leigh scopes out the bedrooms and finds one decorated in too much pink. Definitely not Buck's room.

In the dark, I lower Bridge onto a single-sized bed with lace pillowcases and teddy bears piled at the headboard. I brush her hair away from her face while Leigh brings a trash can from the bathroom.

"*Commere,*" Bridge orders, and slings her arms around my neck. She pulls me in with a strange kind of drunk-girl strength. "I'm so sorry, Wil. I fucked up and I'm so sorry and I *fucked up.*"

I pull away.

"Don't leave her," I tell Leigh roughly. "Do not leave her up here by herself. Got it?"

She nods. "Got it."

I close the door behind me and take the stairs three or four at a time, flying back into the blur that is the party I never wanted to go to in the first place. I almost knock Ana over on the last step.

"*Ooh!* There you are." She holds onto me for balance and doesn't let go. "What're you doing up—"

"We have to go," I tell her.

"You okay? You're sweaty." She slides her hands over my damp T-shirt.

"Yeah. I'm good. I just need to get out of here. Want to get something to eat? Nina's or something?"

She smiles. "Nina's? Yeah, I guess."

"Or wherever you want. Just . . . anywhere but here."

"Okay." She slips her hand into mine, which is humiliating because mine is drenched with sweat. Still, she doesn't pull away. I hate leaving Bridge here because she's not okay. She is so obviously not okay. But I can't help her. I can't save her from drowning under a spinning sky.

# BRIDGE

*Spring, Senior Year*

"LEIGH," I say into the phone. I'm a thousand shards, a useless broken pile on the sidewalk in front of Nina's Diner. The sun is close, the air salty and thick even though it's only April. "Leigh."

Inside, Leonard waves.

"Oh, honey. I hear a blocked heart chakra."

"He *hates* me." My face is swollen and hot, but I can't cry. Crying would feel too good. I pace the bricks, trying not to see KYLIE MITCHELL or DAN & NATALIA. I walk from Nina's to the Surf Shop to Big Mike's bar and back again. People pass with their coffee and dogs and kids and they know the kind of person I am, somehow. "We had a fight and it's so obvious—he hates me, still."

"He's hurting," she says simply, and I remember the millions of reasons I love her, all at the same time. She doesn't ask what happened or what I said or what he said back. She doesn't need the details. She knows they don't matter.

"Yeah," I whisper. I stop in front of Big Mike's. Somebody posted a flyer for a Bob Marley cover band on the door. The neon beer signs on the window bleed red and blue. "I could really use a drink."

"Nope," she says. "We have other plans. Don't move."

I hang up and plant myself outside the door to the bar. If I really needed to, I could get inside in two seconds. It's dark in there. I could probably order a beer and get away with it.

I ran into Wilson in this exact spot, a little more than a year ago. Not in the bar. Outside of it. The sky was bruised a deep purple. Wilson's face looked cartoonish under the neon beer signs. I saw him before he saw me.

"Wilson?"

"Mackinac!" he said, but the word tripped over itself to get to me and it sounded all wrong and we both laughed. "What're you doing here?" He squinted into the streetlight above us.

"Takeout from Nina's. Mom's working late."

"Huh." He bobbed his head. "You coming around anytime soon? Got a new client. Start the work next week."

"I would, it's just—" I didn't know how to finish the sentence. *It's just that I ruined us? It's just that booze makes me stupid? It's just that I'm tired of Wil not wanting us back as much as I do?* "How's he doing?" I didn't mean to ask.

Wilson exhaled and leaned against the door to the bar. "Studying for some test at . . . a friend's place."

The way he said it told me almost everything I needed to know. "Oh."

"You know, Bridge, we're not the things we do." Wilson's voice sounded heavy enough to sink him. "We're not our mistakes. We're more than that."

"Tell that to your son."

"Believe me." He cleared his throat.

I waited for him to finish, but he didn't. He looked too tired to say anything else, old under the dirty yellow pools of light.

"Well," I said. "My order is probably getting cold. Where were you headed?"

"Nina's, too." He forced a smile. His skin was chalky, reminding me of one of Leigh's pastel sketches. He looked like he could be erased with a single stroke. He followed me into the diner and waited with me at the counter while Leonard tossed extra ketchup into the plastic takeout bags. There weren't any bags waiting for Wilson. I didn't mention it.

"Oh, good. You're not bombed yet." Leigh is standing next to me, smelling like coconut oil and a little like the incense place around the corner. "Drink." She hands me a Big Gulp Slurpee with a neon-pink straw.

I take a long sip.

"Here's the plan." She presses her hand into the small of my back and marches me toward Iz, who is idling lazily in the middle of the street. "We're going to school."

"On a Saturday? Leigh—"

"*We're going to school*, and you're gonna help me with the first step of my senior art project, which has to be done by Monday. Call it free therapy. And you're gonna tell me what happened or you aren't." She jerks open Iz's passenger side door. "After you, m'lady."

105

"I guess you decided not to paint the overpass." I settle in and Iz's beaded seat cover pinches my thighs.

"Nah. You were right." She leans in the doorway and glances over the top of her mirrored sunglasses. "Principal okayed the school project, and I decided I don't want to end up in juvie yet." She slams the door.

"Yet?" I pull down the visor. My warped reflection is pale and sweaty in the cracked mirror, a pathetic Picasso.

Leigh coaxes Iz toward school. Wil is in the all details of this town: in the palm tree he climbed on a dare in sixth grade, and in the beach access parking lot where his dad caught us making out sophomore year. I close my eyes, but he's there, too. He's everywhere but here.

"There's something he's not telling me." I wipe a thin layer of sweat from my forehead with my open palm. Another layer surfaces.

"Any idea what it is?" She jumps right in. I like that I can start in the middle with Leigh and work my way out to the frayed edges.

I shake my head. "He just kept saying that there were things he wanted to talk to me about—big things—but he couldn't."

"Because you guys weren't talking then?" she asks.

"I guess."

"So that's what he's pissed about. Not the B-word." She raps an offbeat rhythm on the steering wheel, then whips into the school parking lot at the last second, like it's an afterthought. The lot is empty, except for a father running behind a daughter on a bike. Leigh runs Iz onto the curb in front of the school and kills the engine.

I roll my eyes. "You can say it. Buck." I taste warm Slurpee syrup.

"I choose not to." She gives Iz's console a pat and tells me to grab whatever I can carry from the backseat. I lug a bucket and broom and a bunch of scrub brushes, and she brings dish soap and a paint roller and a couple of paint cans. "Courtyard."

When we get there, I collapse onto one of the benches and Leigh sits next to me. She holds my hand, pressing her fingers between my fingers. A fat tear runs down my cheek and I miss her like hell even though she's not gone yet. I look at the sky, at the shattered white cloud glass littering the blue.

"He asked me to stop, last year. He asked me to leave him alone, to stop apologizing. So I did," I say, resting my head on Leigh's bony shoulder.

"I remember."

"And he's so . . . *angry*, you know, that I did. When really, I thought I was doing what he wanted. I thought if I did what he was asking me to do, maybe it would give us a shot later on, you know? Because I'd listened and given him space."

Leigh rests her head on my head. "Space blows."

"And this time he asked me to go again, and I left again. But this time felt different."

"How?"

"If I didn't leave—" I stop, not sure how to finish the sentence. I don't know what would have happened. He could have hurt himself, could have destroyed the wall or his dad's treasures.

"If you didn't leave, what?" Leigh looks at me expectantly.

I shrug. "I don't know."

"Please. You know Wil Hines better than you know yourself."

"The thing is, I don't. Not anymore." I wriggle away from her. "Ever since—I can't read him like I used to. He's all—I don't know. Cloudy."

"You'll figure it out. Keep shaking that eight ball."

But I'm not sure. I know this: Sadness can make a person strange, unknowable. When Micah's dad left our mother, he broke her, literally—her skin split into rays around the eyes from all the crying, her shoulders knotted. Her brain emptied itself of important details, like how Micah's dad was kind of an asshole who only had a job sometimes and didn't like any of us very much.

I didn't blame her. She was only twenty-four and she was alone again. She was sad and angry, and she felt sorry for herself and for us. Two kids, two dads, and she couldn't seem to pick a good one. Sometimes I'd hear her say under her breath, when she thought no one was listening, *What's wrong with me?* and it felt like my insides had just been ripped out.

Back then, I had this recurring dream: Adult Me in a white coat, surgically removing her grief. It was a shiny black blob that tried to sneak its way back into her again and again, but I was ruthless. I wish I could do that for Wil.

After a long moment, Leigh stands up and stretches. "We interrupt this depressing-as-hell programming to bring you backbreaking labor in the name of graduation credits." She hands me the broom and tells me to sweep. While I drag dead leaves and cigarette butts to the edges of the concrete slab, she pulls the blow-up pool into the grass. It takes both of us to move the stone benches. Leigh fills the bucket with water from a spigot on the back side of the building while I target the spray with my dish soap. We dip the scrub brushes into the bucket and the colors swirl in the soapy water: mauves and yellows and turquoise, the color of Wil's eyes.

"Just scrub the slab down first." Leigh rolls up the sleeves on her T-shirt. "We'll prime it after it dries and I'll start painting tomorrow. You can come, too, if it'll keep you out of dive bars."

We kneel next to each other and she sloshes water on the pavement. I scrub as hard as I can, as angry as I can, as sad as I can.

"I think this might be it." My muscles sting, and I scrub harder. "For us. Between us."

"Okay." Leigh stops scrubbing and pushes her dreads out of her eyes. "So what if this is it?"

"What do you mean?" I sit back on my heels. Hearing her say it is ten times worse than saying it myself.

"I mean, what if this is really it between you and Wil? What if this is the end of your story? What if you were only supposed to come into each other's lives for a certain period of time?"

"Bullshit." My voice cracks. "If we were supposed to come into each other's lives for some big karmic reason, *this* would be that reason. This time, right now. He needs someone *now*, someone to help him pack up his father's . . . books . . . and spare change . . ." I swallow a sob. "And someone to help him take care of his mom. He needs—"

"You," Leigh says.

"Me." I breathe. "I love him." My lips form the words silently, again and again, a pleading prayer to the water and sky. "I've tried not to, but it's fucking useless." I wait for the pinch of surprise. It doesn't come. I have always loved Wil Hines and I always will, and it's no surprise to anybody.

"Of course it is." Leigh sighs and falls back on the shiny, wet concrete. I lie down next to her, and the warm water soaks the back of my T-shirt and gives me goose bumps. "Completely fucking useless. Are you saying you want to be friends again? Or you want to get back together?"

"I don't know," I say, even though I do. "He has a girlfriend. A nice one."

"Fact."

"What am I supposed to do?" I stare at the sun until my field of vision is nothing but gold.

She rolls onto her side. "You can love him from far away."

"I don't want to," I say.

She sighs. "You might have to, though."

And she's right. I know she's right. But I know this, too: I know that Wil and I are bigger than one night on a dock. I know that we're more than a few damn good years. We go longer, farther, deeper. We are not finished yet. We can't be.

# BRIDGE

*Spring, Senior Year*

I don't fall asleep that night until the sun peeks over the water. I dream about Wil, swimming out far past the breakers, and me behind him, screaming his name, begging him to come back. But he keeps swimming, until he's nothing more than a dot or a piece of driftwood or a lost seagull.

When my eyes snap open, the house is quiet. My skin is damp. The room is hot and the sun is too low. I check the clock. Sunday, almost four P.M.

"Oh my God." I sit up and press my feet into the ground. "Mom? Micah?"

Silence.

Downstairs, the light on the coffee maker is still green. I've told Mom a million times she's going to burn the house down one of these days. I pour myself a cup.

I take my coffee to the front stoop and watch barefoot middle-school girls in triangle bikini tops and cutoffs racing up and down the streets on their bikes. They leave the air smelling like strawberry gum and temporary tattoos.

On instinct, I reach for my phone. Nothing from Wil: no apology texts, no calls.

"Hey. Sleeping Beauty!"

Leigh is leaning over the front gate in a black bikini and a gauzy long caftan. Her dreads swing just above her shoulders, and she's wearing purple hippie shades and carrying a giant straw tote. She looks smiley and a little high.

"I just woke up," I admit, raising my coffee mug.

"I can tell." She fiddles with the gate until it springs open. "My mom made me play singles with her this morning. She got an eight A.M. court at the club. Apparently, it was an important opportunity for us to spend quality time together before I abandon my family for the completely inaccessible and faraway land of *Georgia*." She settles next to me on the stoop. "And I got the courtyard primed after lunch, no thanks to you."

I rub my temples. "Sorry. What are you up to tonight?"

"You mean, what are *we* up to? We're going out. This is the obligatory forget-that-man blowout."

I consider arguing and decide against it. I need this, and Leigh knows I need this. Anything to take my mind off Wil. Anything to get out of my head.

"Should I even ask where we're going?" I sip the last of my coffee.

"Bonfi—"

"Nope." I shake my head. "Nothing school related."

"You don't have to drink, but you have to go," she says firmly.

"Wil Hines is having a rough time right now. And we feel for him, but we are not going to stop living our lives."

"Aren't we?" I groan. The space between my sheets beckons.

Her eyes glint like slick river stones. "Get moving."

I shower and shave my legs while Leigh picks out suitable bonfire attire: my good cutoffs, my pink bandeau bikini top, and a black tank top she finds in Mom's closet. I let my hair air-dry and I leave Mom a note that I'm going out.

Leigh and I cross the street to get to the beach access. One of the preteens almost mows Leigh down on her bike, and Leigh yells, "Watch it, Miley!" and the girl curses her out. Up close, the girls don't smell like strawberries and summer. They smell like used cigarettes and older boys. I fire *Your dude's not worth it* thoughts in their direction, but they're too far gone. The thoughts skitter on the asphalt and disappear.

It's prime beach time. We wind our way around surf-seeking dogs and little kids building sand castles and a lot of ugly tattoos. The water is flat and velvet, a faded royal blue. Above it, a faint moon is rising in the afternoon sky. My nerves bubble as we walk. I don't know how to be sober at a bonfire. What if I need something to blur the edges, to melt me just enough? What if Wil shows? What if Ana—or Buck—

I grip Leigh's arm and shake my head.

"I don't think I can do this."

"You can. And if you decide you want to leave, just give me the signal, and we'll leave."

"What's the signal?" My mouth tastes like gritty sand.

"How about 'Get me the fuck out of here'?"

"Hilarious."

The bonfire is at the beachfront house of a senior girl named Loren. Her parents are out of town on business. The house is small, and set far off the beach. It's a tiny tiled bungalow with sandy floors and fake leather couches shoved up against white walls. The galley kitchen is pockmarked beneath fluorescent lighting: scratched countertops, nicked cabinets. The place is run-down but comfortable, and reminds me of home. Someone puts the Allman Brothers on the stereo, a fighting song. I nod at a girl pouring vodka into a coffee mug that says WORLD'S OKAYEST DAD.

"I don't suppose you want a beer?" Leigh asks.

"Nah." I follow her outside. There are fire pits scattered throughout the ratty yard. One of the blazes spotlights Ned Reilly, who was informally voted Most Likely to Die a Virgin junior year. Ned's chatting up Susan, a cute brunette girl from my freshman-year math. She's laughing loudly and leaning in close. She spent a lot of time on her eye makeup, and it looks good. Despite his too-large teeth and plaid short-sleeved button-down, it looks like Ned has a legitimate shot at discarding that superlative tonight.

"Be back." Leigh makes a beeline for the keg, and adrenaline overtakes me. *Calm down*, I tell myself. *It's just a party.*

"Bridge! Hey!" Ned waves me over, and Susan sizes me up and looks unsure. She gives me a too-bright smile.

"Hey, guys. What's going on?" I make sure not to stand too close to Ned and I give Susan a halting hug, which is weird since we don't know each other.

"Haven't seen you out much this year," Ned says. "I saw your brother a while back. A couple of bonfires ago."

"I heard." I groan. "If I can make it through the rest of this year without killing him, we'll consider it a success."

"What are you doing next year?" Susan changes the subject, and I like her.

"I'm going to FIU." I stuff my hands into my pockets. "Miami. Assuming I don't get arrested again."

"I have a friend who goes there actually, and he loves it, so good for you. I guess they don't care if you get arrested, which is awesome. So." Ned's face turns the color of a late-August burn.

"Hey, Ned?" Susan makes her smoky eyes big. "Why don't you get Bridge a drink?"

"Yes. Yes." Ned looks relieved. "Beer? You like beer, right?"

"You've heard, huh?" I raise my eyebrows.

"No! No. Definitely not."

I mercy-interrupt. "How about a Coke, Ned?"

"You got it." Ned zooms across the patio and into the kitchen.

"Oh my *God!*" Susan shakes her head. "I swear, the part of his brain that controls social interactions needs a reboot or something! Like, I picture these frayed wires, just lying around, sparking, connected to nothing."

I laugh. "But he's so sweet. Are you guys—"

"He is, right?" She looks past me and smiles a little. "Kind of. I don't know."

I hear Ana's laugh, followed instantly by Thea's. My stomach dips.

Leigh slides up next to me and gives Susan a nod. "Our democratically chosen leadership has decided to grace us with her presence."

*"Democratically chosen."* Susan snorts. "Do you ever just look

around while you're at school and think *I am living in high-school parody hell and I'm the only one who knows it?*"

"Yes!" Leigh says. "Isn't it so depressing? But you know what helps?"

"Knowing we're almost out of here?" Susan kills the rest of her beer.

"Weed."

"*Aaand* one Coke. Straight up. Virgin. Or whatever." Ned chokes a little on the word *virgin*.

"*Ned.*" Susan sighs.

We decide to head out to the beach. I finish my Coke, and I'm a pleasant combination of loose and awake. In the sand, Leigh plays with my hair. Susan tells us about the gap year she's taking before she applies to college. It's a tradition in her family, taking a year to do community service in Costa Rica.

"The truth is, I don't know what I want to do," she says. "Maybe that makes me kind of uninteresting or unmotivated."

"I think you're interesting," Ned says sweetly. He puts his hand on Susan's knee and she lets him. "And smart."

"I wouldn't care if it was just me, like in a vacuum. I'm only eighteen, right? Who knows what they want at eighteen?" She wiggles her toes in the sand. "But in comparison, when everybody else seems to have the grand life plan laid out, it's like *shit*. I'm behind in this huge race I didn't even know I was running."

We nod, all of us. We are tired, depleted, and we haven't even started yet.

Leigh goes for another round of beers and another Coke for me, disappearing into the party swell behind us. It's getting dark. Susan leans into Ned until they're one shadow. I could lose myself here, with these familiar people I don't actually know at all. Maybe it's just nostalgia, but I suddenly feel a wash of regret. Disappointment that I didn't get to know the Susans and Neds of the high-school universe when I had the chance. I've spent high school bombed with Leigh or wrapped up in Wil.

"Here we go," Leigh announces. She sinks to her knees in the sand and distributes the cups.

I chug my Coke and drop back into the sand and watch the sky, the sweet liquid sloshing around in my stomach. I slide my fingers and my toes under the cool grains and watch the dark navy shift overhead. Leigh lies next to me.

"Don't freak out," she whispers. "But I have to tell you something."

"*Hm?*"

"In a few seconds, please remember that I didn't want to tell you, because we're having such a great time and all. But I figure you'd want to know."

I sit up. Sand slides into my bra. "*Leigh.*"

"Okay, okay." She looks at the sand. "Wil's here with Ana."

Sweetness rises in the back of my throat. I jump up. It's too dark to see, but I would know Wil's lines anywhere. He's leaning next to Ana, sipping a beer. She slides her arm around his neck. I look away.

"They *are* together," Leigh says softly.

"I'd kill for a beer," I tell her without shifting my gaze. "Two, while you're up there."

"Bridge," she pleads. "We should go. I don't think a drink is a good idea."

"I'm not leaving," I say fiercely. "I have just as much of a right to be here as they do."

117

"Okay. Okay." Her eyes shift from Ned to Susan, which is unnecessary.

"He's fine when he's with her," I whimper. "He just can't be around me without losing it."

"Am I missing something?" Ned asks.

"You're not missing anything. I'm just toxic. I'm like this toxic, terrible person that people can't stand being around." My eyes sting.

"Bridge. My darling. Love of my life. Let's go home," Leigh suggests. "It's like my mom always said: Nothing good ever happens after"—she checks her cell—"9:27."

"Fine." I can't tear my eyes away from him. Them. Wil sees me, too. There are history magnets in us, and that's why we always find each other. Wil raises his hand like *can you come here a second?* and I look away. Leigh leans close to my ear.

"Talk it out," she says. "It'll kill you if you don't. I'll catch up with you later." She disappears into the crowd.

I find his eyes and he's still watching me. *Come on*, I tell him silently. His head dips, like he understands. I wander through the house and into the front yard where it's quiet, finally, and I can wait for him. The grass feels good under my feet.

"Hey," he says behind me. I don't turn around.

"Hey." It's killing me that we are the kind of people who just say, *"Hey."* Strangers say, *"Hey."* Not us.

"We should talk," he tells me.

"It's not fair, what you're doing," I say.

"What *I'm* doing?" I hear him behind me, feel his hands on me, warm and rough. He spins me around, gently, and we're so close. This feels right, him and me, the two of us, and he doesn't see it.

"Yes!" I shove him, hard. "What *you're doing*. Pushing me away again and again. Not letting me be there for you. Not being there for *me*! I lost someone when your dad died, too. Whether you want to think that's important or not." I clench my jaw hard enough that my head starts to spin. "I loved him, too. I miss him, too. I think about him and about you all the time."

"That's the thing, Bridge." Color creeps into Wil's face. "You think you loved him. You can think you love a person and it turns out"—he bends over and spits in the grass—"it turns out you didn't know them at all."

"Don't say that to me ever again, Wil. I'm sick of hearing it." I start down the street. "I'm going home." Heat from the asphalt rises. The air smells like beach tar. I think I'm walking toward the water, but all the houses look the same. Wil would know. He's like a human compass who can always find water.

"Hey. Hey." He runs after me and matches my stride. "I'm saying it because it's true. You don't know him. You don't. And I didn't, either." His voice splits like warped wood.

"What are you talking about, Wil?" I stop. I peer into him, try to read the jumbled colors in his eyes and the pulse throbbing beneath his jaw.

"Nothing. I'll walk you home."

"No. Tell me. I'm not going anywhere until you—"

He wrenches away from me. "He hit my mom, okay?" The words explode out of him; rocket into the sky like fireworks. "He was a drunk asshole, and he beat my mother."

Everything stops.

*No. He's lying.*

*Not Wilson.*

*Not*—I close my eyes and claw at the memory of the Wilson I knew. The man who served apple wedges and peanut butter with calloused hands. The man with yellow tulips and Anastasia's doughnuts. Wil is telling me that all these memories are a lie. Everything I knew about Wilson was a lie.

"Wil. Don't," I beg. Hot tears pool behind my lids. It's not fair, what I'm asking. I close my eyes and I picture Wilson, just behind the clouds. I reach for him, for the person I thought he was. "Please don't say that. He couldn't."

"He fucking did. He hit . . . my mom . . . and sometimes I wake up and my very first thought is *I'm glad he's dead.*" A bitter laugh escapes him. "Can you believe that? Can you—" His face shatters into a million shards and then he's crying. And I know it's true. It's been true for I don't know how long, and I wasn't there. It was true when I saw him at Publix, holding tulips. It was true when he held the door open for me at Nina's. Maybe it's been true forever.

The Wilson I knew slips away, just like that. I should have been there. I should have kept Wil close to me, and I failed.

"Wil," I murmur. "I'm sorry. I'm so sorry."

"It's not your fault. It was his." Wil lists forward, a vessel seeking shelter, and I pull him into me. I erase all the space between us. I despise the skin and bones keeping us so far apart. I hug him tight and close. I stroke his wet cheeks.

"I should've told you," he whispers, just loud enough. "I needed you."

I hold him tighter. "You're telling me now. And I'm here now. You've got me."

# WIL

*Summer, Junior Year*

IT'S the dead of August, and I've started running. Early in the mornings, before either of my parents are up. I need to sweat out the acid anger that's bubbling up in my blood. And I can't stand being in my house anymore. My dad has two speeds now: silent and screaming. It's one or the other, one after the other, and no matter which speed he's on, I'm always wishing for him to flip the switch.

My dad has split my mother in half. She's two different people now: Outside Mom and Inside Mom. Outside Mom wears her bright lipsticks and covers her bruises with paint the color of a happy woman. Outside Mom tells strangers in the grocery store that her anniversary is coming up: twenty-five years, and she smiles with a closed mouth like she's hiding the secrets to a happy marriage behind her lips. Outside Mom joined a book club with Mrs. Wilkerson, who lives three doors down. She comes home smelling like white wine. Inside Mom is a deflated balloon. Inside Mom has stopped yelling or arguing or caring about anything. She wanders around the house, not looking at me.

This morning, I'm on the beach early. I'm alone with the water, which is exactly how I like it. I pop my earbuds in and turn the volume on my iPhone as loud as I can take it. I don't recognize the band or the song, but I don't need to. What I need is noise, a noise other than my father screaming at my mother, or the sound of something breaking. I break into a run, following the silver line at the water's edge. The sun worms its way higher in the sky. It's not long before my body is humming.

It's not just anger at my dad that's built up in me, if I'm honest. It's fear. I've always believed that the Real Me and the Real Him were the same. We were beach rats, with sand and salt in our veins. We didn't care about college or better lives or Other People the way my mom did. We cared about real things: varnish and sawdust and a hard day's work.

*Maybe we are the same*, I think as I push harder, sweat stinging my eyes. It's humid, but there's a breeze, and I lift my face toward the sky. *I'll bet I'm just as angry as he is.* I destroyed his boat in the workshop a few months ago. What if I have it in me to hurt people, too? It would make sense. I'm partly him. We have the same hair and eyes. I'm not exactly sure how it works, science-wise, but maybe we have the same anger, coded in our DNA. If that's true, I won't ever escape it. No matter how fast I run.

When I get home, I stand at the back door, my ear pressed against it. Sweat slides into my eyes and down my temples and pools in my ears. My heart is still pounding in my chest.

"He's not here," Mom calls from the breakfast room.

"Good." I find her sitting at the kitchen table, sipping tea that smells too strong. She's still in her bathrobe, even though it's almost eleven. Her hair is messy and she's wearing the shadow of yesterday's makeup. In front of her are all these photographs, hard copies. I'm small in all of them. Dad and me in the ocean. Dad and me in the workshop. Dad and me. It occurs to me that Mom has lived her whole life watching us. Apart from us.

"Where is he?" I pull out the chair next to hers and relax into it. I take my first real breath. Minutes without my father are like deep breaths of ocean air.

"I don't know where he went. I woke up, and . . ." Her voice trails off. She sips her tea.

"Hey." I rest one of my hands on top of one of her hands. It isn't something we do, really, but suddenly I want to slide my arms around her and hug her tightly enough that she becomes a whole person again.

She snaps when I touch her. "What, Wil?"

"Nothing, Mom." I make my voice like air. "Nothing. I'm sorry." I want to ask her the same question I asked her right after it happened the first time, the question she never answered. *Do you think I'm like him? Do you think we're the same?* I don't need to ask. She answers me every time she jumps at the sound of my voice.

"I'm sorry, hon. I'm just—I don't know what I am anymore." She releases a sigh that's been building up for years. Her voice is watery.

"Don't say that."

"It's true." She touches the pictures longingly; traces my little boy face with her fingers.

"Mom. You're . . . you're my mom," I say earnestly, but it comes out sounding thin.

"Did I ever tell you I thought about college and dental school?" She smiles a little, and the skin around her eyes crinkles like tissue paper.

"What, like, you were gonna be a dentist?" I say, surprised.

For the first time in weeks, she's looking directly at me. "I don't know. Maybe it was stupid." Her face goes slack again.

"No. Mom. No. That's what you wanted to do?" I ask.

"I thought about it. My boss said he thought I was smart enough." The storm clouds in her eyes vanish. "It was nice. To hear that somebody smart thinks you're smart, too."

"Yeah. Sure." Suddenly, I wish my dad had said those words to her. Maybe everything in the universe would be different if he had. "I think you're smart, Mom. I do."

But my words are feathery, and they don't land.

"But college is expensive, and we were getting by okay, and time just passed faster than I thought it would." Her face says *My whole life would have been different.*

I want to tell her how sorry I am.

"I don't want you to feel like . . ." I'm digging for the words, stumbling over them, not saying anything right. "I want you to be happy."

"Do you know what I want for you, Wil?" She clenches my hands so tightly, I wince. "Ten years from now, twenty or thirty years from now, I hope you want exactly the kind of life that you want right now." Her voice calcifies. "Look at me."

Her eyes are deep, clear pools, and I can see straight down to the sandy bottom.

"But if there ever comes a time that you need a different kind of life, I want you to be able to go after it. I don't want anything to get in your way. I will die before I let anything get in your way, do you hear me?"

"I hear you," I rasp.

I hadn't realized. I thought she wanted me to go to college for appearance's sake. I thought it was about telling Mrs. Wilkerson where I'd gotten in. Or about being Just As Good As everyone else's sons.

"Good."

There's a force in her that's stronger than anything I've ever felt before. Stronger than gravity or storm winds. Even in her screaming moments, in her thick, sharp, silences, she's never felt this way to me. I wonder who my mother really is. I wonder if I have never seen her before today.

We both jump when the kitchen door slams. Mom clears her throat and I can tell: we feel the same way.

"That you, Wilson?" she says, not loud enough for him to hear. She's disappeared again. I hate him for doing this to her.

*"Dad,"* I say louder. "Is. That. You?"

"Who the hell else would it be?" His voice is runny as he stumbles into the kitchen. "You ladies having tea?" He laughs, like he thinks it's the most hilarious thing anyone has ever said.

"I came back to work on the skiff." My hand finds its way to my mother's arm. "Where were you?"

"None of your damn business." He wipes his meaty mouth with the back of his hand. "Yours, either," he tosses at my mother. His giant ogre body throws a shadow over the table. He doesn't notice the photographs.

"She didn't ask," I mutter. "Besides, I think it's pretty obvious where you've been."

"Wil," Mom murmurs. "Don't be stupid."

"What?" Dad takes a step toward us, then a step back. "What did you say to me?" If he could focus, he'd be glaring at me. But his head is bobbing like a buoy on rough waters.

"Nothing." I stare directly at him. He doesn't scare me. I won't let him.

"Nothing," he spits back. "That's . . . right, nothing."

My stomach surges. I swallow bile. The sight of him is literally making me sick.

"Lunch ready?" Dad's buoy-head sways in Mom's direction.

"You should sober up first," she tells the table.

His nostrils flare. He's a bull, ready to fight.

"Don't you tell me what I should goddamned do first, Henney." He snorts. He lists toward her, but I won't let him touch her. Not this time. She's tired. She needs to rest. Can't he see that? Can't he see us?

"You're drunk, Dad." I shove back my chair and stand face-to-face with him. I am almost as big as he is. Almost. I could take him on a good day. "Go sleep it off or something. Leave her alone."

The air has left my body before I realize it. I'm on the floor before I realize it, staring up at a white ceiling, my chest throbbing.

*He hit me*, I realize, the thought coming from far away. I roll onto my side, curled into myself like a baby, and watch his work boots storm through the kitchen, rattling the glasses and my insides again.

"Wil." Mom kneels down next to me, strokes my hot,

126

embarrassed face with her hands. "Honey. Wil." She bends over me and kisses my forehead and my cheeks, and I pretend to push her away.

"I'm okay." I force the words out, don't meet her eyes.

"He didn't mean it, Wil. He's drunk. He didn't mean it." Her voice is grainy.

I roll onto my back. From here, I can see the words carved into the kitchen table. *We will go together, over the waters of time.* I close my eyes and I let my mother stroke my hair. I'm not in pain. The worst of it is the surprise. Even when I knew who he was, what he could do, the truth is that I never thought he would do it to me.

# BRIDGE

*Spring, Senior Year*

I woke up this morning with secrets under my tongue. The awful truth about Wilson; the long hug between Wil and me last night in the street in front of Buck's house. The secrets make the world seem upside down and backward. I don't know what to make of either of them. They seem so giant and unmanageable that it's safest to hold on to them until I understand them better. Lock them up where no one can see them, even Leigh. And especially not my mother.

Somehow I make it through the school day without saying a word. Wil and I avoid each other's glances, and I try not to wonder what that means. By the time I jam the key in the lock at home, my bones are tired of holding me upright. War sounds leak through the thin windows and the front door. Men killing men; boots on the ground.

"Micah. Turn it down," I bellow as I push through the front door. I let my keys and bag drop, then step over them. The air inside is sticky and still.

He stays hunched over his video game controller.

*"Micah."*

The volume dips. He keeps his gaze fixed on the screen.

"What are you doing home so early?" I fall onto the couch next to him. "No big plans with the girlfriend?" I don't mean to say it. It just slips out.

His forehead creases. "She's not my girlfriend."

"Oh. So what I saw the other day was just a hookup, then. Classy."

"Screw you." He turns the volume up again. On the screen, a cartoon soldier is being split in two.

I dive for the remote and mute the sound. "Come on. Turn it off. I had a weird night last night, and if I sit here in front of the television, I'll just obsess over it." I'll wonder about Wil, about whether he felt what I felt when we hugged. Was he was just looking for someone familiar, or were we becoming something entirely new altogether?

"Me too, kind of." Micah tosses the controller to the other side of the couch. "What kind of weird?"

It's the first time he's asked me a real question in I can't remember how long.

"I guess . . . some stuff came up about Wil's dad last night. Stuff that made me sad to think about. So I tried not to." I twist my hair into a knot at the nape of my neck, so tightly it gives me a headache.

"At least Wil had a dad for a little while." Micah kicks at the coffee table.

"Micah."

"I'm serious, Bridge. Wouldn't you take a not-so-great dad over one who was never there in the first place?" When he turns to look at me, his face looks little boyish in the afternoon light.

I shrug. "I don't know."

But I've felt the way Micah feels before. Once in middle school, Wil and Wilson and I had been working in the shop. When Wil went in for water, Wilson stopped sweeping long enough to ask me, "So what about your dad?"

He'd said it just like that, no extras.

I'd tightened the ridged plastic cap on the varnish can so hard my fingertips burned. "What about him?"

"You ever talk to him?"

I shook my head. "I don't know where he is, really. Neither does Mom. She'd tell me." For as long as I could remember, I'd gone through Mom's drawers, her calendar, her phone, desperate for a clue about my dad. Nothing. I didn't even care about the big questions: why he'd left, where he was, whether he had a real family now. It was the little things that interested me. Did he think the first sip of a Coke Slurpee was the best, or the last? (The last, because there was nothing more to look forward to, so you appreciated it more.) Did roller coasters make him sick? Did he ride them anyway, because he wanted to be the kind of person who loved roller coasters?

Wilson leaned his broom in the corner and sat on the workshop floor next to me. The concrete was clean and cool, and in the background, the stereo played James Taylor. The sunlight filtered through the walls and left a design on the floor. *I'm having a dad moment*, I thought, even though I'd had plenty of dad moments with Wilson before. And I was so intensely jealous of Wil. *What's he done,* I thought, *to deserve this?*

I know the answer now: *absolutely nothing.* Wil has always been a good person, decent. There is nothing he could have done to deserve the father he was dealt. The anger I couldn't see back then.

I shake my head to clear the memory and muss Micah's hair. "Hey. Let's go do something this afternoon. Just you and me. Hang out like we used to."

"Before you got judge-y as hell?" He raises an eyebrow.

"Before you started dry-humping older women."

He makes a gagging sound and promises to hang out with me if I stop using the phrase *dry-humping.*

"We still have a couple of good beach hours left." I tug at my knotted hair and let it fall. "Or we could play Putt-Putt."

*"Putt-Putt?"* Micah frowns at the screen. "What are we, seventh graders going on a second date?" Then his face lights up. "You know what we haven't done in a while? Don't laugh."

I know before he says it. "I won't, I swear."

"Eleanor and Alastair," he says, looking sheepish and pumped at the same time.

"Eleanor and Alastair!" I shriek. "Ten minutes."

Eleanor and Alastair was a game we made up when I was in fourth grade and Micah was in first, and we'd just moved to the beach from Alabama. Mom had just started the job at the resort, and her boss said that we could use the pool and go to the snack bar now and then if we didn't bother the real guests. Everything was so rich there: creamy marble and frozen lemonades so cold they made your brain burn and towels a person could lose herself in. And then there was Micah and me, pinching our toes over the edge of the infinity pool, awkward and out of place in our pilled swimsuits and our new Florida sunburns. So we pretended that we belonged with the kids on vacation. We decided to come up with names for ourselves, the fanciest names we could think of. I came up with Eleanor. Micah picked Alastair, and I still have no idea where he got that name. Eleanor and Alastair swam all day long, like they owned the world. They drank as many frozen lemonades as they wanted, and they never felt out of place. Eleanor and Alastair belonged everywhere.

The lobby at the resort is one of my favorite spots in the whole resort, second only to the pool. The floor is made of miles of white marble streaked with gray, and there are orchids on nearly every surface. At the front desk, Mom is giving a tight smile to a blowhard in a suit and Birkenstocks.

"It's not a difficult question," he says through his nose. "How is it possible to pay these outrageous rates and *not* have access to an in-room masseuse?" He draws his question out slowly, like she doesn't speak English.

I elbow Micah in the gut when he tries to make Mom laugh by crossing his eyes and sticking out his tongue.

"I just don't have an answer for you sir." Mom sighs. "But I'd be happy to suggest the gentleman's club about a mile down Atlantic."

The guy gives up and stalks off.

"No in-room masseuse?" I gasp. "How is it *possible?*"

"Because we're not a whorehouse, jackass," my mom says, her voice low. Then her brow furrows. "You guys okay? You didn't burn down the house or anything, did you?"

Micah tries on his *perfect little angel* voice. "It's just been a while since we stopped by to tell our mother what a beautiful, caring—"

"Eleanor and Alastair?" Mom holds up a finger and answers the phone.

Micah and I give her a wave and skate through the all-white, marble-floored lobby on foam flip-flops. The pool is just on the other side of the glass walls: a saltwater infinity pool that spans the length of the hotel and looks over the ocean. The pool area is almost empty. We sling our bags on the good lounge chairs, the ones with the best view of the ocean and the umbrellas, and I peel off my cover-up and take a running leap. Micah is airborne behind me. If I could freeze us here, I would.

The water is refreshing and the crisp blue moves through me. I dive all the way down, run my fingers over the beautiful blue-glass tiles at the bottom. I torpedo to the surface and catch Micah doing a somersault in the deep end.

"Alastair, darling, is this not simply the most *divine* resort you've ever been to? Including that peach of a place in St. Tropez?"

"Magnificent, Eleanor." Micah tips his nose to the sky. "Although I must say, the European girls do know how to party."

"Yes, well, no need for details, Alastair."

We swim until we're wrinkled, and then I order frozen lemonades while Micah sets up our towels. The lemonade is fresh and blended with vanilla ice cream. I take a too-long sip, and my tongue shrinks at the taste of sour.

When we're staring at the water, Micah says: "Hey."

"What's up?"

He squints at the water. "I wanted to say sorry? For the whole thing with Emilie the other day. We shouldn't have—I'm just sorry."

"Look at you, with your mature apologies." I grin.

"I'm serious, Bridge. That was a douchebag move."

"Just make sure it doesn't happen again."

He doesn't say anything for a while. Then: "I don't know if we're together, still, actually."

I tread carefully. "What do you mean?"

"I heard this rumor about Emilie Simpson."

"What kind of rumor?"

"I heard she was hanging out with some college guy. With a scorpion tattoo." He blinks pool water out of his eyes. "You haven't heard anything like that, have you?"

I shake my head. "Just because people are saying it doesn't make it true."

"Doesn't make it a lie, either." His jaw pulses.

"That's also true," I concede.

He sighs and shrinks into the chair. Crosses his arms over his chest as if he just squeezes hard enough, he can keep her out of his heart. "It's not like we said we were exclusive or anything. Maybe she's been looking for someone better this whole time."

My heart shrinks. "Micah."

"I like her," he blurts. "I know you don't think she's that great, but she's really funny, Bridge. She is. You'd get it if you got to know her. And I'm, like—"

"You're, like, this awesome guy," I insist, sitting up.

His face is splotchy with red. "My dad left for someone better than us. Your dad, too, probably."

"That has nothing to do with us," I say fiercely. "And if Emilie Simpson is hanging out with a college guy, that's on her. That's not on you."

"Yeah." He flips onto his back and stares up at the sky. "Maybe I'll text her later and if she texts back right away—"

I groan. "You are so. Fifteen."

"Whatever."

"Hey. Micah." I sit up. I wait until I know he sees me, until we're so still that I can see the tiniest flecks of light buzzing in his eyes. "You. Deserve. Good things."

He looks at me, and he is thirsty to believe it. But then his eyes glaze over and he says he's tired. We're too old for games like this, he says, and we should just go home. I get it. It's easier that way. But he's breaking my heart in a whole new way.

# BRIDGE

*Spring, Senior Year*

MICAH heads home after we swim. I decide to shower at the resort, under a gushing waterfall faucet, because resort water feels like velvet. The shower is tiled with mother of pearl, and the shampoo here makes my scalp tingle. I watch shampoo lather circle the drain and disappear. Then I wrap myself in a fluffy resort robe and blow-dry my hair. I change into a fresh pair of jeans and a tank top, and I slip on the MAMA P'S cap. Wearing it makes me feel closer to Wil.

In the lobby, I pilfer sea salt caramel chocolates at the front desk.

"What are your dinner plans?" Mom murmurs, scanning her computer screen. "I think there's some cash in my purse, if you guys want pizza."

I shrug. "I'll probably just grab some takeout from Nina's."

*And sit on the couch and wonder what it all means and why Wil*
*hasn't called or texted or sent a carrier pigeon with a note explaining*
*how he's feeling about this and me.*

The phone bleats and Mom lifts the receiver. "Front desk, this is Christine." She lifts her eyebrows and twirls her finger, motioning for me to turn around. In the center of the lobby, dressed in jeans and a T-shirt that matches his eyes, is Wil. Without warning, my body is warm and soft, made of melting wax. As awful as last night was, I want to hug him that way again.

"Hey," I say carefully.

"Hey," he says. His Adam's apple bobs in his throat. "We should talk."

"Yeah. Okay." For a boy I used to know inside out, he is unreadable. His eyes are cast down but his body is loose, relaxed. He takes a few steps and swats the bill of my hat. My body floods with relief.

"Come on," he says. "I want to show you something."

I follow him outside. Wilson's truck is idling in the parking lot. A canoe rests in the bed, tailgate down. It's long, sleek, made entirely of wood that changes to different shades of amber as the pink light moves.

"Whoa." I push myself into the truck bed and run my hand over the curves of the wood. "Beautiful. Have you taken her out yet?"

"Nah. I just finished her."

"You made this? *Wil*."

He tosses his hair out of his eyes. "Would you, ah—you want to try her out?"

* * *

We don't speak on the way to the beach. I watch the lines of his jaw pulse in an odd rhythm, watch his lips move slightly. He's far away, someplace I may never be able to find. When we get to the beach access, we carry the canoe across the sand. It's lighter than I expected. Wil rests the boat on one shoulder and two paddles on the other. There are almost no waves and the sun is slinking red beside us.

"One, two, three," Wil says, and we ease the boat onto the wet sand. I kick off my flip-flops and roll my jeans up. I wade in up to mid-calf, tugging the boat with me as I go.

I jump in and Wil wades a little deeper before he jumps in, too. We're quiet. I've done this enough to know that a boat meeting water for the first time is a sacred thing. Wil hands me a paddle and settles in behind me. I wish I could see his face. I imagine it instead. I make it soft, with no harsh lines. I pretend that he has nothing to worry about except a quiz in science or a mother who wants him to go to college more than he wants to go. We fall into rhythm, sliding across the water. It doesn't take long for everything in me to sync with our strokes. My breath, my heartbeat. We head north.

Wil speaks first, with a voice like uneven pavement. "Do you . . . do you hate me?"

"What? Wil!" I know better than to turn around. "Of course not. How could you think that?"

"After what I told you about my dad. It's embarrassing, Bridge." He pauses. "That's not even the word. It's humiliating, the kind of person he was."

"That has nothing to do with you," I tell him. "That's on him."

138

"It has everything to do with me." The canoe rockets forward. "I'm part of him. I have him in me. And I don't want you to think—I fucking care what you think, Bridge."

"Listen to me. It doesn't mean anything about you." The breeze carries my words back to him. "No matter what kind of person he was. You're different. You aren't your dad."

"Really, though?" His laugh has an edge. He stabs the water with his paddle and spins us in a perfect circle. The beach and horizon replace each other. My stomach swoops.

"Really."

"See, I'm not so sure. I'm part of him, or he's part of me, or however that works."

"But you're not the things your father *did*," I say fiercely.

"Maybe a man can't separate who he is from what he does. Apparently, I'm the kind of guy who puts his fist through a wall, right? You saw that. Tell me I'm not just another angry Hines asshole."

I swivel until we're knee to knee. The color has drained from his face.

"No," I say emphatically. "Hell no." I take his hands in mine. They are damp. "I think you're pissed because your dad wasn't who you wanted him to be, and then he died."

His face buckles, and he glances out at the water. No doubt he wishes he could slide beneath the surface, release the oceans behind his eyes. "What are the odds?" he asks me.

"What do you mean?"

"The mathematical odds of something like this happening to a person's family."

"You can't think about it like that." I squeeze his hands tighter. He's shaking.

"There are billions of other people out there—billions, right?"

"Seven billion."

"Seven billion other people out there, and this thing, this thing that has ruined my life forever, happened in my house. To me and not somebody else. How is that possible? I'm just this little speck in the universe. And I never wanted to be more than a speck. I just wanted to be happy, that's it. Simple, right?" He shakes his head. Pulls away from me.

I remember a bulletin board in fifth grade. In sweeping glitter letters at the top, Mrs. Gilkey had written *Fifth graders flying high!* She'd stapled bunches of Tootsie Pops over construction paper baskets, and we were supposed to write about our dreams in our candy hot-air balloons. Where did we want to live one day? Who did we want to be? I think I said *Someplace exotic* and *The woman who ends world hunger.* Wil's basket had two words.

*Here. Me.*

"Simple," I echo.

"But I don't get simple anymore. Not after this." Wil shakes his head suddenly, violently, like he's trying to fling the memory of that night from the folds of his brain.

"Look at me," I tell him.

His eyes are bottomless worlds of green. They hold everything I've missed. *Tell me. Tell me what happened that night.* I wish I could unlock his skull. Draw out the memory parasite in thick coils. Remove it from his body. I'd make it mine, if it would just give him some relief.

"I'm sorry. I am so sorry." My body is made of thousands of tiny magnets, opposing forces, propelling me into him and holding me back. "You don't deserve this. I wish I could take it away. I wish—" My eyes fill.

His head drops.

There's a heavy silence between us. I can't hold this inside me for another second.

"I fucking *miss you*. I've *missed* you, Wil. I miss us." Saying it out loud makes my insides firework: turquoise and gold and scarlet rocketing inside me.

He sort of collides with me, slides his arms around my waist and buries his face in my neck and makes a sobbing sound. My eyes are hot and wet. If there is a breath somewhere, a full, deep breath anywhere on earth, I can't find it.

He pulls back and the space between us is unbearable, and before I can wonder, he covers my mouth with his.

He tastes like boy and salt, like Wil. I have been parched for him, for the way his mouth fits with mine, for his hands on my arms, my waist, in my hair. My hands search him, remembering every little detail, every familiar inch. Wil Hines is a story I know by heart, a story that comes racing back to me, all at once. Now that he's close again, I'll never let him go.

# BRIDGE

*Spring, Senior Year*

THE next morning, my skin is still vibrating from the kiss. I race across the tennis court during PE, wanting to shriek the words to Leigh. But I can't. Not until I know what we are.

"So, what'd you do last night?" Leigh lobs an easy ball my way, a neon sun backspinning over the net. Despite having a general policy against a heart rate over 130, Leigh is somehow good at tennis.

"Hung out with Micah. And, ah—" I whack the ball as hard as I can, and it hits the fence behind her and rolls two courts down. "Sorry."

She waits until the gym teacher at the other end of the court isn't looking. Then she gives me the finger and takes her sweet time interrupting the game next to us—two sophomore stoners, and the game next to them: Ana and Thea.

I watch Ana scurry for my ball and my whole body tingles like I've been under the sun for days. I watch her laugh and toss the ball back to Leigh, and my brain shifts into overdrive. *They aren't a good match, Wil and Ana, not the way we are. She'll find someone next year, someone who wants college and a tie collection and a golf membership. I didn't ask for this. He needs me.* But my excuses are thin, and beneath them is simmering guilt. The feeling that I've done wrong by her. I look away. I pretend to stretch. I am sweat-soaked under low clouds.

"Seventy-six–love," Leigh bellows before she serves. She's been making up scores all period.

We lob the ball back and forth until she gets bored and decides to end the game, punishing me, point after point. We meet at the net and slurp the Big Gulp Leigh filled with gas-station iced coffee on the way to school.

"What's going on with you?" She squints sweat out of her eyes.

"Nothing. What do you mean?"

"You're, like, smiling. It's weird."

"I can't smile?"

"Not lately, you can't."

I reach for the Big Gulp and suck the last of the syrupy dregs through the straw. "Maybe I'm just having a good morning."

"It's fucking *PE*." Leigh shakes her head. "Nobody on earth is this happy this early in the morning unless—" A sly grin crosses her face.

"Leigh." I cut my eyes down the court. "Shut up."

"Ohmygod." She socks my bicep, hard.

"*Leigh.*"

"You got laid! For the first time in, like, a year!" She yelps loud enough that the stoners on the next court burst out laughing. Ana and Thea glance over.

"I. Did. Not." I grab her arm and drag her across the court, toward the locker rooms.

"Ladies?" the gym teacher yells.

"Feminine issue!" I yell back. We hustle off the courts, Leigh squawking the whole way. When we get to the locker room, I shove through the double doors and I check beneath the bathroom stall doors before I say, "Okay. I did *not* get laid."

"*Buuut—*" Leigh pulls me down to the bench in front of my locker. "Spit it out, Hawking."

"I kissed Wil. Last night," I blurt.

Leigh's eyes go big. "You kissed Wil. Like, *your* Wil. You kissed your Wil."

I bob my head.

"Who happens to be Ana's Wil, at the moment." Her forehead crinkles.

"Don't remind me." I kick off my sneakers and peel off my socks.

Leigh sits there with her mouth slightly open, silent.

"*Say* something," I order.

"No, I mean, this is . . . Are you getting back together?" Her disapproval lines get deeper.

"I don't know. We haven't talked about it. I was going to find him after Spanish so we could talk."

Leigh twists one of her dreads around her index finger. She looks past me. "This is huge."

"I *know*, Leigh. That's what I'm telling you." I search her.

144

Stormy eyes are not what I expected. "Would you look at me? What are you, pissed?"

She shakes her head. "No. No way."

"Well? Aren't you going to say, *Do your thing, whatever makes you feel good*, some bullshit about my goddamned heart chakra?" My stomach surges.

"No way. This is *you guys*."

"So?" There's an edge to my voice.

"So . . ." She lets her head fall back against the locker. It makes a tinny thud. "If it was just some guy, and you were just hooking up, then hell yeah. Do what makes you feel good. But you and Wil . . ."

"So what am I supposed to do, then?"

"You're supposed to think, Bridge. I mean, like, now? With all he's got going on? With Ana?"

"Can we not talk about Ana?" I stretch out on the bench and stare into the fluorescent lights overhead.

"Not really." She reaches over and squeezes my ankle. "She's kind of an important part of this."

I press my palms over my eyes until everything goes black. "Yeah. I know."

"Bridge. I didn't—"

The locker room doors swing open again, and I sit up and rub the spots from my eyes. Ana and Thea traipse in and lean their rackets against the wall.

"Hi." Ana's face tightens when she sees me.

"Hey." I nod.

"I'm just saying, you've been there for him," Thea tells Ana. She bends over one of the sinks and splashes her face with water.

"And I know he's sad and everything, but that doesn't give him the right to forget you completely."

"Are you guys talking about Wil?" I ask before I can stop myself. The knot in my stomach gives me the answer.

Thea turns from the sink and blinks, wet-faced, like she's seeing me for the first time.

"I just wish this whole thing was over, you know?" Ana tells Thea quietly as a few freshmen girls trickle in. "It's just been hard, and I know that's selfish or whatever. But Wil just isn't . . . *there* anymore."

Thea sighs, leaving pity fog on the mirror.

"There is no *over*, you know." I just can't stop myself.

Ana turns. "What?" She launches the word directly at me, hard.

"I don't think you ever get over not having a dad anymore."

"Right. Obviously, I know that, Bridge." Ana's face is red. She looks at Thea. "You're not the only one who—"

The shriek of the bell cuts through the locker room. Head down, I follow Leigh through the double doors. I don't expect to see Wil on the other side of the hall. Just like that, the sadness, my disappointment in Leigh's reaction, drain from my body.

He opens his mouth like he's going to shout something across the hall, and then he sees Ana. He edges through the crowd and he leans close to her in a way that I understand, in a way that kills me. She lights up. I watch his lips.

*We have to talk*, he tells her.

Wil doesn't get to Spanish until there are *doce minutos* left in the period. When he comes in, he looks at Señora Thompson and we all look at Señora Thompson and she gives him this *poor baby* look and she keeps teaching, but now it sounds like there is something caught in her throat. Anyone else, and she would have sent them straight to the office.

Wil slides into his seat without turning around. I want to stare into him, through his pupils into the wires that power the Wil machine, and read his mind. To know what he's thinking, and know where we stand.

When the bell rings and everyone else has left, Wil says, "I'm sorry I was, uh, *tardes*, Señora."

I want to hug him and say, *God, you're so bad at Spanish.*

"I'm sure you had a good reason, Wil. Try to be on time tomorrow," she says.

"*Gracias.*"

In the hall, he pulls me into the corner by the stairs. A group of sophomore guys takes a break from shoving one another into the closest row of lockers to stare. I edge even closer. I'm desperate to kiss him again, but I won't. Not here. His eyes are brighter than I've ever seen them.

"Hey," he says.

"Hey," I say.

He rests his hands on my hips and he falters, as if he isn't sure. I rocket *yes* vibes. I guide his hands with mine. Our movements are halting, like a song that fades in and out from a station that's far away.

"I ended it with Ana," he says.

"Oh, Wil." I collide with him. Slide my hands over his warm, solid chest and rest my head against his collarbone. I've missed the sound of his heartbeat, the smell of his skin. I drink him in. I want all of him. I want to make up for lost time.

I curl my fingers around his fingers. "Is she okay?" I murmur.

He shakes his head. "Nah."

I pull back. "What'd you say?"

"That it wasn't working. That we would have broken up after graduation anyway. Which is true." His eyes are cloudy.

"Oh. Okay." I wonder if he said my name, or she did. I wonder if Ana Acevedo has ever lost anything precious. She seems like the kind of person who might be able to take all the right turns in the life maze. Who might get through unscathed. I hope she is. Real loss is like water: Over the years, it erodes. Slowly makes full things hollow.

*I'm sorry. I am,* I tell her.

"I didn't say anything about—about last night," he admits. "I didn't want to make it worse for Ana."

I shake my head. "Yeah! Yeah. Of course." I look at him and he looks at me. Ana's name hangs between us.

"I want to go somewhere with you," he says, reading my mind.

"Anywhere," I say.

# BRIDGE

*Spring, Senior Year*

**WE** rocket through the double doors, blowing through the barrier between school and the outside world. We surge down the steps, and when our feet touch the asphalt, we break into a sprint, my hair whipping behind us. We leave Ana's hurt and Leigh's furrowed brow and the curious boy stares behind us. We run toward us.

"I've never skipped school!" I screech, barely sidestepping a Vespa. "If I get busted for this, you're dead, mister."

Wil takes my hand. "Truck's that way." Urgently, he pulls me toward his dad's pickup. We both lunge for the passenger side, and he throws open the door for me. "Get in." His body dips toward mine, and he pulls me into him. We press our noses together and breathe into each other and then we let our lips touch, lighting each other on fire.

He kisses me once more, quick, and slams the door.

I lean back in my seat and close my eyes. My phone dings, and I ignore it. It's probably Leigh, texting all the way from the land of *Do you think you should?*

"Where are we going?" I ask when he slides into the driver's side seat.

"Don't know." He throws the truck into reverse and peels out of the parking lot. In under a minute, we're leaping down Atlantic, windows down. I was expecting the beach, but we're headed west, away from the water. The wind whips through the truck, tickling my damp skin. In here, with his fingers wrapped around mine and propped on the console, we're safe.

We barrel down Atlantic, and at the last minute, he whips the truck across three lanes and we're speeding down his block. He pulls into the empty driveway and kills the engine.

I thrust open the car door, and I hit the pavement on shaky legs. Inside, the house is silent. There are still a few boxes in the front hall, neatly labeled.

"More of his stuff," Wil says before I have to ask.

I can't imagine what it would be like to live in a house alongside Wilson's ghost. I slip my hand into his, and he tugs me down the hall and into the breakfast nook. The only sound is the hum of the ancient refrigerator, the one Wilson refused to replace. Wil told me once that his mom wanted one of the sleek silver refrigerators, the kind that spits crushed ice and has a special drawer for things like kale.

I wander into the kitchen. There's a grocery list pinned to the fridge in Wilson's small, boxy handwriting. I recognize the letters from the napkin notes he would leave in Wil's lunchbox: *This is the last of the Halloween candy. Make it last. Or six more days till summer, buddy.*

Wil catches me looking. "I can't take it down."

I turn and slide my arms around his waist, kissing his collarbone, tracing his lines with my mouth. With every kiss, I remember him. Our lips find each other's slowly. I kick off my sandals, and he lifts me onto the kitchen counter. His warm hand slides up my leg and over my thigh. He takes his time reading me with his lips and hands. He rediscovers the small bump on my wrist, never the same after I broke it falling off my bike in fifth grade. I close my eyes and trace the long scar on his middle finger. We know all the places where the other has been broken. We know the unspoken details no one else can hear.

His mouth covers mine and a hot tear slips down my temple and follows my jawline. Kissing him, feeling his hands on me is like taking a first breath after years underwater: necessary, and almost painful. I have been desperate, aching for him.

And then the door slams. Wil lunges for a knife from the butcher block. His face electrifies.

"Wil! Don't!" I shriek. I bolt upright and jump off the counter. My heels collide with the icy tile floor, sending aftershocks through me. My skin is damp, my heart electric.

We are gulping air when Henney appears in the doorway between the hall and the kitchen. She's bundled tight in work clothes: black scrubs under a pink pastel blazer. She looks different, now that I know what Wilson did to her. I don't want her to look different, but she does. Smaller somehow.

Henney clutches her chest. "What in the world?"

Behind her, two cops clomp into the kitchen: a tall black woman with close-cropped hair and a pudgy white balding man. It takes me a second to recognize them. They were standing at the back of the church during Wilson's funeral.

"You doing okay, Wil?" The female detective gives me a brief nod.

"Uh, sure, Detective Porter." Wil's fist curls next to mine. He slides the knife onto the counter, behind us. "What's going on?"

"Answer me, Wil," Henney demands. "Why aren't you in school?" She doesn't look at me.

"We just needed a break, Mom. I'm sorry." Wil's glance shudders between the two detectives, uncertain, like a moth caught between two searing bulbs.

"Mrs. Hines, this is my fault," I say, pushing the words past my cottony tongue. "Wil seemed stressed, and I thought—"

"Wil." Henney closes her eyes. "I can't deal with this now, you understand?"

"I know, Mom. I'm really sorry. This was stupid." He looks at the balding detective. "Seriously, Detective Yancey. What are you guys doing here?"

The balding detective hooks his fingers around his belt loops and hikes up his pants. "We have a little more information on the suspect's history. Wanted to ask you about a few details, see if everything fits."

"No. No. He should be in school." Henney turns to stand next to Wil. She holds on tight, like she's about to fall. "I'm happy to answer your questions, but Wil should get back."

"Besides, we've gone through this already, right?" Wil says. "I've told you everything I know."

*I wish he would talk to me.*

I can't help it: The thought bobs to the surface before I can stop it. It's a selfish thought, but it's real. I wish he could tell me what happened that night. I want to be the person who lightens him, who carries his thoughts. He is so heavy with the weight of it all. But I wonder if he will ever let me share that weight. Wil has always been one to carry his burdens silently, without complaint. The kind of guy his dad used to call *a man's man*. I blink and remember the morning I helped him pack his father's things. I remember his pained expression, the cracks in the skin around his eyes like he might come unstitched if he spoke a single word about that night.

Detective Porter is smiling at me. I look away.

"This shouldn't take long," she says.

"I don't get it." Wil's voice is too loud for this room, for these people. "We've told you everything, and it's like it's not good enough or something."

"How do you mean, son?" Yancey cocks his head to one side.

Wil cringes. "We shouldn't have to talk about it over and over again. That's *fucked up*, man."

"*Wil,*" Henney hisses.

My breath catches in my throat.

Detective Yancey is chuckling, muttering something about how he's heard worse.

"I'm serious!" Wil shakes off Henney's hand. "Every time you come over, every time we have to tell the story again, it—it messes with your head. I—my mom can't sleep, she has nightmares." His skin is the color of fog. I watch the grays pulse, move, like there's a wind inside him that won't be still.

"I should go," I say. "I should get back." My words are a whisper in the middle of a hurricane.

"We're trying to find him, Wil." Detective Porter says evenly. "You have my word on that."

"Try harder. Try someplace else. Leave us alone. We're done." He storms out of the kitchen. Henney follows, calling after him, and the kitchen door slams. I'm left alone in this old gray kitchen with two cops and the Wilson ghosts.

Detective Yancey clears his throat. "We'll give them a second."

"Um, I'm Bridget," I tell the detectives. "Bridge." I prop my hands on the counter behind me, but they slide off. I can hear Henney and Wil in the side yard, muffled sadness and anger. I swallow the lump in my throat.

"You two go to the same school?" Porter asks. She gives me a reassuring smile.

"We grew up together," I whisper.

"So you know the family pretty well." Yancey's voice is talking-about-the-weather light, but something in me knows better.

I don't know what Wil has told them about who Wilson was and what he did. I don't know if cops go after the killers of violent men the same way. I don't even know if they should. "Yeah. It's been hard for them." I'm dizzy, unsteady on my feet. My skin is hot and damp where Wil's lips were. I don't want to cry in front of these cops. But it's too much, all of it, and I can't stop the silent tears.

"Sure, sure," says Yancey. "This is tough." He gives Porter the same look Micah gives me when Mom cries in front of us: helplessness mixed with discomfort.

"I should get back to school." I sniff, wiping my eyes with my

T-shirt. I glance through the kitchen door window. In the yard, Wil is holding his mother in a way that makes my bones ache for them. I want the cops to leave them in peace. Maybe peace is what they need, more than justice or a trial or casseroles.

"I'd be happy to drive you," Detective Porter offers.

"No! No. I'll walk. Thanks." I slip past the cops and hurry down the hall. I can feel the detectives' eyes on me as I push through the front door and start across the lawn, my stride longer than usual. When I hit Atlantic, I run. Away from the sick, sour death air that has invaded that house and snuck into my lungs. Away from the nagging feeling deep in my gut that peace, real, deep, still-water peace, is something Wil may never find again.

# BRIDGE

*Spring, Senior Year*

I slow to a walk on Atlantic, my skull pulsing with the beginnings of a migraine. Every step is harder. There is an invisible string between Wil and me, and that string is pulling me back to him, back to that house. I hate that I left him there with the cops and the ghosts and the grief he can't share with me, or won't.

"*Smile, sweetheart,*" yells a man in a chicken suit on the other side of the street, spinning a LUNCH SPECIALS sign, even though it's only 10:45. "*It can't be all that bad.*" The sky is gray, the kind of day that looks cold until you step into it. The storefronts and cracked sidewalks and neon signs sag under a cloudy sky.

"*You have no idea, asshole,*" I yell back, but it doesn't make me feel any better.

My phone dings yet again, and this time I reach into my backpack and check it. Leigh has sent a zillion texts—all of them containing the phrase *where the hell?*—but nothing from Wil. I stuff my phone in my back pocket. I don't want to think about Leigh. Free-spirited, dowhateverthefuckmakesyouhappy, art school Leigh. She should understand Wil and me better than anybody. She's watched me love him for years.

I turn for home without stopping by school for my truck. I want to stretch out on the couch in the dark and wait for Wil to call. I want a beer. The thing about me, the awful, secret thing about me is this: In the first three years of high school, I didn't drink to look cool. I didn't force down watery beer because everyone else was doing it. I did it because I loved the after. I loved the warmth, how heavy and loose it made me. Alcohol undid me. Sometimes I miss being undone.

It's silent when I step inside. I flop onto the couch and pick at the cushion seams, where the gray ikat pattern doesn't quite line up. Mom and I reupholstered the sofa with extra fabric from the resort's most recent makeover, and it's obvious to anyone who's looking closely. I reach for the remote and let daytime television dull the uneasiness that needles me. I go for three minutes without checking my phone, then four. Micah comes home too early, and he doesn't ask, and I don't, either. He dives onto the couch next to me with a box of sugar cereal and tilts it in my direction.

"Sick day in quotes?" he says over a mouthful of dried marshmallows.

"Sort of," I say. I pick out a green clover and crack it between my teeth.

"I heard you and Wil made out in the hall today."

"False."

"Just telling you what I heard." He shrugs. "Dude. Don't hog the pinks." He chucks a pillow into my lap and lets his head drop. "Sugar crash."

My eyes burn as I watch the tough boy lines in his face wriggle down deep, out of view. I want to stroke his hair, its sunset colors, the way I did when we were kids and he couldn't sleep. I miss him being this close.

"Quit being psycho," he tells the television.

"Huh?"

"You're watching me sleep, like Mom. That is creepy. Quit." His lips part slightly.

"Sorry." I touch the end of a single lock of his hair with my ring finger. "You want to order some food?"

"Pizza. Pineapple and ham. And orange soda." His eyes snap open at the mention of food.

"I feel as if it's my duty as an older sister to inform you that that meal will take at least six to ten years off your life."

"If you don't want it, maybe I'll call Emilie." He sits up and shoots a devlish boy grin my way.

"Gross. I'll call." I sigh. "But for the record, I don't appreciate blackmail." I reach for my cell. The screen is blank. *Please. Wil.* I think. *Please.*

Nothing.

I scroll through my contacts, highlight Wil's name.

"Oh my *God*, Bridge!" Micah sighs. "Just call him already, okay? I'll order the damn pizza." He launches off the couch and thumps up the stairs in bare feet.

"And breadsticks!" I yell.

I'm staring at Wil's name when there's a knock at the door.

"Hi." He's standing on the porch, all formal, straight lines.

"Hey! Hey." I fall into his chest, and he slides his arms around me. "I've been worried about you. I've been—I hope everything's okay."

"It's been a long afternoon," he murmurs into my hair. "You smell good. I missed your shampoo."

"Get a room!" Micah yells from my bedroom window.

Wil coughs.

"Come on in," I say. "Micah and I were doing some family bonding." I grab his hand and pull him inside.

"I actually came by to see if you wanted to go out." He grins when he sees the empty sugar cereal box on its side on the coffee table. "Busy afternoon around here?"

"Important things have been accomplished on this couch." I wait for him to tell me about Porter and Yancey, to say the word *Mom*. But he just gives me a quick, soft kiss.

"So Micah and I were just about to have dinner." I scour his ocean eyes for clues. "You in the mood for pizza?"

"Actually I'm kind of family-timed out," Micah announces from the top of the banister. "I could use a little alone time. Hey, dude." He gives Wil a wave and disappears again.

Wil says, "Looks like you're free."

We go outside and sit in the truck. Wil leaves the keys in his lap and stares straight ahead, his mouth the tiniest bit open. I wait, because I know him. Everything in his own time. I close my eyes and I remember what it was like to be in this truck and think sunburn was the worst of it.

"I'm sorry you were there this morning." Wil's voice is like cracked leather: soft in some places (*sorry* and *you*), hardened in others (*there*). "I know it was weird for you. I should've taken you back to school first. I should've gotten you out of there."

"Wil. You don't have to explain."

"I know they're just doing their jobs," he says it like he's trying to convince someone. "But they don't have to live with my mom the other twenty-three hours every day." He swallows. "Not that I mind—"

"I know you love your mom, Wil."

"Right. Right. And I really don't mind being there for her when she's having a hard time. Like with the nightmares and stuff. But every time the cops show up, I know it'll start all over for her. It's like the first night after it happened, all over again."

He makes a noise I don't understand. In my lap, the phone buzzes. *Leigh*. I silence it.

"And it never stops," Wil continues. The veins in his neck are shadowy lines beneath his skin, like petrified wood. "If we're not talking to the cops, we're trying to make sense of the shitty records my dad kept for the business, or I'm doing the math on the mortgage. I know it hasn't been that long since—but it just feels like it'll never be over, and I need it to be over, Bridge. I need it to be over." His chin drops to his chest.

I put a hand on his knee as he murmurs the phrase again and again. I wish I could end it for him, just like he wishes he could end it for his mom. Maybe that's the worst part of tragedy: realizing how small we are. Wanting to end another person's pain and being completely powerless to do it.

"My mom thinks we shouldn't be dating right now," he blurts. He sucks in a quick breath, like he's surprised himself.

A lump bobs in my throat. "What?"

"No. It's not—she likes you. She just thinks that we have too much going on right now for me to be dating." He scrunches his face muscles like *shiiiit*.

*Dating*. The word makes us smaller than we are.

"I shouldn't have said anything." He reaches for me. Pushes my hair out of my face. "God, that was so stupid." He shakes his head.

"No. I guess that makes sense, why she would feel that way." My heart beats *nonono*. "I get it."

"Hey." He leans in, nudges his forehead against mine. "I told her she was crazy. I told her that you're the only thing that makes sense right now. Just because she doesn't know what it's like to have something good—"

"Tell me you didn't say that," I say, relieved.

"I didn't say that." He presses his lips against mine, hard. "But you are, Bridge. You're everything good in my life. You know that, right?" He searches my face.

I answer him with another kiss.

"Good." His face breaks into a smile, and we settle back into our seats. He pulls away from the curb but curls his hand around mine and leaves it there.

"Where do you want to go?" I squeeze his hand.

"Wherever you want," he says. "Just don't want to go anywhere that reminds me of Dad. That okay?"

"Yeah, sure. What about Nina's? We could get dessert."

He shakes his head. "My dad and I had kind of a hard conversation in there once. Right before."

"Got it. No Nina's. So you probably don't want to do an after-dinner beach walk, then. Or take out the canoe?"

"Ahh." He looks pained. "Sorry."

"Wil, it's okay." I don't want to say it, and I don't have to. *There is no escaping your father.* Wilson is everywhere. Wil won't ever outrun him.

I get an idea. "If you want, I know a place down Atlantic you've never been. Has pretty good tea and cookies, actually."

"Tea and cookies?" He looks at me with a crooked smile. "Sign me up."

We pull into the Sandy Shores entrance during the commercial break between *Jeopardy!* and *Wheel of Fortune*, which buys us ninety seconds of focused, productive Rita. When Rita sees me with a boy, she stage-winks at me, as if he's not sitting between us. Then something clicks and I watch her recognize Wil. She bows her head when she presses the button to let us in.

"One of these days, I could have plans, you know," Minna says when she opens the door. She's Joni Mitchell cool in bare feet, loose hair, and a caftan that Leigh would pay too much for at Vintage Vixens.

"We took a shot in the dark," I say. "Wil, this is my friend Minna."

"Oh." Wil can't hide his surprise. "Ah, hi. I'm Wil."

Minna bobs her head. "Hello, William." I say a silent *thank you* that she doesn't talk too loud or with a lilt to her voice or tilt to her head, the way everyone does around Wil these days.

"It's short for Wilson, actually."

"Don't be ridiculous." She shakes her head and waves us inside. "Anyone up for Dirty Scrabble?"

Wil elbows me. "We are most definitely up for Dirty Scrabble."

"Minna. I don't think this is appropriate," I tell her once we're seated in the living room with the Scrabble board, lavender tea, and the tin of caramel popcorn I gave her for her birthday.

"Dirty Scrabble is always inappropriate, Bridget. That's the point."

"So, how do you guys know each other?" Wil wrestles with the popcorn tin.

Minna puckers her lips at her tiles. "We met during Bridget's juvenile delinquent phase."

"Minna. God." I reach for popcorn. "I was never a juvenile delinquent."

"I seem to recall an arrest warrant that begs to differ." Minna slides too many tiles onto the board. "JOHNSON."

Wil laughs and Minna smiles big enough that her face breaks like dried Earth.

"I can't argue with that." Wil fist-bumps Minna. She goes along with it.

"No! That—no." I shake my head. Wil records the points anyway. "Whatever. I forfeit."

"So I guess you're retired now?" Wil says to Minna, shuffling his tiles.

She nods.

"What did you do before?"

"Oh, lots of things. Receptionist work, mostly."

"My mom does that. At a dentist's office. Did you like it?"

She nods. "You know something, I did. And people liked me, because I could make them laugh over the phone."

"I'll bet." Wil slides his hand across the settee and takes mine.

"And you. You go to high school and build boats," Minna says.

I should have known better: she would never pretend to know nothing about him. Unlike Henney, Minna says exactly what she's thinking, exactly when she's thinking it.

"We—I—do repairs, mostly. But I want to get into building. My dad owned the business and he was more into the repair side of things. Small-scale projects. But I like the idea of making something brand-new, instead of spending all my time fixing what's broken."

"I was on a sailboat once," Minna says. "A Catalina 52. A friend and I sailed up the California coast for a few days after my husband and I split."

"A Catalina." Wil's voice catches. "I've always wanted to work on one of those."

"*Hm.*" Minna pauses. "I suppose the past few weeks have been hell for you."

Wil pulls back a little, surprised. "Ah—"

"Minna." I squeeze his hand. It's damp. "He doesn't want to talk about it."

Minna shrugs. "He doesn't have to. But I won't pretend."

"It's okay," Wil assures me. "It's actually kind of nice . . . People always ask, *You doing okay?* which feels like it only has one right answer. Or they say, *How are you feeling?* Which is just stupid."

*Wait. Have I asked those things?* I wonder.

"How are you feeling? You're feeling like shit," Minna volunteers.

"Yes! Exactly. Most of the time, I'm feeling like shit."

I look at Wil, at the storm brewing in his eyes.

"Actually, I'm feeling . . . complicated these days." Wil stacks his Scrabble tiles in a tiny high-rise, then breaks them down again. "I only just told Bridge, but it turns out my dad was kind of an asshole."

My brain wrestles with his words. *Wilson* and *asshole* have never belonged in the same sentence before.

"But, like, I didn't know it for a long time. I really loved him for almost all his life."

"You could even love him, still," Minna says gently.

"I do." Wil's face twists into an unreadable mosaic. "Most of the time, I'm wrecked about what happened to him and I'm pissed and at the same time I love him, you know? He is—was—my *dad*, and he was a complicated guy."

"Of course." Minna glances at me. "The people we love are never just one thing."

"And he was trying to do better. He *was* doing better, for a while. He just—"

Watching Wil is like watching the face of someone who is dreaming. His colors and lines shift slowly. If you didn't look closely enough, you would miss it.

Minna is saying: "My husband was, like you say, an *asshole*. And I left. That was years ago, and it saved my life, but sometimes I wake up in the middle of the night and I miss having him there next to me. But only with my heart, and only for a second. Then I remember that—" Her voice breaks.

Wil's breathing gets loud.

I say nothing, because something is happening between them, something Wil needs.

"I remember that I loved the man I wanted him to be."

"Did you ever think that if you wanted him to be that way, if you wanted it enough, you could make it happen?" Wil's bangs cling to his forehead. It glints in the lamp light, damp with sweat.

"Oh, for years." Minna's sigh is a single note, never ending. "But turning someone into what you want them to be is no more possible than willing someone back from the dead. We don't have that power. We are not that kind of magic."

I lean into Wil, rest my head on his shoulder. We want the same thing: for Minna to be wrong. I want to take every last bit of my strength, every molecule of energy, and I want to transform the person Wilson was into someone entirely different. I would trade all my childhood wishes about my own dad for this one wish. I would do that for him—use everything I have to change the shadows in Wil's life.

# WIL

*Winter, Senior Year*

FOR months now, he's been trying to convince me that he's changed. That he is someone other than the man he is. But people don't change. He said it himself, last year. We are who we are, down deep.

I've accepted it: He is part of me. But there are plenty of pieces of me, the Real Me, that have nothing to do with him. This morning, I stare into the bathroom mirror and count the ways we aren't the same. My eyes have more gray in them. My hair is just a little bit lighter, or maybe that's the light in here. There are these grainy freckles on my shoulders, where the sun stays all summer. I am not him.

"Wil? You in there?" Dad's fist slams against the door, and I jump.

"Just give me a second to shower," I yell back. I turn on

the shower and sit on the tile floor, a rolling wave of nausea overtaking me. Maybe it's the godawful smell of the candle my mom put on the back of a doily on the toilet tank. *Lavender Serenity.* More likely it's the fact that my dad is six foot three inches of rage, and I'm not immune.

By the time I lurch into the shower, the water's only lukewarm. I wash my hair with the same shampoo he uses. I scrub my chest extra hard, the spot where he put his jackass hands on me months ago. I want to slide dripping wet between my cool sheets and sleep until the world is upright again. But I can't, because it's a school day and a person shows up to play, no matter what.

I've barely finished getting dressed when Dad comes into my bedroom without knocking. I brace myself for I don't know what.

"You sleep okay?" he asks, which is not what I expected. I still can't look at him. But the little boy part of me senses him sitting on my bed, fingers laced together like he's a reasonable man and we're about to have a father-son talk about sailing or something embarrassing like sex. And I'm so pathetic that it takes everything I have not to bury my face in his chest and make him swear that he didn't mean it, any of it. He'll never do *it* again to me or to my mom. *Swear, Dad. And then let's go out to the workshop and listen to some Steely Dan.*

"Haven't slept well lately, that's all," I say.

From the corner of my eye, I think I see his head dip. "Listen." He clears his throat. "I know you've got to get to school, but I want to have breakfast together first. Out. Nina's."

"I, ah—" I check the clock radio next to my bed. "It's getting late, you know? I've got Econ."

"I know, son. I'm asking." His voice is a soft I've never heard.

168

I don't ever remember him asking instead of telling. I let myself hope a little.

"Fine. Meet you at the truck," I say. A *guy's gotta eat*, I think. I hate myself for giving in so easy. I wish I could cut the ties between us, a single swift slice of a knife. But it's harder than it should be. He is my dad, after all. And that means more than it should at a time like this.

At Nina's, everyone is staring. Ned Reilly from school is there with his Bible study group, plus Leonard who runs the place, and I swear each and every one of them can look over and tell *that man is a wife abuser, and the son's probably messed up, too*. We are transparent. Anyone who wants to can see through our reptile skins to our ugly insides.

Dad doesn't seem to notice. He just walks in and orders two coffees, even though you're supposed to wait for menus. We find a booth with empty booths around it.

We eat for a while before anyone says anything. I won't be the first to speak, that's for sure. I could sit here for years without saying anything. I sip my coffee between bites, soak my pancakes in broken yolks. I stuff syrupy bite after syrupy bite, and dissolve it all with black coffee.

"I have something to say to you," Dad says finally. "And I need you to look at me"—he takes a flimsy breath, which surprises me enough to look up—"while I say it."

I look at him for the first time in months. I expect him to look broken or angry or even ashamed. I expect him to look like someone else. But he just looks like my dad. It's like my brain won't let me think too long about the terrible things he's done.

Instead, I see the guy who taught me to bodysurf, who carried me on his shoulders on the beach at night. I want to hate him. He deserves that.

"Look at me," he says again. "I want you to know that no kind of man should do what I—it wasn't right to do what I did to you. I haven't been acting right for a while, especially toward your mom. I want you to know that I know that. I know that it doesn't matter how mad she makes me or how much damn pressure I feel sometimes."

"Okay."

"Your mom and me—" He closes his eyes. "You know. We don't get along sometimes. We get upset. We fight. She's—marriage is hard, son. I think you'll understand that when you're older."

"I understand now, Dad." I squeeze my coffee mug. "I understand that plenty of people have hard marriages and don't punch their—"

He almost yells, "I *never*—" People are staring now, actually staring, and Dad must see it, too. He leans in and lowers his voice. "I have never punched her, Wil."

"Right. Hit," I say under my breath. "Or whatever. That's better." I've never talked to him this way. The fact that I'm getting away with it tells me: something is very wrong. I check the clock over the counter. I'm late. I'm going to miss Econ. Econ is now the most important thing in the world.

"I'm sorry. I'm sorry. This isn't how I—" He tilts his head from side to side, and I wince at the cracking sound. "What I'm trying to say is that nobody's perfect. Not your mom and not me."

"Okay. Nobody's perfect. Got it." I slide out of the booth.

"Wil. *Please*. Please, boy, sit down."

170

When I look down at him, his eyes are like mirrors. A fat tear worms its way to the edge of his nose and hangs there, suspended. It's the first one I've seen from him. I want to wipe it away and I want to leave it there. I want to shove him and I want to pull him into me. I sit. People are looking.

"I'm not saying what I need to say." The tear slips into a pool of syrup and disappears. "What I mean. I'm saying the exact same things my old man said to me."

"What?" I go cold. "What?"

"My dad, ah . . ." He looks up at the water-stained ceiling. "You never met him, of course, but he wasn't very nice to my mom and me. And that's not an excuse. It's just the way it was. He drank, and . . ." He works hard to straighten out his face. "He got pissed off a lot, and he didn't know what to do with it. So." He interlaces his fingers together on the table so tightly they go white. "So," he almost whispers.

"Dad," I say, my face hot and twisty.

"Anyway." He clears his throat once. Twice. "It's not an excuse, like I said."

I don't know what it is, but it's something. Why didn't he tell me?

"When your mom and I were younger, before you were around"—he smiles a little when he says *you*, and it makes me feel good—"we had a couple of bad fights, and we decided to stop drinking. Both of us. So we did, cold turkey. And things haven't been perfect, of course, but I haven't—I haven't messed up in a long time." He slides his hands across the table and grips my arms so hard I wince. His fingers are sticky with syrup. "I'm going to fix this, son. I swear to God. I want a clean slate for all of us. I'm going to be better, for you and for your mom."

171

He looks at me like the rest of his life depends on what I say in the next three seconds.

"What do you want me to say, Dad?" I take shallow breaths, feeling like I might throw up everything I just ate.

"I want you to say you'll forgive me," he says, still holding on. "Or that you'll think about it. Your mother will come around. I know her. But I need you on board, son. I need your support."

I close my eyes. My head is hurricaning with things I didn't know before: This is not new, he's done this before, and I am third in a line of pissed-off men. Maybe even fourth or tenth. Violence is imprinted in me. In my father. In his father.

I say, "Tell me it won't happen again."

"I won't hurt you again, son. You have my word."

I keep my eyes closed, through the cash register ringing in the background and plates being slid onto tables and change being released into the tip jar.

"I don't care about me." I open my eyes. "But don't you hurt her again."

Dad's face is solemn. "Never." We slide out of the booth, and I stick out my hand. The air whooshes out of our lungs when he hugs me instead. Finally, I say, "I have to get to class," and he releases me. He says, "Good man," and I jog to school, because if I don't burn off these feelings, who knows what I'll do. I am genetically capable of despicable things.

My feet pound past KYLIE MITCHELL and a brick that is too bright to be old, IN MEMORY OF OUR PAL ROOSTER, and I think about a fresh start.

There are ties to cut, and things to let go. I picture myself sawing through waterlogged rope. I will release everything that has held our family back. The things I didn't even know about: my dad's past and the hurt he caused my mother. The things that are mine to release: anger that he isn't who I thought he was and so maybe I'm not who I think I am. I hold my breath and I sink beneath the surface. With my next breath, I break above the waterline.

For the first time in months, I can see the shadow of land. The *maybe* of a new beginning. For the first time, I believe that he wants to make us new. The kind of family we should have been from the start.

# BRIDGE

*Spring, Senior Year*

EVERYTHING in my room glows with the blue-gray light of morning: the shapeless bathrobe draped over my desk chair; the nearly perfect fossilized starfish Wil found in the front yard when he dropped me off last night after Minna's. He gave it to me like a regular boy gives a flower away. The abstract painting hanging over my dresser, an early graduation present from Leigh.

"Shit." I sweep my hand over my bedside table, my fingers closing over my phone. I stab the screen until it lights up. There are three texts from Leigh.

6:37 P.M.
Where were you today? Worried. For real.

7:13 P.M.
Sending search party soon.

11:14 P.M.
Micah says you're out. Thanks for telling me.


I fall back on my pillow, deflated. This is my fault. I don't want Leigh and I to erode at the same time that Wil and I are rooting into each other.

I text her back.

6:13 A.M.
So sorry I missed these. Phone was off.

6:14 A.M.
No it wasn't. I'm just an asshole.


When the sun comes up, I drag our enormous cooler from its resting place behind the house and I scrub and rinse it with the garden hose three times. I make a Publix run, and with most of my gas money for the week, I buy the things I never buy: subs loaded with everything, so fat they are spilling open, and the potato chips that taste like Old Bay. I buy a six-pack of Coke in the doll-sized glass bottles because Coke tastes better that way. Dried mango and fresh fruit salad in a plastic container.

I text Leigh and Wil separately. I tell them that we need a *sick day in quotes*. I tell them to meet me at the First Street access.

Beach day. Wil texts back *in* and Leigh texts *history quiz, can't.* I tell her there will be Pub Subs and groveling, and she caves and says fine, the last few weeks of high school don't count anyway.

I'm making my last trip from the house to the truck when Mom stirs on the fold-out. Her real estate exam study guide is tucked next to her. I cap a pink highlighter that's peeking out from under the bed.

"Mom," I say.

"What're you doing, offspring?" she sleep-asks, without opening her eyes.

"Sorry, maternal unit," I whisper. "But I need a favor."

"It's fine," she says into her pillow. "What's up?"

"Can you call me in sick? For a beach day with Wil and Leigh," I tell her.

This time, she opens her eyes. "Just a beach day? Nothing future-jeopardizing, right?"

"Just a beach day. I—we all need a break."

Her brow furrows. "Something going on with you and Wil again?" she asks, trying to make her voice even, the way moms do when they're pretending that something is NO BIG DEAL. "You guys have been hanging out a lot lately."

"Um, I don't know," I say, and then I say, "Yeah. I think so," because Mom and I don't lie to each other. That's important to her. *Hawkings are real. Hawkings tell the truth, even when the truth sucks,* she always says. When I was a kid, I used to wish that she would lie to me about the adult things. I didn't want to know about account balances and how she had no idea where my dad was, that asshole.

"Good." She yawns. "Is he doing okay?"

"I guess," I say. "As well as you could expect. I think his mom's having a pretty tough time, so he's worried about her."

"We should have the two of them over for dinner." Mom sits up and hugs one of the couch pillows to her chest. Her hair is a shock of warmth around her face. "We could make a casserole or something."

"A casserole? Here?" I don't think Wil could eat another casserole in his lifetime.

She shakes her head. "You misheard me. I said bring them *takeout*, which *sounds* a little like *casserole*."

"My mistake. I don't think they're up for company right now, but you and I could have dinner. It's been a while."

"Done," she says.

"Great. Okay. So . . . *sick day in quotes?*" I flash my most responsible smile.

"I'll call the school." She yawns.

I blow her a kiss and tote an armful of beach towels out the door.

I listen to Lynyrd Skynyrd on the way, cranked up too loud. *Wilson taught me that's the only way to listen to Lynyrd Skynyrd*, I think, and then I get pissed and change the station. The day is bright and hot and cloudless. I park near the beach access and lug everything onto the sand. I smooth the towels a million times, and when I'm dripping with sweat, I crack open a Coke and kill it in a single gulp. I'm nearly alone on the smooth sand; near the waterline, there's a mother trailing behind an unsteady toddler and an elderly man casting a fishing line beyond the waves.

Wil shows up first, and then Leigh not a minute later, and when they see each other, they both try not to get caught giving me a look.

"*Surpriiise!*" I say. "Happy beach day!"

"Happy beach day?" Wil's face is crooked. "Hey, Leigh."

"You are smiling too big, Bridget," Leigh tells me. "Like, religious cult big." She gives Wil an awkward back pat. "Doing okay today?"

"Sure." Wil gives her an obligatory nod.

"I just—I wanted us to hang out, is all. Together, since the school year's almost over," I say. I want to hug Leigh, but she's all angles: arms crossed, shoulder pointing in my direction.

"Great," Wil says. "Definitely beats spending the day boxing up the last of my dead father's shit, which I was supposed to do after school."

I put a hand on his shoulder.

"Sorry." Wil's cheeks redden.

"Hey. No judgment," Leigh says.

Wil peels off his T-shirt. "I'm gonna go in real quick." He jogs toward the ocean, and I watch him disappear beneath the waves.

"Rough." Leigh unhooks her frayed denim overalls and shimmies out of them. Beneath them is a bikini she must have tie-dyed herself.

"So. You guys are banging," she says matter-of-factly.

"We are not," I say, pitching a bottle of sunscreen in her direction.

"You are such a liar! Wil Hines is drowning his sorrows in your—"

"Leigh. Gross. And no, he isn't." I chuck my cutoffs and tank top and stretch out on my stomach. Leigh drops next to me. I perch on my elbows.

"I heard Wil broke it off with Ana."

I try to stare through her mirrored shades.

"Yeah," I say. "Objectively, they weren't a good match."

"Objectively?"

"Okay. I'm not the most objective person," I admit. "But you know they weren't good together."

"Everybody knows they weren't good together."

"I'm sorry," I say. "For being so—" I make a face. "For disappearing yesterday."

"You scared me," she says, and she makes the same face. "In a big way. And you didn't call or text or anything."

"I know." I drop to my side. "It just pissed me off, the way you reacted when I told you about Wil."

She nudges her sunglasses down the bridge of her nose. "What do you mean?"

I hold my breath for a few seconds, and the words tumble out. "I wanted you to be excited for us. Because even with all the shitty stuff that's happened lately, I'm excited. I'm happy. I've wanted Wil back for a long time. This is a big deal."

Leigh rests on her side, too, and takes her sunglasses off and scoots so close that we're almost touching. I can hear the ocean rushing beneath the towel, beneath the hardened sand.

"Listen," she says. "I know this is big." I see my reflection in her eyes. "And I'm sorry for not reacting the right way or whatever. It's just that I love you. And I know what a fucking hard time this is for him."

"No, I get it."

"But you don't," she pushes back. "I don't, either. No one but Wil knows what Wil is going through right now."

I'm silent. I wish I could tell her about Wil's dad. It feels lonely, having that kind of secret, and I think of how Wil had to carry it alone for so long.

"I guess I just didn't think it was a good idea for you guys to try to get back together when he must be in such a dark place." Her lips are still pressed together like a tiny bud, worried.

"You don't want me to get hurt," I say quietly.

"But it's more than that," she argues. "You can get over being hurt. You're tough."

I flex my bicep.

"But what if you and Wil had one last shot to get back together? And what if you tried to make that happen right after his dad was killed, and it was just too much for both of you and you lost your chance?" Finally, Leigh blinks, her eyes bright and glassy.

"That's a lot of what ifs." I reach for her hand, feeling a pinch in the pit of my stomach. "What's going on with you? I'm usually the neurotic one between us."

She shrugs. "End-of-senior-year existential crisis, I guess. Sorry."

"You're forgiven." I lean over and give her a sandy kiss.

We flop onto our backs and watch the universe hurtle by in slow motion.

"I know I don't get what he's going through, exactly. And sometimes it feels like he's a million miles away." I think about the shadows that cross him when I ask if he wants to talk about that night. "But I don't care, Leigh. I don't think you have to understand every little corner of a person to love them. I think you can love them first, and you spend the time you have trying to learn the parts you don't know."

"And how much time do you have?"

I feel Wil's footfall in the sand and I shush Leigh. When he gets close, he shakes his hair, raining on my too-hot skin.

I flip over, grab his wrists, and pull him next to me. "You look good out there."

"Buddha, beam me up." Leigh groans, opening her arms wide. "Thank God school is almost over."

"Can you believe we only have a few weeks of classes left?" I say, and it sounds wrong. Seniors finish classes a week before the rest of the school, which gives us a week to decompress before graduation.

"Three weeks, baby!" Leigh high-fives the nearest cloud. "Which means three weeks until I unveil my senior art project. You guys'll come, right? The Saturday before graduation. Just me and the other AP Art nerds."

"Definitely," I tell her. "We love AP Art nerds."

"So, Leigh." Wil turns onto his side. "What's your plan? College, I'm guessing?"

"Art school." Leigh opens the cooler and unearths one of the subs. "At SCAD."

"Cool," he says.

"Are you staying here?" she asks.

He nods. "Running my dad's shop. I would've done it anyway, but now that—" He stares past us, at the ocean. "I want to keep an eye on my mom for a while, and she'll be at the house, so—"

"Plus, you've always wanted to build boats," I say.

"Right," he says. He turns to me. "When are you supposed to leave for Miami?"

"Orientation is in August," I say.

"August?" A shadow changes Wil's face.

I scratch at the sand. I've been planning on Miami for months now. I've worked hard for four years, and I almost lost it all last summer. Now, next to Wil, I can't imagine being without him. Losing him again. For the first time, the word *stay* flits across my consciousness, then zooms out of reach, piercing the folds of the bright sky.

# BRIDGE

*Summer, Senior Year*

MAY brings sticky, slick-skinned days, each one reminding me that my hours with Wil are numbered. I know that I am leaving soon. I have to, no matter how much I'll miss Wil. Miami is only six hours away. We've overcome wider distances than that.

At school, we're careful. I feel Ana's eyes on me—on us—throughout the day, and when we're both at our lockers at the same time or when Wil loses his pencil and has to turn around to ask me for another, the space around us gets quiet.

We spend our afternoons relearning each other, sitting in our old booth at Nina's and bribing Leonard to make iced coffee. Leonard says it's a trend that will never last, but obliges, since we're *graduating this year and all*. We are giddy with caffeine and almost summer and each other. I remember how much I love his different laughs, even the fake ones when he thinks my joke is lame. I'd forgotten how his eyes change color with the seasons.

At the start of our last week of classes, I'm hanging in the parking lot after school, fiddling with the radio dial, when Mom texts. *Code S*, which means she needs help at the resort. Depending on which one of us you ask, *Code S* either means *Short-staffed* (me) or *Shitshow* (Mom).

*On my way.* I hit SEND just as a set of knuckles collides with my passenger window.

"Wil!" I screech.

*Sorry*, he mouths. His grin is lopsided.

The passenger side window only rolls down successfully once every six months or so, and I don't want to risk it. I lean across the console and pull at the handle so the door swings open.

"You scared me," I accuse as he slides into the front seat.

"Still haven't fixed that window yet?"

"Shouldn't I be asking you that question?" I let him meet me most of the way for a kiss and another and another.

"You headed home?" he asks into my neck. "Want to go to the beach?"

A shiver runs through me. "I wish. Mom needs my help at work."

"Doing what?"

I twist the keys in the ignition. "Answering the phone maybe, or setting the tables at blu. I don't know. She didn't say."

"Count me in."

I pull out of the lot and we drive the few blocks to the resort. We park in the staff lot and sneak another kiss before we duck into the lobby.

Mom is standing behind the front desk, with the phone lodged between her shoulder and ear. I like seeing my mother when she's at work. She looks contained in her black knit dress and black pumps. Her red bob is smooth.

When Mom sees us, her eyebrows leap behind her bangs. She smiles and waves us over.

"You're absolutely right, sir. That's unacceptable." Mom rolls her eyes as we approach the desk. "Listen, as long as I'm sending someone up, I hope you won't mind a bottle of the Pinot you enjoyed so much at dinner last night? On us, of course. My pleasure." She hangs up, flutters her lashes, and mouths, *Asshole*.

"Another pleasant day at the office?" I lean over the desk and blow her a kiss.

"That's one way to put it." She comes around the desk and pulls Wil in for a hug.

"Mom," I say.

"Well!" she says, with a giant grin on her face. Apparently, my mother hasn't gotten the memo from Wil's mother that says now is not a good time for us.

"Here's the deal," she says, releasing Wil. "My best housekeeper called in sick, and she brings her sister to work, which means I'm short two." She chews on her bottom lip. "You can have dinner at blu as a thank-you."

"What's the special tonight?" I half tease.

"Seared ahi tuna with roasted-garlic-and-wasabi mashed potatoes and a grilled heart of romaine salad," she says. "What do you have at home?"

"Granola." I roll my eyes. "We're in."

"Okay, then." She tells us where to find the cleaning supplies and gives us both key cards. She has special instructions for each of the rooms we're supposed to clean, the kinds of details that only she could remember. The Freemans don't like the smell of lemon, so we have to dust room 301 with the lavender-scented spray. Mr. Kildaire likes to come home to a chilled bottle of champagne. The Eddys need an extra pillow for the annoying-as-hell Jack Russell they're not supposed to keep here.

"Got it?" The phone rings again, and Mom waves us off.

We start with the ocean-view penthouse, where this young stockbroker hotshot named Mr. Kildaire lives three months out of the year. Wil drags the cleaning cart inside and I shut the door behind him. The place is a disaster: dirty laundry everywhere; ties slung over the back of the leather armchair, and a skimpy red thong that Wil lifts from the pillow with the handle of the toilet plunger.

"Ten bucks say it's his." He grins.

"Nah. Bet it belongs to the . . . girlfriend? Mistress?" I unwind a pair of fishnet stockings from around an empty champagne bottle. "Wife?"

"Uh, I'm going with girlfriend or mistress." Wil catapults the thong in my direction, and I bat it away with the bottle. "Wives wear ratty flannel bathrobes."

"According to who?"

"My mom's laundry basket." Wil laughs. "I guess your mom's too young to wear that kind of stuff?"

I scoop a pair of high heels from under the bed and line them up next to the dresser. "My mom's never been a wife, so—"

"Oh." I pretend not to notice that Wil's face is red. "Well. It's probably not all it's cracked up to be, if you ask my mom."

186

I don't know what to say to that.

Wil's muscles look taut as he picks up a bucket of cleaning supplies. I strip the sheets and make the bed while Wil tackles the bathroom. Every now and then he yells, "Gross!" and I yell, "What?!" and he yells, "Trust me, you don't want to know." Eventually, he emerges, red-faced, yellow rubber gloves up to his elbows, holding a stuffed clear trash bag.

"This guy," he says, with a look that somehow contains disdain and admiration.

"You're right. Definitely don't want to know." I turn my back to him, spritzing window cleaner on the balcony doors.

Behind me, Wil hums cheesy porn music until I'm laughing so hard I brace myself against the glass door and have to clean it all over again.

I vacuum while he dusts and then I wedge a fresh bottle of champagne in the bucket on the glass coffee table. When we're finished, Wil reaches for the remote and flops onto the bed.

"No. No way. We have to get to the other rooms." I reach for his hand and try to pull him up, but he's too strong. With one quick tug, I'm facedown in a pile of pillow shams. I inhale ocean breeze fabric softener before I flip onto my back and blow the hair out of my eyes. "We have to get out of here. What if Kinky Kildaire catches us?"

"Just for a few minutes." Before I can argue, he's on top of me, trailing kisses from my lips to my chin, down my neck. My body burns with want for him, for the softness of his lips and the roughness of his hands. I kiss him back, map the muscular lines of his back with my fingertips.

"Wil," I whisper as he tugs at my T-shirt. "I want to. But not here. We can't."

"Just for a second," he murmurs, kissing my stomach.

I can't catch my breath. "Seriously." I laugh. "Not here."

He groans and rolls us over so that I'm on top now. "Whatever you say, boss." He looks deep into my eyes and everything is suddenly quiet and still. I run my fingers through his hair. I want to slow time. I want to live in this room, in this exact second in time, with him forever.

"Do you ever wonder what it would be like to live like this?" I ask him, pointing and flexing my toes. "To come home and have everything look perfect?" I slide next to him, tucking into his body.

"*Look* perfect." He sighs. "That's the thing. You never know what peoples' real lives are like." He kisses the tip of my nose.

"I know," I murmur. "But sometimes I wonder what it would be like to have everything just . . . taken care of."

"You'd hate it," he insists with a smile.

"Says you." I shove him playfully, and he pulls me in even closer, fast.

"That's what you like best. Taking care of people. You're good at it."

"Thanks." I smile.

Wil says, "Besides, living with all this stuff doesn't make a person happier. It's just noise." Cloud cover passes through him. Then his eyes are clear again.

"That view, though." I prop myself up and watch the ocean colors pulse.

"I can see the ocean any time I want. I can see it up close, the way it's supposed to be seen." Wil moves closer. "Beautiful things are meant to be seen up close."

"Really?" I murmur. "You're going with that line?"

"I have to. It's out there now." His lips spread into a smile in the second before we kiss.

The phone bleats a shrill tone, and Wil jumps to his feet, accidentally knocking a glass off the side table. It hits the floor and shatters.

"Shit!" He stumbles back, his head colliding with the window. It makes a dull cracking sound. His hand flies to the back of his head and his breath comes out in short, rapid breaths.

I jump off the bed. "Wil!" I try to take his hand, but he is frozen. His eyes are distant, unfocused, like he's miles away. "Wil!"

"I'm okay," he finally says, sinking against the foot of the bed. I watch the adrenaline drain from him, until he's nothing more than an empty vessel.

"You're not *okay*." My voice breaks. I kneel close to him. Not too close.

"I'm fine. I guess I scare easy these days." He closes his eyes, shutting me out. "Sorry. That was so stupid."

"No. No. It's okay, Wil. Can I get you something, or—" He shrinks when I touch him.

The words *Tell me, please* hover on my tongue. But I am not the girl who wants to know the way everyone else wants to know. I've waited for him this long.

"Don't. Just give me a second." He slides his hands through his hair. His breath is thready. I watch his eyes race back and forth beneath his lids. "I'm fine. Sorry. I'm fine."

I pull away. "It's okay, Wil." I am helpless, watching a storm inside him that I don't understand. When his breath is slow again, I try to touch him. First on the knee. Then the arm.

"Talking about it could help," I say. "You can tell me anything. Everything."

"I can't, Bridge." His eyes are closed, still. I need to see them. "I want to. I just—I can't."

I settle back against the bed. The comforter smells like lavender. Leigh was right. I'll never really know what Wil went through that night. No matter how close we are, no matter how much I love him, he will always have rooms I couldn't possibly enter. Dark, hidden corners I won't be able to find.

# WIL

*Spring, Senior Year*

STORM clouds sink toward Dad's truck as we pull out of the grocery store parking lot. Ana and I are wedged into the corner of the truck bed. I take off my jacket and wrap it around Ana's shoulders in case we can't outrun the storm.

"First senior bonfire, babe," Ana whispers, her mouth close to my ear. Our run-in with Bridge in the grocery store flower aisle doesn't bother Ana at all, apparently. "Can you believe we're graduating in a couple of months?" She scoots closer, and I check Dad's rearview to make sure he's not spying.

"It'll be fun." I focus on the road. Even with my girlfriend so close, I can't get Bridge's colors out of my mind. Somehow I forgot that her hair is all the different shades of fire. Wind streams through the truck bed as Dad zigzags us toward home. "We should stay at the anniversary party for a while, though. Hang out with my parents."

"Oh. Sure. It's just that I've been wanting to go since I was a freshman," Ana says. "Don't you think it's a rite of passage?"

I smile and nod and think, *Really? You've been thinking about sitting around a fire for three years?*

I need Ana to understand: Tonight is more than some stupid excuse to chug beer around an open fire like cave people. Tonight is the night that my mother will understand: My father is exactly the man we need him to be. It's been months since Dad squeezed the air out of me at Nina's, and he's kept his promises. The most unbelievable thing has started to happen to our family. I'd never believe it, if it weren't for the sea cucumbers.

I learned about sea cucumbers when I was six, in the middle of the night, on the National Geographic channel. I used to keep the television on at night, three bars above *Mute*, just loud enough to drown out the arguing or the silence in my parents' bedroom. I liked the shows about the creatures from the deepest, blackest part of the ocean. Like the sea cucumbers, who could do this thing called regeneration. Cut a sea cucumber in half, and the halves will grow into wholes. The damn things can heal themselves.

Ever since that morning at Nina's, ever since Dad promised to be better, it feels like the same thing has happened to our family. We're becoming whole again. Only it's not science or magic. It's my dad. He's been working on becoming the man I've always known. He goes to church on Sundays now, which I don't get, but I don't have to. Sometimes Mom goes. My dad touches her now—on the back while she's doing the dishes or he'll squeeze her feet while we're all watching TV. When he gets pissed off, he goes out to the workshop and he doesn't come back in until he's cooled down. One time, he stayed out there all night.

I've never seen him work harder at anything, and Mom is starting to feel different, too. She smiles out the window while he works in the shop. She's started power walking around the neighborhood with Mrs. Wilkerson from her book club, and she says that she's lost a couple of pounds. She even bought a new pair of jeans. (*Skinny jeans*, Ana tells me.) When Dad saw those jeans, he smacked her butt with a stack of catalogues and she laughed out loud. A real laugh that came from her belly.

If there's any part of her that wonders still, she'll understand tonight. It's their anniversary. Dad and I have the whole night planned: Ana and I will have a snack (*appetizers*, Ana keeps correcting me) with them on a twenty-five-foot Catalina he's just finished working on for a friend. After that, Ana and I will jump ship for the bonfire and leave my folks to sail to the Shoreline, the restaurant where they had their first date. We've never gone out for their anniversary before. But we're different now—the kind of family that thinks being a family is something to celebrate.

"You know, your dad is adorable." Ana leans into me. My arm is slung over her shoulder, and her hand rests on my thigh. We've been running around town for supplies since school let out. "I wish my dad did stuff like this for my mom. Last year, he had his assistant send her flowers."

"He hasn't always been like this," I say for some reason.

"Huh?"

"Yeah. He's a good guy."

She nods. "Well, he made you, didn't he?" She kisses my

193

neck in a way that makes me wish we were alone.

We pull into the driveway just after six. Dad throws the truck into park and asks, "You kids ready?" over the idling engine.

"Flowers—check." I hold up the bouquet of flowers like a torch. Tulips, which Dad knows are Mom's favorite flowers.

"Appetizers—check!" Ana pats the bags of cheese and crackers.

Ana slides her hand up and down my thigh, sexy without trying. I respond exactly the way she wants me to, and she grins and all of a sudden the bonfire seems like an okay idea.

"Okay. Here we go." Dad leans on the horn in rhythm until Mom throws open the front door with a *what the*—? look on her face.

"Get in, Mom!" I yell. "We're going out."

"Wilson? What in the world—" She comes over to the truck bed, and when she leans over the edge, I see her at seventeen, getting into this same truck. It's enough to make me look away. She smiles at Ana.

I hand Mom the flowers. "Happy anniversary," I say. "We're going out. All of us."

Her eyes get wet. "Oh my God."

"You didn't forget, did you?"

"I—" Mom buries her nose in the flowers, and when she comes back up for air, they're beaded as if we're standing in the rain. "I guess I'm just surprised, is all."

I give her a squeeze and she holds on tighter and longer than usual, until Dad lays on the horn again and shouts, "Sun's going down before you know it!" When we pull away, we're both kind of foggy eyed. I think we've all been waiting for tonight, each of us in our own way.

* * *

Ana and I follow my parents to the marina in her car. We listen to a boy band covering a Queen song, and Ana talks about how some guy I don't know is an amazing songwriter. I don't say anything, because if there's one thing I've learned from my dad lately, it's that loving someone means sometimes not saying what you want to say ("It's *Queen!*") when you want to say it.

Last week, Ana told me she loved me. I don't know if I love her or not. She's a nice girl, sweet, and I like that she doesn't know how pretty she is. I said, "I love you, too," because I do *like* Ana, and I don't want to be an asshole since we've been dating for coming up on a year now. The way she said it—as if she was stepping on hot coals—made me think she'd said it lots of times before, and gotten lots of asshole answers.

The Catalina is a beautiful boat, with graceful lines that would slice the water like a blade. When we get to the slip, my parents are settled on the boat's stern. My dad's laugh slides over the water, bigger than I've ever heard it before.

"Permission to board?" I call.

Dad waves us over, and we slip off our shoes and climb aboard. I love the way the boat moves beneath us.

"We've got snacks," I say. "Appetizers." I slide in next to Mom, whose eyes are still unfocused, and damp. I break open the cheese and crackers and a little plastic knife, and Ana arranges everything on the brown grocery bag. Behind my father, the sun is sinking low. This is my favorite time of day on the water. Everything in the world is on fire. Everything is gold.

"You boys," my mother says. She glances back and forth between us. "You really didn't have to do this."

"Well, happy anniversary," Dad says, and he makes a special point of leaning over to kiss her on the cheek.

"Hey. Tell us about your first date," I say to Mom. She shakes her head and says, "Wilson?" softly.

"Let's see. I picked her up at her parents' place in that same truck," Dad says proudly.

Ana giggles. "Seriously?"

Dad's eyes gleam. "I picked her up in the truck, and she came out and she was wearing white jeans and this shirt that looked like she'd shrunk it in the dryer—"

"A *crop top*, Wilson." Mom smiles a little. Her eyes are still wet. "It was in style."

I try to picture my mother young.

"Half a shirt, which was just fine by me, and her hair was real long then." Dad rubs his hands together like he's making fire. "I knew her from school and such. I'd asked her out because one of my buddies was too chickenshit—"

"Wilson!" Mom rolls her eyes.

"Fine. Too much of a wuss to do it himself. When I saw her walk out of her folks' house that night, I thought to myself, *Damn. That is one beautiful girl.*"

"That's really sweet," Ana chirps. My mother is crying now.

"Anyway, I'd been working on a boat for the principal of the high school—"

"Dr. Berman." Mom wipes her eyes.

"And even after I dropped out and started the business, he let me keep working on it. When I finished up, I went to his office and we were just talking, and I just happened to mention that I wanted to take your mother out."

"Just happened to slip that in there." Mom sniffs.

"What'd he say?" I am hungry for this. I realize that I know nothing about them, about their history or who said hello first or why.

Dad grunts. "He told me I could take her out on his boat," he says, disbelieving. "He made me swear on the keys that I'd bring her back safe, and I said I would and I told him, *I think I really like this girl, sir,* and he said—" Dad tilts his face toward Mom, and his beard grazes her cheek. She pulls back a little. It's a reflex: quick, but I see it. "You remember?"

They say it together: *"I was talking about the boat, son."*

I laugh louder than anyone.

"Well," Ana announces. "You guys don't need us cramping your style. But first, I brought some wine, for a little toast."

"Ana," I say as she unearths the bottle from a bag at her feet. I've told her.

"Oh. We don't drink, dear." Mom's voice is stiff. Her eyes dart from my dad to me and back again.

"I told her," I say quietly.

"Henney." Dad reaches for the bottle. "The girl brought wine. Let's thank her."

I am instantly wearing damp skin. "Dad?"

*"Wilson,"* Mom says without moving her lips.

"One glass of wine. On our wedding anniversary. On the evening I planned for you." Dad's voice has an edge.

*"Dad,"* I say again. I beg him silently not to do this. It's been such a nice time. It's the only thing I want from him in the whole world. I'll never ask for anything again.

Finally, he puts the bottle down. "Coke it is." He disappears into the galley, and Mom and I exchange looks.

"Um—" Ana says, and I have to take a slow, deep breath, and I can't look at her.

He resurfaces a few minutes later, and he's his old self again, cradling a two-liter bottle of Coke and four plastic cups. He pours a few sips into each cup and passes them around in the silence.

"To my wife," he says. He opens his mouth like he has more to say. I *know* he does, words buried under his skin, tucked between all the years they have together. But after a few seconds, he tosses back the drink like it's a shot, and we all do the same.

We drive to the bonfire in silence. Ana tries a few times—*Aren't they so cute?* and *Seriously, I wish my parents . . .* —but after a while, she gives up and turns on the radio.

The bonfire is exactly what I expect: a bunch of kids I don't care about chugging watery beer in somebody's backyard because that's how they want to remember high school. When we get there, Ana finds her friends, and I stand at the edge of the yard, watching.

I get a beer to have something to hold on to, and I retreat back to my spot at the edge of the world. I don't see Bridge. I'm not looking for her or anything, but I don't see her. I do see her brother, buzzing around Emilie Simpson. If Bridge and I were speaking, I'd drag Micah home right now, myself.

"Wil Hines!" Ana comes winding back to me. "Wil Hines, don't you know not to leave a girl alone at a party?" She leans into me, her mouth so close to my skin, her body touching mine.

"This is kind of lame, don't you think?" I ask, but I don't think she hears me. I wish I knew what my parents were doing now—I'm hoping for laughter and calm seas beneath them.

Ana sighs into me. "Do you ever think about when we're old like our parents, how we'll look back on this time in our lives and wish we could do it again? If you think about it, it's kind of amazing: *We are living the best part of our lives right this very second. It will never be this good again.*"

I look into my red cup of beer. I have never felt more alone.

"I kind of think I'll like being older," I tell the beer. I'm not one of those people who thinks, *Everything will be different when* . . . I am who I am—*a simple kind of man*—and my life probably won't change much. But I can't stand the idea that this is it.

"Oh. Me too," Ana says quickly, and her eyes get sharp all of a sudden. "College will be fun."

That's not what I meant.

"Hey." I brush her hair away from her face. "Do you maybe want to get out of here?"

"Wil Hines!" She slaps my chest with her free hand. "It's *early*. Thea's not even here yet."

"Okay, well." I set my beer down. "I think I'm going to head back to my place. I'm kind of tired. Big day." It's such a lame excuse that I close my eyes for a second, so I don't have to see her expression. But I feel a pull toward home. "You gonna be okay?"

"Um, yeah." She looks past me. "Sure."

"Thea's coming soon, right?"

"Probably." She shrugs. She scans the crowd.

"Okay. I'll, ah—I'll text you." I lean in to kiss her, and she turns her head at the last second. "Okay."

I walk for a while before I know which way is home, before the neon lights of Atlantic appear against the dusty purple. By the time I turn onto my street, it's dark. The walk has unscrewed me, and everything I've been holding on to floats outside of me and drifts into the trees. I let go of Ana's blank face and the line of her jaw when she turned away. I release my dad's weirdness on the boat and the thoughts about Bridge and the gone look on her brother's face. By the time I shove the key in the lock, I feel good.

"You guys home?" The house is dark. Once my eyes adjust, I can see shadows that don't belong here. I see the edges of a pink suitcase I haven't seen in years. Some hanging clothes: dresses and coats I've never seen Mom wear before. I sidestep Dad's golf clubs, leaning against the table in the entrance hall. (*Dad has golf clubs?*) I feel my way to the wall, and I flip the light switch. *Dad wouldn't like this*, I think. *It's messy. She should put her things away.* I fight the heaviness that is filling me up, because I don't know what this is yet. I don't know.

"Wil?" My mother's voice is thick, coming from the kitchen.

*Dad wouldn't like this*, I think again. It's the only thought I can manage.

My mother is leaning over the island in the kitchen. She's my mother but somebody has rearranged her features. Her lips are puffy and I can barely see her eyes, and her face is inflated and red, like a horrible doll. She's been crying, hard.

"What?" I snap, even though I know. I already know. "What?"

"I asked him to leave," the strange doll tells me. "I want a divorce."

200

# BRIDGE

*Summer, Senior Year*

THERE are two Wils now. I think that's what happens to a person after the worst day of his life: There's the before and the after. I want more of Before Wil, whose eyes were clear and whose laugh came easily. But loving Wil means loving After Wil, too. His sudden twitches and unexplained shadows. That's what I tell Minna early Sunday morning. She answered the door in her bathrobe and slippers, with a long white braid snaking down her back, looking like an old woman in a pioneer movie. Now we're tucked in her bedroom, Minna under the sheets in an antique sleigh bed and me on a cream-colored club chair with a small stain that looks like red wine.

"I get it," I say. "He's not the same guy he was before. I can't expect him to be the same."

Minna gives me a look that is the old lady equivalent of *no shit*.

"What's the *but?*" She yawns. The coffee I brought her sits untouched on her bedside table.

"There's no *but.*"

"There's always a *but.* You have three seconds, or I'm going back to sleep."

"Okay, okay. But I don't know how to help him. When he gets . . . far away." I think about his face in the hotel room the other day. He was gone, too far away from me. Buried so deep beneath his shell that I was afraid he might never come back. "I don't know what to do to make it okay."

She doesn't answer because she doesn't need to.

"And before you tell me that there's nothing I can do to change this or make it okay, I *know.* I can't."

"You can't."

"But it makes you crazy, watching somebody hurt so badly and not being able to do shit about it." I sip my coffee.

"Of course it does. Grief itself is a kind of temporary insanity. We are crazy when we are suffering and when we are watching loved ones suffer. We're animals. We snap, and wound, and snarl."

I think about Wil in his kitchen, nipping at the detectives.

"If I knew what happened that night," I say. "Maybe then."

"You think knowing the details will change how helpless you feel." Minna tilts her face toward mine. The early morning light makes her look younger. "Trust me. It will only make you feel worse."

She's wrong. There are only three people in the universe who are carrying the weight of what happened that night: Wil, Henney, and the man who killed Wilson. If Wil would just tell me, his load would be lighter. I would do that for him. I want to.

"Wil's told me some of the details already." I sound defensive. "Not about the night of the murder. About the kind of guy his dad was."

"An asshole, if I remember correctly."

"Which"—I rub my temples—"still doesn't make sense, entirely. I guess I always thought Wil's family was kind of perfect."

Minna says, "No family is perfect, and it's dangerous to think so. Do they still teach Tolstoy in school? 'Happy families are all alike; every unhappy family is unhappy in its own way.' It's the first line of *Anna Karenina*."

"Depressing."

"Not depressing. Realistic. No family is happy all the time. Families are living, breathing, flawed organisms."

"You never talk about yours, you know. Your daughter?" I press my lips together as soon as the words slip out. Maybe I shouldn't have asked.

"You want to know about my Virgina," she says, and her voice tells me it's okay. She pulls the covers up to her chin, cocooning herself. I have the sudden urge to slide under the covers next to her.

"When I was young, I married a very charming, very intelligent, very handsome man who happened to love money and hate women. He was very smart. He didn't show me who he was until after we'd married. And then it started, small things at first. He'd take the money I made in my receptionist job. For safekeeping, he said. So that I didn't have to worry my pretty, little head about it. Finances were the man's job."

I can't imagine anyone speaking to Minna that way. Not now, not then.

"Remember, it was a long time ago, and I'd been raised to believe that he was right."

I picture Young Minna with smooth skin and jewel eyes.

"And then, as time went on, something else started to happen. My family, my friends, everyone I held close, started to drift away. I didn't notice it at first. When I wanted to have my mother for dinner, he'd say he wanted me all to himself. When I wanted to see friends, he'd say I wasn't being a caring wife. I needed to devote more time to him. And one day, I woke up and I realized: I was completely alone."

"Scary." I swallow.

"Terrifying. And so I did the stupidest, most wonderful thing I could have done."

I bite my lip. "You had a kid."

"I had a kid." Her voice thins with the words, and they come faster now. "I felt sure that things would change once I had the baby, but they only got worse. He started calling me names. *Stupid. Useless. Whore.* He said no one could love me, not even my own child." She is trembling.

"Minna," I whisper.

But she doesn't stop. "After a while, I became so depressed that I considered ending it all. The only thing keeping me on earth was Virginia. So I went to a psychiatrist, who prescribed me medication for depression. And I was in therapy for *years.*" She sits up suddenly, laughs. "It was my favorite hour out of the week. Other than bedtime for V, of course."

I am wordless. Minna has had thousands of other lifetimes before this one. There is so much I don't know.

"And things got better, but only because I built up a sanctuary in my head. When things got bad, when he got angry, I would disappear into myself and I would think about escaping to the mountains with my girl. I saved money on the sly. And when Virginia was three, I was ready to file for divorce." She reaches for her coffee and takes a sip. Then she sets the mug on the bedside table. "Horseshit," she announces.

"Divorce," I remind her.

She nods. "When I filed, Virginia's father told the judge I was an unfit mother."

I bolt upright. "*That* is horseshit."

"He said I was unstable, and told the judge I'd been on medication. He went through my things and found a journal I'd written in just after Virginia was born. I'd been sleep deprived and depressed, but we didn't have a name for it then. I'd written some things that made it seem . . ."

"But that's not fair!" I lunge forward and squeeze her arm. "Minna!"

"He got full custody. I had visitation, but it wasn't enough. He told her that I was unwell. That I didn't . . ." Her voice wavers. "That I didn't . . . want . . . her. And she believed him." Her lips freeze. She can't even form the words. "By the time she was old enough to choose . . ."

"Minna! She can't believe him, still!"

Minna hushes me and nods at the clock. "It's early, Bridget. There are cranky old people around here for miles, you know."

"Sorry."

"It is truly amazing, the damage one human being can do to another human being without ever raising a hand," she tells me.

I think about my dad, whoever and wherever he is, and I

wonder if he understands the damage he inflicted just by walking away. I wonder if he knows what it feels like to walk around knowing that you are unwanted.

"But she hasn't responded to any of your letters? Even as an adult, she hasn't—"

Minna holds up a hand. "Enough, Bridget. I'm tired."

"Right. Sorry." I crawl into bed next to her. I don't think she minds, because she closes her eyes without saying anything. The light from the bedside table settles in the valleys around her eyes and mouth.

When Minna's breaths are slow and even, I slip out from under the covers. I swallow a yelp when my toe slams into a clear plastic container beneath the bed, the kind Mom stores her sweaters in. I'm nudging it back into place when I see the name on an envelope in uneven script, pressed against the plastic from the inside: *Virginia*.

Instinctively, I know what this is, and I know I should leave it. Instead, I slide the container from beneath the bed and I pop open the top. The container is filled with envelopes. Letters, all of them addressed to Virginia. Stamped but not dated. Some of the envelopes are yellowed and old. There are hundreds, thousands, maybe, years and years worth, and there are three identical containers jammed behind this one. The letters show addresses in California, in Colorado, in Florida, a few hours south of here. Minna has followed her daughter through childhood into adulthood, across the country. But she's never mailed a word.

The room tilts a little. All of Minna's years are here, faded and tucked away. Unwitnessed. Maybe the letters are apologies, explanations. Or maybe they are crammed full of the small details that make up a day: rude comments from an ignorant boss, a whole paragraph on the best doughnut in the world. There is a whole life here. Shoved under the bed like a secret.

I take one of the newer envelopes. Its edges are still sharp. I stuff it into my back pocket and shove the bin under the bed again. I move quickly down the hallway and out the front door. I twist the lock in the knob before I pull it closed behind me. In the sunlight, I look at the envelope again. Minna's handwriting is tired. Minna is tired. Life has wrung her out. How much more time does she have to find her way back to Virginia?

I jump in the truck and balance the envelope on my thigh. It wasn't mine to take. But this is my chance to do something for her, before a life storm swoops in and wrecks the possibility of Minna connecting with her only child.

*And Virginia,* I think as I back out of the parking lot. I couldn't stand wandering the world without the mother who made me. In this world, there are men hitting their wives and sons. There are mothers deserting their babies. Parents who don't deserve to watch their children grow. But Minna is not that parent. She deserves to find her way back to Virginia.

I roll down the window and slow to a near stop as I approach the guard gate. There's a mailbox there. I could do it. It would only take a second. There are so many broken families in this world, and maybe Minna is right. Maybe every family is broken in its own way. But not every family is beyond repair.

I pull open the slot, close my eyes, and slip the letter inside.

# BRIDGE

*Summer, Senior Year*

**ALL** day, I think about Minna and Virginia and Wil and me and what it means to be a real family. In the evening, after Mom heads to work and Micah ditches me for his friends, I drag our bedsheets and towels to the Laundromat downtown and camp out in the orange plastic chairs by the window while I wait. I stare at the bricks that carry the names of people who love one another now, or did once. The more I think about the bones of what it means to love another human being, the more I know: There can be no secrets. You have to know everything: the darks and the lights, the befores and the afters. To love Wil, all of Wil, I have to understand what happened that night.

When the buzzer goes off, I pull the hot sheets from the dryer. I don't bother folding them, just stuff them in Mom's wicker laundry basket and heave the basket into the passenger seat of the truck. I drive to Wil's house, my skin damp with early evening heat and adrenaline. My hands slip against the steering wheel. I'm going to ask him.

I see him the second I turn down his street. He doesn't notice me right away. He's standing in the bed of Wilson's old truck, sweeping dead leaves into precise piles and then spilling them into the drive. He's neat like Wilson was. Watching him, my inside seams might burst. My throat gets tight and my eyes get full. He is good to his depths. There should be more of him. It strikes me as the saddest thing in the world that there are people on this earth who don't know Wil Hines.

I pull up to the curb and he spins around to face me. He shields his eyes with one hand and gives me a wave. I roll down the window.

"Getting your Sunday chores done?" I tease. "Good boy."

"*Actually* . . ." He draws out the word in a way that makes me shivery and warm at the same time. "I was on my way to see you."

"Me?" I flutter my lashes like a coy girl in an old movie.

He nods. "I want to take you out tonight. On a real date. Not a bonfire, and not your old lady friend's house. You and me and a beach, and nobody else."

"That sounds really good," I say.

"Only one condition." He jumps down from the truck bed, and doesn't even wince when his bare feet hit the cement. He leans through my open window, and the truck is filled with the warm, earthy smell of him.

"What?" *Anything. Everything. Always.*

"No talk about any of the big stuff. Off-limit topics include graduation, next year, and my dad," he says. "Deal?"

I nod. Instantly, everything outside of us can wait.

"Deal," I say, and we kiss on it.

I park my truck on the street and wait for Wil in the yard while he tells his mom we're going out. Summer is ripening quickly. I close my eyes and listen to the reedy thrum of the cicadas. The sound reminds me of summer nights when I was a kid. Mom would prop my bedroom window open with an old dictionary, and the cicadas' mating calls mixed with the sound of the waves would lull me to sleep.

I hear the crunch of Wil's feet on the grass.

"Making a wish?"

I open my eyes. "I guess you could say that. I was just thinking that I like it here. With you."

He smiles. "I like it here with you."

"I've been thinking that I want to get out of here, start a new life someplace else, but I don't mind this place, as long as you're here."

He brushes my hair from my eyes and rests his hand against my neck. I know that he can feel my heartbeat through my skin. "I like everywhere you are," he says, and kisses my neck. I could sink into the grass with him and never come up for air.

He opens the passenger door of the truck and pulls a black backpack from the seat.

"Hold this," he says. "But don't open it."

"Or what?" I get in, and he kisses me roughly. My heart leaps through my chest.

"Better not, Hawking."

He starts the truck and takes us in the direction of the highway. It's not long before we're driving too fast on an empty two-lane road. Someone has wrung out the sun, and it drips pink into the mirrored river.

"Where are we going?" I ask.

"Little Talbot."

Little Talbot Island is one of the small barrier islands not far from home. It's wild, still—nothing but untouched beaches and salt marshes and dunes. I raise an eyebrow. "Scheming to get me all alone, mister?"

"Definitely. Just you and me and the stars and the ocean. That's all I've ever wanted, actually. Since the first day of fourth grade." He looks at me with a face that has broken wide open. Finally, I see all of him: his colors and shades, his pain and the way he loves me.

I don't say anything back. Some words deserve to stand alone.

We drive the rest of the way in the kind of silence that feels like a warm bath. When we get to the park, Wil takes a back entrance. He's sailing buddies with the guy who works the gate during the day, the guy who conveniently left the entrance unlocked tonight. Sand spins under the tires, and he maneuvers the truck onto the beach.

"Pass me that bag?" he asks.

I heave it in his direction.

"Okay. Now stay here until I tell you to come out."

"Got it." I slide back in the seat and close my eyes, listening to Wil's sounds behind the truck: his bare feet against the wet sand and the way he clears his throat every few seconds because he's nervous, which makes me nervous. Soon he opens my door, and extends a hand.

"Come on," he says quietly, and leads me around the truck bed.

He's blanketed the sand with colorful quilts his mother made with his old Little League and sailing camp T-shirts. Around the perimeter of the quilts are glowing pillar candles, like the beach is on fire. We are the only ones here, and the only sounds are the lapping ocean and the pop of the candles.

"Wil." I let his name rest on my tongue as we settle onto the blanket. I can't pull away from us. Wil's face is shadowed and blazing in the most beautiful way.

"I love you, Bridge," he tells me. "I've loved you for a long time."

"I've loved you forever."

His fingers are trembling when he touches my collarbone. When he curls them around my tank top and pulls me into him. A breeze swoops down the beach, extinguishing some of the candles. But we are ignited by shared sunburns and workshop afternoons. Handstand contests and hours spent bouncing around in a truck bed. All these things make us who we are. The things I don't know about him don't define him. I was silly to think I had to know them all. I don't need them to see the real Wil Hines. He is right here, in front of me. He slides over me, pressing me into the sand, anchoring me to this life, to us.

# BRIDGE

*Summer, Senior Year*

THE next morning, I stand at the foot of the stairs in the filtered morning light. I blink furiously, just to be sure. But every time I open my eyes, Wil is there, lounging in the living room with Mom and Micah, an open box of bagels on the coffee table. He looks good, sprawled in the middle of my family portrait. I press my lips together. They are still swollen with him.

"Hey there, Sleeping Beauty," he says.

Micah makes a gagging sound.

"Hey!" I lock eyes with Wil. "How long have you been here?"

"This boy was sweet enough to show up at the door with bagels and coffee this morning." Mom tightens the sash on her waffled robe. "Just a little celebration, since the two of you are out of school this week."

Micah scowls. "I hate my life."

I drop between Wil and Mom on the couch and give him a kiss on the cheek.

"That was really sweet." I brush Wil's hair away from his eyes.

"That *was* really sweet, Wil," Micah says in a girly voice.

"Dude. Not cool," Wil jokes, handing me a latté in a paper cup.

"You guys have big plans for today?" Mom asks. "Graduation rehearsal?"

"Not until tomorrow," I tell her.

"Yeah, so . . . kind of a free day today," Wil says, sliding a glance in my direction. His cell rings, and he checks the screen. "Sorry. It's my mom." He ducks outside.

"*Sooo* . . ." Mom leans back. "How was Little Talbot last night?"

"How did you know?"

"Wil told me. Unlike some people, he tells me things," Mom chides me.

I ignore her tone and sip my coffee. "It's really romantic out there."

"Age-appropriately romantic, I hope." She looks straight through me.

"Oh, age-appropriately, for sure." I switch to a chug.

Wil pushes through the door, silent. He is blank-faced and gray.

"They got him." His voice is thin, like water. "They got him."

"Got who?"

"Honey? Wil?" Mom tenses.

"The guy who killed my dad. He broke into another place last night, and they got him." His face twists, and he lets out a half sob.

"Oh my God." I'm frozen. I don't know whether to laugh or cry or scream. I jump up and hug him hard. "Wil. Oh my God."

"Yancey and Porter want to talk to Mom and me. At the station." He blinks. "I have to go to the station." His eyes are unfocused. He is too quiet for a moment like this.

"When?"

"Now. I don't know. Now." Finally, he finds my eyes. His are begging. *Help.*

"Give me the keys. I'm driving." On the way out the door, I jam my feet into an old pair of Micah's flip-flops.

Wil pitches the keys my way. I follow him outside, where he stops in the middle of the sidewalk and bends over.

"Wil? You okay? What's—"

He dry heaves, then pukes in the grass. The air smells like rancid coffee.

"Fine," he rasps, without looking at me. "I'm fine."

I rest my hand on his back, rub it in slow circles. When I pull back, my palm is laced in his sweat. "Just take a few deep breaths, okay? It's gonna be okay." Already, the air is hot enough to split my skin. I steer him to his truck and help him into the passenger seat.

"I know. I know. I know." He tilts his seat back and closes his eyes. His lips are moving, and suddenly, he punches the dashboard. I close his door gently and sprint around the truck to the driver's side, my heart pounding. I roll down the windows, because this space can't contain us.

"It's the station on Seminole," Wil instructs me. He turns away, toward the window.

"So the guy tried to break into another house? Did anybody get hurt?" I peel away from the curb.

"I don't know yet. She didn't—"

"But they know it's the guy, for sure?"

"Bridge!" Wil sags out the open window. "Can you just—"

"Sorry." I keep my eyes on the road.

The station is a low concrete rectangle only a few blocks away. When we pull into the parking lot, Henney is standing outside, pacing in front of a set of double doors.

"Mom? Mom." Wil jumps out before the truck comes to a stop. I park and kill the engine, watch him envelop her in a hug. Guttural sobs rumble in her, or in him, I can't tell. I look away. I take my time rolling up the truck windows. Closing the door quietly. Locking the doors. I wander in a wide arc around them. I pretend to read a plaque near the door in memory of a K9 officer.

Finally, Wil releases Henney to the ground. Both of their eyes are red-rimmed. He smoothes her hair and I read *It's okay* on his lips. He steers Henney through the double doors and I trail a few steps behind. Inside the station, the chilled air makes my skin pucker. I take a seat in the first of a line of plastic chairs near the door. It is unremarkable: white walled and quiet. It doesn't seem like the kind of room where entire lives can begin again or end. There is an officer sitting behind a desk, and behind him is an American flag. To the left of the desk is a door. Wil goes to the desk and asks for Detectives Porter and Yancey.

"Just a moment." The front desk cop makes a call, and in a few minutes, Detective Porter steps into the waiting room. She's taller than I remember. Her gun gleams under the sterile lights. I wonder if she's ever killed anyone, and then I try to un-wonder.

"Good morning, folks. So, this is a big day." Porter shakes

Wil's and Henney's hands. "A good day." She catches sight of me near the doors and presses her lips together. I do the same.

"What, ah, what's next?" Wil can't stand still. Henney hangs from his arm. She is suddenly, instantly an ancient woman. "Is he back there?"

Porter nods. "He is. We got a call through the Crime Stoppers hotline this morning. A woman in Jax Beach saw this guy and thought he matched the description on the flyers."

I watch the muscles in the back of Wil's neck go taut. My body twitches with every *tick* of the second hand on the clock over the doors. *The man who killed Wilson Hines is in this building.* It feels unreal, impossible. I imagine Wil staring through one-way glass at the man who has changed his life.

"What, ah—" Wil's face goes dark. "What happens next?"

"In terms of next steps, we'll need you to make an identification." Porter speaks slowly. "We don't have much to hold him on yet, so we need you to confirm that this is the man who broke into your home and killed your father. If we can get a positive ID from your mother, we can hold him while we investigate."

"Wait. Will she have to see the guy?" Wil blanches.

"You can be with her. And you'll see him, but he won't see you," Porter says gently.

"Wil. I—I can't," Henney bleats. "We can't."

Wil buckles under his mother's weight. Detective Porter steadies them both.

"I don't think she can do this." Wil's voice is full, a rushing current. "It's too much for her right now."

"We can take our time." Porter tilts her head and nods at Wil.

*She learned that in cop school*, I think.

"Could I get you both some water?" Porter offers.

"I *said*, she can't do this," Wil says again, his voice dangerously soft. "We're the victims, right? We don't have to do it if it's too much."

"You're under no obligation to make an ID." Porter's features calcify. "However, I would strongly encourage you to at least take a look at the lineup. If we don't get an ID, we won't be able to hold him."

"Wil?" I'm on my feet, confused. "If it'll help them keep the guy in jail? Your mom got a good look, right?"

"It was dark, and she was fucking scared." Wil doesn't turn around.

"Take me home." Henney is sucking short, horrible breaths that are not enough. "I can't breathe, Wilson. I can't breathe." Her hand flies to her throat.

"I'm getting her out of here. I'm not putting her through this anymore." Wil wraps his arms around Henney's waist and guides her back through the waiting room, past me without even a glance.

"Wil!" I push through the doors, run after them. "What the hell?"

"Go home, Bridge," Wil yells over his shoulder. "I'll call you later." He jerks open the passenger side door of Henney's sedan and scoops her into it.

"Hey. Hey. I'll take both of you," I argue. "You can't drive like this."

"I'm fine, Bridge. I just have to get her home." Wil's brow is sweat-soaked.

"Just—tell me what happened in there," I plead. "Don't you want this guy locked up? This is your one chance!" I smack my palm against Henney's back window. Inside, she shrieks. "Fuck! I'm sorry."

"It's okay. You didn't mean it." Wil's jaw pulses. "Of course I want him locked up. But it isn't that easy, Bridge."

"I *know* it will be hard for her, but—"

"I can't force her, Bridge. It's just too hard for her right now."

"*Wil*," I protest.

"I can't. *She* can't." He pulls me close. Kisses the top of my head, and I let my eyes flutter closed to the sound of his heartbeat. It's unfinished, like the jagged edge of a knife. Like a truth only partially spoken.

# WIL

*Spring, Junior Year*

SHE'S lying. Or maybe this is some kind of sick joke.

"I want a divorce," she says again.

I laugh, and the musty air around me smells like stale beer. My laugh is this awful, bleating sound that shoots out of me and pins my mother to the oven. She takes a step back, like she's afraid. Maybe she is, and I don't blame her. I am Wilson Hines, after all.

"What? You what?" Her outline goes grainy in the dark. "Mom. What are you telling me?"

She moves around the island, murmuring, weak, until I slap the countertop with the kind of force that should crack it and me.

"Don't," I tell her. "Don't."

"Wil," she says, pleading. "I didn't mean for it to happen like this."

"You didn't mean for it to happen like this?" My voice is not my voice. "Like what, Mom? Like right after he plans the best anniversary of your life? Like months after he's been trying to make things better?" I am bigger, sadder, angrier than my body can contain. I am going to burst. I imagine little bits of my flesh on the floor, scattered like confetti.

"I didn't know," she says, and when she starts to cry, I hate her deeper than I ever thought I could. "I had everything packed this afternoon, and I didn't know that you and your dad . . . And then I came outside, and Ana was here, and I just . . . I couldn't."

I am not hearing this, these impossible words that she's saying. "So you went along with it? You fucking went along with it? Do you have any idea how *insane* that is?" I have to find my father. He is everywhere here: leaning against the walls in small, contained stacks. But I need the real him. I dive from one room to the next, searching. "Where is he? Where's Dad?"

"He's not here, Wil. He went out," she says behind me. "I don't know if he's coming back."

My breath comes in gasps, so short and shallow that the room is starting to spin. "He was trying," I say to the living room wall. "We were getting better. What have you done? What have you done to fix it?"

"It can't be fixed, Wil." Her voice is too steady. "He showed me that when he hit me again, after all those years. He cannot be fixed. He is an angry man who does not love me."

I turn and we're so close that *I could just—*

"I deserve better than that," she says as if she's trying to convince me . . . or herself.

"You're a liar," I tell her. "You don't want him to be better.

You're giving up." I feel so stupid! *Why didn't we know?* The smiling and the power walking and the new jeans: Those weren't for us. She was gone months ago.

"I have waited for your father to change my whole life," she says sadly. "Don't you dare."

I shove past her. This house is a maze, walled in with his things, and I can't find my way out. "I can't wait to get out of this sick, fucking house." I toss the words over my shoulder like tiny grenades. She doesn't try to stop me.

I slam my bedroom door. Dive into my bed face-first and suck hot, wet breaths through my pillow. The worst of this isn't that she wants a divorce. My parents have been unhappy since the beginning of time. The worst of it is that I let myself believe for a minute tonight that we were a completely different family. A family who shared first date stories and ate cheese and crackers on a *sailboat* while the sun set over the water! What kind of a family does that? But I let myself believe it.

I sock my pillow again and again and again. I hate her for doing this to our family. I hate myself for wanting us to be different people. I hate Ronnie Van Zant for convincing me that it was possible, to be a simple kind of man. I'll leave this place, I decide. I'll drop out of school. I'll start my own workshop on another plot of land near another ocean. I will fix things for a living, without them. I'll tell them tonight. She's not the only one who can leave.

I take my pillow and I drag it to the floor, next to my bedroom door. I lie down and listen past my heartbeat, past my storming brain, for the vibrations of his work boots on the hardwood. Waiting for life as I know it to end.

* * *

I feel him in the house. My breath catches with the door slam. He'll come this way. I sit up and lean against my bed, and I try to make sense of the glowing red slashes on my clock. They're a foreign language, I think, until I flip the clock over and then I understand: 3:28. I hear my father say my mother's name and I hear my mother say my father's name. I wait to hear him coming for me.

Instead, I hear their underwater voices getting louder, louder until I can make out some of the words. I hear: *"You fucking bitch,"* but it's warbled, like he's having trouble getting the words out (*Oh no,* my body feels). I hear: the shattering of glass on the kitchen floor. I hear: my mother screaming, *"Wilson, don't, Wilson, you're drunk, Wilson, I'll call the cops."* I hear: the soft sounds of water lapping the bottom of a boat, and then I hear: the crack of a skull against the wall. The sharp intake of breath, like the fizz of a just-lit match.

# BRIDGE

*Summer, Senior Year*

TOO early the next morning, I take the turn into Sandy Shores.
I haven't slept. I snuck out of the house as soon as the tiniest bit
of light crept into my room, Mom and Micah still sleeping on
the couch with last night's Chinese takeout containers open
and the television blaring.

I need Minna. I need to talk to her, to let her untangle the
word webs in my brain. I need her to tell me that I'm being
paranoid, that the way Wil and Henney bolted from the
substation yesterday was a normal part of grief. But still, I don't
understand it. If I were Wil, if a strange man had ended my family,
I'd want him locked up. I'd want him dead. How could Wil and
Henney just let him go? *Trust him*, I tell myself. But the feeling I
had yesterday remains: doubt twisting in my gut. Something was
strange. Something was wrong.

I roll to a stop at the guard's cottage and tilt the rearview toward me. Minna will tell me I look like shit, which is accurate. I should look better than this on the morning of graduation rehearsal. I should look fresh-faced and excited and ready for The Future. My hair is swept into a nest on top of my head, and I'm so pale that I can see the tiny purple veins branching across my eyelids.

I look out the window. It's too early for Rita, too: She's curled up in her folding chair in her tiny fake cottage, her salt-and-pepper bun rising and falling with her breath. On the black-and-white *Today* show, Matt Lauer is staring into the camera, reporting a shooting on a military base in Texas. He is trying to give it the gravity it deserves—people are dead, and that means something—but he's read the same story hundreds of times, replacing the words *military base* with *school* or *department store* or *bedroom at high-school party*; replacing *armed assailant* with *suspected terrorist*; with *bullied teen* or *frat boy asshole*. Minna was right. Violence happens everywhere.

"Welcome to Sandy Shores!" Rita sleep-blurts too loudly. I sit up. "Oh," she says with a yawn. "Bridge. I thought it was somebody."

"Nope. Nobody. Just me." I give Rita a weak smile. "I know it's early, but do you think she'd mind? More than usual, I mean."

"Enter at your own risk is what I always say." Rita leans over to flip the switch, but she stops halfway. "Oh," she says, and her face gets cloudy.

"What's up?"

"I, ah . . ." Rita's mouth pinches into a frown. "I can't let you in, actually. Miss Minna came up here last night and told me."

"What?" I shake my head.

"You sent a letter? To her daughter, without asking her first?" Rita studies her chipped manicure. "I didn't even know she had a daughter."

"Well, yeah, but that was a good thing, actually." My heart is lead. She couldn't be angry. Maybe the Minna kind of angry, the kind that blazes fast and fades. But not a real, lasting kind of angry. "She hadn't spoken with her daughter in years, Rita, and her daughter didn't even know she was living here. So I wanted to—I thought—"

"She didn't even yell, Bridge," Rita says quietly. "She just walked up here last night, real calm, and said to tell you not to come back again. Said your services were no longer required."

*No longer required.* I swallow the lump in my throat, but it bobs right up again. "Rita. You have to let me in. Please. I was trying to do something good for her. If she understood where I was coming from, maybe—"

Rita shakes her head. "I can't, baby. I'll lose my job."

"Right." A weird strangled sound is trying to force its way up. "I wouldn't want—I get it."

"Plus she told me if I let you in, she'd come up here and personally kick my ass, and I think we both know she could do it." She says it to make me laugh, but I don't and neither does she.

"Will you tell her I stopped by, though? Will you tell her this is all one big misunderstanding?"

Rita nods. "I'll tell her."

I have to do a nine-point turn to get the truck headed in the right direction, and I stop fighting the tears on the fourth point. Rita is sweet, and pretends not to see me coming apart.

\* \* \*

I'm late for graduation rehearsal. Late enough that Señora Thompson decides to stop talking entirely and breathe into her wireless microphone like a phone stalker while I slap across the shiny gym floor. The walk to the bleachers is long enough that I have time to think about things, like how I never realized that the gym is thousands of miles long, or how flip-flops are much louder on buffed wood than any logical person would guess. I sweep the crowd for Leigh or Wil or even Ned Reilly or Susan, but all the student-blobs look exactly the same.

"As I was saying. You'll arrive here at school *promptly* at eight-thirty this Saturday morning." Señora is staring at me, and I blink back, like, *Nine-fifteen, then?* "Caps and gowns will be distributed in classrooms M-102, M-103, and M-104, alphabetically by last name. We will line up just outside the double doors and process down the hall and into the gym. Mr. Reilly and Ms. Choudry, your valedictorian and salutatorian, will lead."

"*Ned Reilly!*" someone hoots, and half of the senior class chants, "*Ned. Ned. Ned,*" until Señora Thompson thumps the microphone.

"*Followed* by your senior class, again in alphabetical order. The faculty will bring up the rear." She says something about how showing up bombed or naked underneath our graduation robes will *seriously jeopardize* receipt of our diploma, which everyone knows is bullshit. That kind of warning didn't exist before the legendary Chaz Foster, who was a senior here when we were in middle school. Chaz reportedly showed up to graduation bombed *and* naked under his robe, and he flashed the crowd after the principal handed over his diploma. Now he works at his dad's investment banking firm in New York City and makes quadruple Señora Thompson's salary. So.

"Here we go. Let's see if we can line up in six minutes or less." She releases us and we clog the exits immediately.

"Hawking, right? So we're probably next to each other." Wil's breath on my ear sends a molten shiver through me. I don't mean to jump.

"Ohmygod. You scared me."

He gives me a confused smile and slips his arm around my waist, tight. "You okay? I stopped by this morning, to see if you wanted a ride."

"I'm fine. It's been a weird morning, so . . ." I study him. There is no trace of yesterday's exchange in the parking lot. "Is everything okay . . . with your mom?" I ask carefully. "I've been thinking about you guys. I was kind of worried, actually."

"Oh. Yeah." A shadow stains his features and then disappears as quickly as it came, like an afternoon storm. "I don't think we realized how hard it would be to think about seeing the guy again."

"I'm sure," I say carefully.

"I just feel like I have to protect my mom, you know? Make sure nothing bad happens to her." Wil's brow furrows, drawing into familiar lines. They're the same lines that surfaced when he cheated on a math test in fifth grade; when he invited me to his twelfth birthday party and conveniently forgot to tell me I was the only girl guest.

*He's lying.*

"From—" I start.

"Huh?"

"Protect her from what?"

"Just . . . emotionally," he says vaguely. "You know."

But I don't. I don't because he won't tell me. I let him guide me through the crowd. I tell myself, I *know* this boy. I know him deep. He's not lying about wanting to protect his mother. I've watched him carry her through this. He's calmed her; he's stood between the cops and her; he's spoken for her. And all to protect her. From what?

"You cold?" Wil rubs my shoulders.

"I'm fine."

"Bridge?"

"Huh?"

"I asked what you were doing after this. I have something I want to show you," he says.

"Sure. Okay." I catch a flash of Leigh's dreads, the tips dyed purple. "Hold my place for a sec?" I push through a swaying circle of stoned beach rats and grab her embroidered sleeve. "Hey. Hey."

Her face hardens when she turns around. "Oh. *Hey.*"

"What's—" I try to decode her. "What's wrong?"

"You cannot be serious, Bridge." She drags her fingers through her hair. "You're like—I don't know. Unbelievable." She whips her head around, like *Is anyone seeing this?*

"Leigh. Just tell me."

"That's just it, Bridge," she says. "I shouldn't have to tell you. I shouldn't have to say that you missed the unveiling of my art project Saturday morning."

My stomach bottoms out. I can't breathe.

"Oh, shit. Leigh." I told her I'd be there. I'd promised.

"I shouldn't have to tell you that it's not friendship when you drift in and out at your goddamned convenience." She crosses her arms over her chest.

"*Leigh*," I say again. Like if she would just give me a second, I could explain! Everything would make sense! Only we both know that I won't be able to fill that silence.

"What, Bridge?" she snaps. "It's just . . . I'm *here*. And unlike Wil, I've been here the whole time. All of high school. I'm not his understudy, you know? I'm not."

"Leigh," I say again. "You're not an understudy. You're not—"

One of the beach rats yells, "Ooooooh, tell her," and I whip around to tell him off. By the time I turn around again, Leigh and her purple hair are gone, and Señora Thompson is steering me toward the H section, where I belong.

When rehearsal is over, I find Wil's truck in the parking lot. I lean against the tailgate and the metal burns through my T-shirt and bra strap. I'm the sick kind of tired. I don't know whether to accuse Wil of hiding something from me or fall into his arms. The kid part of me wants to slide into the cab and hide there. Burrow into the ripped cloth seats because it's safe. Or at least I used to feel that way, wedged between my best friend and the father I didn't get to have, as though, for a few minutes after school every day, we were a family. But that wasn't real, because Wilson wasn't real. He's made my memories fiction, wiped them out with his fist.

"Sorry." Wil comes up behind me. "Señora pulled me aside asked how I was doing and then she started crying, so I couldn't really—"

I crumple under his hand.

"Bridge?" He turns me and pulls me into him, and that's a

mistake because now I'm sobbing into his T-shirt, and I have no right.

"I screwed up," I bleat into his chest. "With Minna and Leigh—I really screwed up."

"Here." He holds me steady with one hand and unlocks the truck with the other. He helps me inside and then jogs around the back. I catch his reflection in the rearview: a flash of a young Wilson.

"Okay. Tell me," Wil says when he's next to me again.

I shake my head. "I don't—you have too much going on."

"Not for you," he says. "Not ever for you. Got it?"

My face crumples like I'm going to cry again, but there's nothing there.

"Got it?" he says again, and I nod.

"Still." I rub the stiffness from my face. On the other side of the window, a circle of girls is hugging and wiping single diamond tears from one another's perfect cheeks. This is what high school should have been. "I don't really want to talk about it. Later."

"Yeah. Sure. You just—let me know."

"Thanks." I sniff.

"Here. I want to show you something." Wil leans over my lap and pulls a wrinkled yellow legal pad from beneath the seat. He flips to a page with a rectangle drawn on it. Inside the rectangle are our names.

BRIDGE & WIL

There's an etching of a canoe beneath the words.

"It's kind of a graduation present," he says. All of a sudden, he

231

looks shy. We're kids who don't know each other yet, but want to. We are the old versions of ourselves.

"It's, ah . . . what it is?" I ask. My insides flutter.

"It's a brick! For downtown. I ordered it this morning. Should be installed in a couple of weeks." He looks proud, and he should. This is the sweetest thing. We have a brick. Wil and I will stay here together forever. We will be cemented into this place, no matter what. The faucet in me twists again.

"Wil. It's so . . . It's really . . . Thank you." I lean across the seat and wrap my arms around his neck. I inhale him. I don't know how I could have doubted him. He loves me. He would never lie to me. I know it, but it's more than that. I can feel it.

"Yeah? You like it?"

"I love it, Wil." I lean into him. Press my ear against his chest. Touching him quiets the buzzing doubts in the back of my mind.

# BRIDGE

*Summer, Senior Year*

I wake up the next morning in my bed, my ear pressed against Wil's bare chest. But the steady chant I've heard before is absent. I hold my breath.

Silence.

"Wil?" I sit up in bed.

His skin is the color of almost night. He is rigid, stiff lips and dripping curls sealed tightly to his forehead. He smells like the ocean. His skin is transparent, showing his insides. Beneath his skin is a pulsing, living thing. Oil-black grief, curled around his heart. Blocking his throat. Pulsing in his fingertips.

"Wil?" Sour sick rises in the back of my throat. "Wil?"

His eyes snap open.

"Help. It's killing me," he says.

A never-ending scream rises up in me. I scream until there is nothing left inside me.

"Bridge!" Mom's face looms over me, dull at first, then sharper. "Bridget!" She pulls me into her lap and holds me so tight, I can't move. "It's okay, baby. It's okay."

"Mom?" Micah hovers in the doorway, wide-eyed.

"It's okay, honey. Bridge just had a bad dream. Give us a second?"

Micah looks relieved to shut the door.

I shudder against her. She's solid and warm. "Mom," I moan.

"I'm here, sweetie. You're safe." She rocks me slowly. I wish I could stay here, curled against her, forever.

"Want to talk about it?" She brushes damp hair from my forehead.

I shake my head violently. "I can't. I just . . . I don't want to think about it anymore, okay? Please."

Mom kisses the top of my head. "I'm always here, you know. Always."

"I know," I whisper into her collarbone. I want to stay here with her forever. Slowly, she is becoming one of the only people I have left.

I shower under an ice-cold faucet and throw on the first pair of jeans and T-shirt I find on the floor. My hair is still dripping down my back when I jump into the truck and speed out of the driveway, headed for the Mini Mart. I buy two giant coffees and start out again, all the while thinking of anything, everything other than a cold, dead Wil.

My gas light flickers on, then off again as I pull onto Leigh's block. Her parents built the pretty stucco house when she was four. It's the kind of house that whispers *A beautiful family lives here.* The kind of house that belongs on the cover of a decorating magazine, if readers could overlook the ugly-ass VW van parked in the driveway. The house has a widow's walk, which has always been my favorite part. Stand up there and you can see the Intracoastal snaking to the end of the world, and the ocean beyond that.

I park my truck on the street and walk up the bricked drive, past the flower beds that are wet and throbbing with color. I can see through the front windows to the water on the other side. I knock. Louder, more insistent, with every passing second.

Finally, Leigh's mother appears on the stoop. She's wearing a plush bathrobe with matching slippers, and just the right amount of makeup to make her look awake but soft. The coffee she's holding smells like hazelnut.

Leigh's mom gives me a look like *Good morning, sweetheart,* and then she holds up her index finger and disappears inside. *Leigh . . . your . . .* underprivileged *friend is here,* I imagine.

Leigh appears on the stoop a few seconds later, in boxers and a purple T-shirt that matches the tips of her hair.

"Hey," I say.

She squints into the sun.

"I'm, ah . . . here." I hold out her coffee. At first I think she's not going to take it, but she does, because she's Leigh and she believes in caffeine even more than she believes in grudges.

She takes a sip. "You pick terrible coffee. What is this, pineapple?" She sticks out her tongue.

"Hawaiian flavor, I think." I take another step toward her. "What you said yesterday. You were right."

"Okay."

"I've let everything in my life take a backseat to Wil. Including you. And that really sucks, and I'm sorry. And also I've screwed up a lot of things lately, so it's not just you, if you were wondering." My voice wobbles.

"You know my mom thinks you're high," she informs me. "Or, as she likes to put it, 'taking the pot.'"

I try a small smile, and she smiles back.

"We can get real coffee at Nina's," she says. "You probably shouldn't come inside while I change, though. Unless you want a lecture on the dangers of the pot." She gives me a real smile, like *Forgiven*, and disappears inside for a few minutes. When she reappears, she's wearing cutoffs that are short enough to show the pockets from the inside and a T-shirt that she's clearly spray-painted in.

"Nice shorts," I say.

"Yeah, well. My best friend's a bad influence." She elbows me. "On account of taking the pot."

Iz takes us to Nina's, and we slide into our usual booth by the window. Leonard gives us a wave and goes back to the television on the counter.

"Just coffee, thanks, Leonard," Leigh yells.

"So . . ." I tug a napkin from the dispenser and start tearing it into ribbons. "What's new . . . with you? How did the unveiling go?"

She rolls her eyes. "Stop being weird. We can talk about you. Or Wil or whatever you want."

My face gets hot. "Sorry."

She shrugs. We are not us yet.

236

I don't know where to start. I want her to know about my dream without my having to speak it. Leigh would say that the dream is my subconscious, trying to send me a message. Only there are so many messages blinking on and off in my brain— *Wil is lying; Wil would never lie to me; trust no one; he's hiding something, for sure*—that I don't know which to hold on to.

"Hello?" Leigh waves a plastic-coated menu in my face.

"Okay. Minna's pissed," I say carefully.

"Minna's always pissed."

"No. I mean, like, for real." I tell her about Minna's history, about the letter I sent to Virginia. "Maybe her daughter called and they had a fight or something," I decide. "So she's mad about that."

Leigh's whole face squints at me. "Are you serious?"

"Yeah. I'm guessing it didn't go well."

"Maybe it went well and maybe it didn't. But that's not the point. You know that, right?" Leigh says.

Leonard comes over with coffee, and I pretend like we have to stop talking while I stir in cream and sugar.

"Tell me you know that." Leigh's eyes narrow. "Tell me you understand that this was absolutely inappropriate and an inexcusable invasion of privacy."

"Leigh. The woman hasn't spoken to her daughter in thirty years! It isn't fair!"

"Oh, but you know what is fair? Stealing her personal property and sending it without her permission. Changing her life without asking first."

"It wasn't like that," I protest. The coffee is too hot, too sweet, but I chug it anyway.

"It was exactly like that. Here. Put your coffee down." She reaches for my hands and squeezes them. "Look at me. For real."

I look everywhere else, until there is nowhere else to look. Her eyes are a near black today, burning coals.

"Thing is, Minna is an adult. She's been running her own life since the Stone Age."

"Well." I blink.

"And deciding when, or if, to speak to her daughter is one hundred percent her business. It's so far from being your business that if you were standing in your business, you'd need a telescope."

"Okay. I get it." I pull away and stare out the window.

"So far from being your business that you'd have to take three flights, a train, and a ferry to get even close."

"*Okay*." I rub my temples. "I'm an asshole."

"That is appropriate."

I laugh and cry a little and ask Leonard for a refill.

"So . . ." I say.

"So . . ." Leigh says.

"Maybe I should write her a letter or something. To apologize, since she's not talking to me."

"That'd be a start. As long as you make it clear that this was not a misunderstanding. She didn't take it wrong or miss the point. This was just you being the worst court-ordered gal pal Minna has ever had."

I let my head thunk against the window.

"Onward. So what's going on with you and Wil?" Leigh starts to build a small standing house with artificial sweetener packets. This is the thing about Leigh: She can be mad about Wil one second and ask about him the next. It's a kind of goodness that

238

isn't in most people. "You guys looked kind of weird at rehearsal yesterday. Scratch that. *You* looked weird at rehearsal."

"He's, ah . . ." I want to tell her. I do. I want her to tell me that I'm ridiculous, over-involved, reading everything wrong. "I love him."

It's the only truth I know.

I spend the rest of the morning at home on the couch, trying a letter to Minna. But everything comes out the wrong way, the way Leigh warned me.

*It's just that my family is broken, too, and—*

*I know how much you love your daughter, so—*

*I only meant to—*

"Bridge." I snap out loud. Leigh was right. I should never have sent that letter in the first place. And believing that I was doing Minna a favor was nothing short of delusional. I crack my neck, hunch over the legal pad, and write an apology. A real apology. I ask for her forgiveness. I tell her that it's okay if she doesn't want to give it. It's her choice. I mean the things that I say. When I'm finished, I press a stamp into the corner and shove it in our mailbox.

Inside, I slink onto the couch again and turn on the television. A talk show host I don't recognize is delivering paternity test results. Cartoons. A woman in an apron is moaning over the apple crisp she just made. A local news anchor is bringing breaking news, live from Atlantic Beach. The helmet blonde from the newscast I watch with Minna. From Wil's street, the night Wilson was killed. The house behind her is Wil's house. I sit up.

239

"I'm here in front of the Hines residence with breaking news in the ongoing investigation into the death of Wilson Hines, the Atlantic Beach husband and father who was murdered in cold blood during a break-in back in early April."

I turn up the volume.

"Police have been investigating the murder as part of a string of break-ins in recent months. A second victim, twenty-four year-old Dana York, died due to complications from a separate, but police believe related, attack."

"Get on with it, get *on* with it." I turn the volume louder. Louder.

"According to reports from the Atlantic Beach Police Department, detectives in the case have, just minutes ago, arrested a suspect."

My stomach launches into my throat.

"Police say twenty-one-year-old Timothy Pelle, seen here, has been charged with two counts of second-degree murder in the beating deaths of Wilson Hines and Dana York. Additional charges are reportedly being considered by the state attorney."

*Beating deaths.* I taste sour.

"ABPD says that they apprehended Pelle in the middle of yet another burglary and police say they are confident that Pelle is responsible for both attacks. Channel Five will bring you more information on this ongoing investigation as we have it. This is—"

I kill the sound, and then the picture. And I fly to Wil's, my heart miles ahead of the rest of me, searching for Wil's heart.

# BRIDGE

*Summer, Senior Year*

I park one street over from Wil's, my front tires wedged in a random yard. I run the rest of the way, my sneakers slamming into the glittering pavement. Wil's block is choked with fat painted news vans, each with thick silver poles and satellite dishes scraping the sky. Sweating cameramen and reporters in too-bright suits lean against the vans, fanning themselves with scripts.

I skirt the vans and pass the neighbors who are suddenly interested in Wil's family again. There's a cruiser in his driveway. *Porter and Yancey.* I sprint across the yard. I find him where I knew I'd find him, with his saws and stains and the stereo with the cord bound with a garbage tie. He's sitting on the workshop floor. His knees are up; his head is down. He is curled into a ball, sealed up tight.

"Hey," I breathe. I wipe the sweat from my upper lip.

"They got the guy," he says to the floor. "Without our ID, so."

"It's on the news." I sit next to him without touching him. When Wil is sad, he has to be the one to touch first. You have to be patient. In fifth grade, when he lost the election for president of our chapter of the St. Johns Riverkeepers club, it was days before I could play-punch him in the arm without having to duck.

He shows me his face finally. It is streaked with red and not-so-red and so much pain that I swear it is rolling off him like choppy September waves. He's been crying. "There's gonna be a trial. We'll have to testify."

I nod.

"I don't know how to feel," he says, and he pulls my arm around his shoulder. This is real pain, meaty grief for the father Wilson was and maybe for the father he wasn't.

"That's okay," I say. "You don't need to know."

"I mean, he's still dead, and I—" He straightens out and scoops me up, the way men carry their wives into new homes. He cradles me against him like I'm nothing, a feather. His heart is getting louder. Searching for a way out of his body.

I think about staying here, with him, forever. I think about wearing a fine layer of Atlantic Beach sand from all my Mays to the rest of my Septembers.

"I can't stay trapped in here all day." Wil's head jerks toward the door, and he lets go of me. "I can't breathe in here, Bridge."

"We'll go." I scramble to my feet and pull him up. "I'll go with you. Wherever you want."

He closes his eyes. "Goddamned reporters." His breath reminds me of splintered wood.

"Screw the reporters. Hey." I grip his head in my hands. "Screw them. They can't keep you here. You're not a prisoner."

He mumbles something.

"Give me your keys."

He digs his keys out of his back pocket and dumps them into my palm. I hold them so tightly it hurts.

"Stay here," I tell him. "I'll pull the truck close." I drag open the workshop door, leaving Wil in the corner. I walk slowly, casually, across the lawn. It isn't until I'm diving into the truck and gunning across the lawn that I catch a reporter's curious face in the rearview.

Wil launches out of the workshop the second I pull up to the doors. He jumps into the car before I've come to a stop.

"Go!" he yells as he slams the door.

I press my foot on the gas and the truck leaps across the yard. We whip around the caravan of journalists and the wheels screech as they hit the pavement. We leave everyone else behind.

Wil tells me to drive to the marina. His breathing is even rougher now. By the time I pull into the parking lot, I don't think I've heard him take a breath in minutes.

"Do you want to sit here or . . ." I let the words hang as I throw the truck into park.

"My dad refinished the deck on this beautiful—" His face is pinched. I look away out the window. The boats are bobbing, eager for him. "I thought we could take her out. *Annemarie.*"

"Sure. Anything you want."

But we don't move. I roll down the windows and kill the

engine. The sounds of the marina should soothe me, but the slap of the water against the hulls startles me, again and again.

"Timothy Pelle. Guy sounds fake, doesn't he?" Wil's voice is thick with tears. I don't look at him, because he needs me not to. "You know what I've been thinking all day, since the detectives came by to tell us?"

"What?" I ask quietly.

"I've been thinking about how the guy was a baby once. About how his parents probably loved him and maybe they thought he'd be president someday. I'll bet he has a family, too, you know? And now that's two families. Ruined." His breath is like wind through a straw.

"He should've thought about that." I tilt my face toward the window. There's no breeze. "Before."

"His life is over, Bridge. Starting today. I feel—it doesn't feel right." His body is tense; his lines bolded. His tears leave silvery lines on his cheeks. He is breaking, slowly.

"He took your dad's life. It's only fair." I cup his face in my hands, turn him toward me. "It's not your fault. It was his choice."

"There's no fair in this, Bridge. Nothing about this is fucking *fair*." He twists away from me, and the heel of his hand collides with the dashboard, turning on the radio. Static-laced jazz fills the truck until I twist the volume dial down.

"Okay. I know." I don't understand the storm that's happening in him. He should be glad that his father's killer was caught. That this part of the nightmare is over. If Minna was speaking to me, she'd tell me that Wil doesn't have to be logical. That he gets to thrash around with the meaning of his dad's death. That he should be breathless and angry and dizzy with the unfairness of it all.

I wait for Wil to speak. I watch the sailboats bob on the surface of the water. Their movement makes me feel sick, like I've just stepped off a roller coaster.

"He wasn't all bad," Wil says while I'm studying a neglected, listing sailboat. He rubs the heel of his hand. "My dad. He had bad in him for sure, but he had good in him, too."

"I know there was," I say, and it's the truth. "That good isn't gone. It's in you, still. You're the best guy I know, Wil." Finally, I turn to look at him. His face is a kind of pale I've never seen, except in my terrible dream.

"Don't say that," he mumbles.

"It's true. You *are*." Anger rises up in me. "Why can't I say that? Why can't you accept that?"

"Because it's not fucking true!" he wails. "Because you wouldn't say that if you *knew*!" He rests his forehead against the glove box, takes labored breaths.

"Knew what? Knew *what*?" I beg. "Please, Wil. Tell me. Whatever it is, whatever you don't want to say out loud—" I stroke the damp curls glued to his neck. "I want you to tell me."

"I can't," he whispers. "It was because . . ." He wraps his arms around his middle like he's going to be sick. "It was because of me. I could have stopped it somehow, and I didn't. He's dead because of me." He releases a slow, painful noise that dies slowly.

"Listen." I scoot close to him. I wrap my arms around his solid, safe body, and rest my chin on his shoulder. He heaves bottomless breaths between sobs. "Whatever you think you could have done, whatever you think you didn't do, nothing that happened that night was your fault. It was out of your control, Wil. It was a freak accident that guy picked your house."

"You don't know. You don't," he says.

"So tell me." I hold him tighter. "It's me, Wil. It's just me."

He tilts his head to one side. His tears have made well-traveled roads across his cheeks, down his neck. I stroke his hair and his lips, and I rest my palm against his neck.

Wil rolls up the windows so we are alone. "It was so dark when he got home," he begins.

I hold my breath. Steady myself. I'll hold the weight, no matter how heavy. I'll do anything for him.

# WIL

*Spring, Senior Year*

I can't feel my body.

One minute, I'm on the floor listening for him and the next I'm shedding my Generic Teenager skin, leaving it slumped on the floor next to the bed. I fly out the door and over the box maze and into the kitchen, waiting to feel my feet on the ground or hear the heart engine inside me (*tickticktick*). I feel nothing. I wonder if I am here at all.

The sick *crack* of a skull against the plaster wall makes everything sharp again. Real. I'm standing on the other side of the island, squinting through the dark. My dad palms my mother's head like she's a basketball. There are tulips and glass and water in the sink.

He throws her against the wall next to the stove again. Again. She isn't screaming. Why isn't she screaming? There is a thin river of blood creeping from her mouth. Her eyes are dead.

He says, "I love you, I love you. Why would you—I love you."

It sounds like: *Die, bitch.*

I say, "Dad! Don't! Stop!"

It sounds like: silence.

His back is shaking, heaving. He is crying.

"Dad!" I scream again. (Or maybe for the first time.)

I lunge for him, hurl the weight of my body over the island and collide with a cement man. I drag myself up with his shirt and wrap my arms around his neck and I squeeze, and for a second, he releases her. I see her and she sees me and then I watch her slide down the wall into a heap on the floor. She is shedding her skin, too. She is becoming unreal like me.

I squeeze harder. He throws me back, sends me flying—we're in the public pool he took me to a few times as a kid. It's bright and the water is blue and cold. He's standing in the shallow end and he launches me up, like he is giving me to the universe. I slam into the refrigerator.

It takes too long to find my breath. By the time I'm up again, he has her by the neck. I am screaming for all three of us.

He holds her against the wall again, holds her by the neck, so high that her feet don't touch the ground. So high that I can see the life leaking from her eyes, rolling down her cheeks in jeweled beads. Her mouth lolls open, searching for air. In the silent dark, she is the only sound. Gasping, gulping, straining for air. Until the moment her face relaxes. She goes slack. He is turning her from a human into a doll.

I search the kitchen for something to stop him, something that will press PAUSE, and there is nothing. It's because of him that there is nothing—because clutter makes him insane, because the countertops must be clear at all times *or else*. Maybe this is ironic. I don't know.

Now I am flying again, but it is harder this time. I am heavier this time. In the entrance hall, my hands find the golf clubs—find a single golf club with a bulb at the end—and I run back into the kitchen. They are on the floor now and he is on top of her, slowly turning off her life switch. Dimming her.

I want to stop him.

I only want to stop him.

I raise the golf club up and I bring it down between his shoulder blades. He crumples like paper and he curses. I bring it down again. He collapses on top of her. I was wrong about him when I was a kid. All this time, he's never been anything more than a man.

My mother's eyes are wide.

"It's o—it's o—" I wheeze. *That's it*, I think. *For now*. And I let myself suck deep breaths like I will never see the surface again.

"You . . . sonofa . . . bitch." My dad is up again, off her, swaying toward me. I can't find his eyes. "I'll kill you, too."

I smell booze: sugar and sick.

"Back! Back!" The only words I can manage. I raise the club over my head.

I think, *He never taught me how to play golf.*

He comes for me and comes for me again, and I swing the club like a baseball bat. It slices through the air and collides with his temple.

He stumbles back, surprised. The corners of his mouth curl up like a smile. And he falls back into the island. His skull on the corner is the loudest noise I have ever heard.

We are all silent, all of us now.

My mother's eyes are still frozen open, and I try to remember, try to remember whether people die with their eyes open or closed. I should have paid attention in class.

"Mom? Mom?" I drop the club and I sink next to her and I should scoop her up, kiss her, breathe into her, but her wax skin and open mouth terrify me. I slip my hand into her hand, and it is damp. She squeezes slowly three times, and I know.

# BRIDGE

*Summer, Senior Year*

"NO," I say. I say it again and again, until the word itself starts to sound wrong. It is an incantation. A desperate attempt to undo what has already been done. But Minna told me: I am not that kind of magic. "Wil. No." Every part of me rejects the story he's just told: my sour stomach and ocean-filled eyes, my tight fists and wet, panicked skin. I knew there was something. I never knew it was this.

*Wil Hines killed his father.* My mouth fills with bile, and I gulp it down. Wil's face thrashes in choppy waters in front of me.

"I did it. I killed him." He turns toward me so abruptly it scares me. And then I remember: It's him. It's still him, right? "I had to, Bridge. He was gonna *kill* me." The word *kill* is pinched.

"You killed him," I echo. I look up and see everything in the bleeding sky: the color of Mom's cheeks when she's been laughing too hard. Micah's hair, unruly fire. But mostly I see Wil and me as cloudkids, racing out past the breakers, arcing back to catch a wave to shore. I see Wilson in the surf, holding me, holding me, holding me until just the right time. Rocketing me into the crest of the wave, whooping and clapping as I ride until the sand scrapes my belly. I see the three of us on the hot sand, water-beaded and spent. Wilson covering us up with beach towels like blankets, and saying, G'night, kids, until one of us cracked up and blew the whole game.

I propel myself back, away from Wil, pressing myself against the driver's side door. I don't mean to. It just happens.

"And then what?" I moan. "Why didn't you call the cops, Wil? Why didn't you—"

"Fuck! I wanted to!" he sobs. "But my mom—my mom said—" He's crying too hard to speak, and almost all of me wants to hold him. And I'm watching his fists clench tighter and tighter and I think about it. I think about the fact that those hands have ended a life.

"Okay. Okay," I say, and I don't know who I'm talking to, exactly. I can feel it worming its way up from my gut: a deep, low moan that turns into a sob. Into a scream.

"I wish you didn't know!" Wils shouts at the windshield. "I didn't want to tell you. I didn't want to tell you any of it!"

"Okay." I wipe my face, making space for more tears. "It's not too late. You can go to the cops, still. Turn yourself in. Explain what happened! It wasn't your fault!"

"I can't. If it had just happened—but we've done too many things to make it go away." He curls into a ball, his voice muffled. "We wiped my prints from the golf club. We put the club in Dad's

252

hands. We broke the glass door from the outside to make it look like a break-in. We lied to the cops!"

"So tell them now!"

"Tell them what?" he wails. "Tell them that I let my mother convince me to lie to save my own ass? Tell them that the story about my dad coming home from the bar to find an intruder is total bullshit? Thank them for all the news stories about the break-ins?"

"I don't know!" I scream. "I don't know what you're supposed to tell them!" I don't know how to fix this for them, for us. I hate Henney for convincing her son to lie. I hate Wilson for what he did to his family. The only person I can't bring myself to hate is Wil.

"She said our lives would be over." He closes his eyes, and his voice gets soft. "She said with my dad gone, we could start over and have the lives we were supposed to have. And I'm sorry, but I wanted to give her that. After all the bullshit he put her through—" Fresh tears slide down his cheeks. "She deserved that."

I reach for his hand and I take it. He lets me.

"I believe," I say fiercely, "that you did what you had to do to save your life. And your mom's life. And I know that anyone else, anyone who knows you, would see it the same way."

He shakes his head. "It's too late."

"Timothy Pelle," I say. I squeeze his hand.

"He killed that other lady. He broke into those houses, right?" Wil's eyes are big and wild. He is grasping for something to make this okay. There is nothing there but dead air.

"But he didn't kill your dad."

"He should be off the street," Wil argues. "He's a murderer."

"He didn't murder your dad."

"No," he says finally. His body crumples in the seat. "He didn't murder my dad."

I am suddenly and completely empty. I want to curl up in his lap and sleep for years. I sink back against the window. The warm glass tugs at my skin.

"What about Porter and Yancey? They have no idea?"

He covers his face with his hands. "That guy's been on the news for a long time now. I remembered some of the details. I told Porter and Yancey that my dad saved my mom's life."

"And they just . . ."

He nods. "They believed us," he murmurs into his palms. "We said Dad had been out drinking at Big Mike's, and hadn't been home too long when a guy broke the front door. We said Mom had surprised him, and when he'd attacked her, my dad had tried to hit the guy with a golf club. We said the guy was wearing gloves, and after he attacked my dad, he just . . . He ran."

This is too much. I can't hold this. I thought I could. I pull my knees into my chest and squeeze until I can't feel my arms anymore.

"Anyway, next couple of days when the cops were asking us to go over the details, we'd seen the sketch of the guy they were looking for. So we knew what to say." Finally, Wil lifts his head for a fraction of a second before his chin drops to his chest again. "We're such fucking liars."

"Don't say that. Did they check with the bar?"

Wil nods. "Yup. He was there that night, just like Mom thought." His mouth withers. "He'd been hanging out there a lot lately. Drunk piece of shit."

When I blink I see Wilson, leaning outside the bar as I'm on my way into Nina's. *Fuck.* Maybe if I'd said something. Maybe.

On Atlantic, a siren screams past. An electric charge runs through me, and Wil stiffens, too.

"They'll figure it out," I tell Wil gently. "When they don't find the guy's DNA, when you slip up and say something different—they'll figure it out. You should have—"

"Don't do that. Don't you sit there and judge me." There is venom in his voice. "I had to. For her."

A new wave rises in me. I let the tears leak. I'm too tired to cry.

"I didn't—" He looks out the window. "You can't tell the cops. It'll end me, Bridge. You can't. I love you. You can't."

"I have to go home." My head is throbbing. I'll go home and I'll sleep, and when I wake up, this won't be true. Wil Hines will be Wil Hines again. Our biggest worry will be a long-distance relationship. I'll bitch about an eight A.M. class, and he'll tell me about this customer he had who was kind of a jerk. But we won't talk about this. Nothing like this.

"I have to graduate. For my mom. I don't care what happens to me after that, but I have to graduate this weekend."

"I know, Wil. I just—I need to think." I pull out of the lot. He rolls down his window silently. The breeze can't cool my fevered skin.

"You have to tell the cops," I say.

He doesn't respond. I close my eyes and let the neon lights bleed over me.

"I love you," I say.

# BRIDGE

*Summer, Senior Year*

"YOU have to let me see her," I tell Rita the next morning. "Please. I know it's early, and I know she hates me, but I have to talk to her. I'll do anything, Rita. Please." My face feels like rubber and my head is full of hot air, three times its usual size. I am one of those giant blow-up people, bobbing and waving from the parking lot of a dealership on Atlantic. A flimsy cartoon version of a distraught girl. My eyes are bloodshot. My tongue is thick. I haven't slept. Eaten. I have to talk to her. She is the only person in the world who can help me.

Rita sucks in a deep breath and releases it slowly, ballooning her cheeks and then deflating them. Life has wrung her out. She turns off the television. The metal chair shrieks when she pushes herself to standing. She leans into the truck and pats my arm. There is a red lipstick gash on her front teeth.

"You can't talk to her, honey."

"No. I know. I know she's mad, but this is an emergency." I want to shake her.

She closes her eyes. "I mean, you really can't talk to her. Miss Minna had a fall last night and hit her head. They haven't been able to wake her."

My blood runs cold. "But she's going to wake up, right? People don't just fall and not wake up." I feel better as soon as I say it. Women like Minna don't expire this way. She is bigger than that. She'll go out fighting, in some sweeping, grand way. Giving the world the finger. Spelling LATER, MOTHERFUCKERS on a giant Scrabble board.

"I'm real sorry, honey." Rita rests her hand on my arm and leaves it there.

"Can I at least see her?" I close my eyes and picture the truck mowing through the gate. I'll do it. I am just sad and lonely and crazy enough to do it.

She squeezes my arm. "Let me call up to the nurse's station and see what I can do." She ducks back into the cottage and closes a door I didn't know existed. I watch her red lips move.

Rita opens the door again. "Her daughter said you're welcome to stop in."

"Her daughter?" I parrot back.

"Yeah. Lady from Winter Park, drove up late last night when we called. Brought the granddaughter, too." Rita winks. "I guess somebody's letter did some good, after all."

I shake my head. Lift my hand and block the words. I won't take them.

"Anyway, Miss Minna's in room 302. Just follow this road past her place to the center of the development. She's in the—"

"Epicenter of Death," I mumble.

She squints at me. "Hospital."

"Right."

"Hold on." Rita rummages around her desk and unearths a bag of mini chocolate chip cookies. "Take these. Just in case she wakes up. The Jell-O around here is shit."

I pull through the gate and wind around and around until the hospital looms up, several stories high. I take the elevator to the third floor. It opens directly to a nurse's station. It's quieter than I expected. Slower. Nothing like the hospitals on television. There's a nurse on the phone, sipping Starbucks, and when she sees me, she raises her index finger, like *Just a second*. But the call is personal, so obviously personal, the way she's smiling into the receiver and laughing like Minna isn't somewhere on this floor, not waking up.

Finally, the nurse slides the phone into its cradle. "Here for Mrs. Asher?"

"*Ms.* Asher, I think," I say.

"Second room on your left, there."

Outside room 302 are a few plastic chairs, the kind we use for assemblies at school. The kind in the police station. I wonder how many people have sat in these chairs and cried. Waited. Sipped bad coffee. I wonder how many people were sitting here when they heard that their mother or father or grandmother or great-uncle was never coming back.

The door is open a crack, and I knock lightly. There's no answer. The crack is person-sized, and I slip through it and

258

close the door behind me. She is lying in a hospital bed, eyes closed. Her hair is down, pretty but tangled. She looks like Minna sleeping, like the morning I slipped into bed with her, only there's a deep purple mark on her forehead. A small cut, and a teeny bit of dried blood. I pull a tissue from the dispenser on the bed and I wet it with my tongue. I dab the blood away. I can't find a trash can, so I stuff the tissue in my back pocket.

"Hey, Minna," I say out loud, and I feel stupid and embarrassed.

There's a chair pulled next to the bed, and I sit. She is plugged into too many things. Recharging. My eyes fill with angry tears and I want to sprint into the hall and yell that there is *someone in here who needs help, does anybody know that?*

"I don't know if you can hear me," I say. I pat her hair. "Or if you got my letter? But just in case, it said how sorry I was for mailing that letter to your daughter. It was, ah, stupid, and just . . . I didn't think. Which isn't an excuse."

I think I see her lips move.

"Leigh says I stick my nose into other peoples' business. Micah says that, too. Like, all the time. He says I'm controlling." I exhale, and it comes out sounding like a laugh. "That's not an excuse, either."

I lean back in the chair. I am so tired. I want to twist the blinds shut and crawl into bed with her and sleep until we both wake up. I want her to tell me the right thing, because she will know the right thing. This is the one decision I can't make on my own, the one time I don't want to make the call.

"I have to tell you something." I lean close, and lower my voice. I get it over with, fast. "Wil killed his dad. Did you know that already? On the way over here, I was thinking that maybe you had a feeling. I didn't. I didn't know.

"He asked me not to tell." My face is hot and full again. "And I don't know what to do, because I know he had to do it. And I know what kind of person he is, and I just wish he'd told the truth from the very beginning, because I don't think I can carry this secret around. What am I supposed to do? Go off to college without saying anything? Come back on weekends, and have breakfast at Nina's and sit across from each other and talk about pancakes?"

I watch her for a sign, but her face is blank. Empty.

"And the other thing is, I just keep thinking about how unfair this is. No matter what, he'll have to walk around with this for the rest . . . of his life." My lungs crumple at the thought. "And I don't blame him for that. I blame Wilson." I want to punch something. Shatter something. Ruin something, but too much is ruined already. I close my eyes, only for a second, and I see Wil bringing the golf club down. I force my eyes open at the moment of impact. Launch out of the chair and pace next to the window. Beyond the blinds is a parking lot. I wonder if there are ocean views on higher floors. I'll tell someone: She should have an ocean view.

"I came here so you could tell me the right thing to do, and you can't tell me the right thing to do. I don't even know what you'd say." I screw my eyes shut again, and I listen hard. But there is nothing, only the sound of my own breath and a nurse's laughter outside.

"He didn't have a *choice*," I whisper. "He had to. And if I tell, it will ruin him."

There's a light knock on the door, and I jump.

A young nurse pokes her head in. She's holding a clipboard. "Hi there. You the granddaughter?"

I nod. "No," I say. "Just a friend."

She pauses. "Well, whoever you are, I need to check on her. Mind stepping out for just a moment?"

"Okay." I squeeze Minna's hand and give her a kiss on the cheek. Her skin is papery, thin and dry. "Do you know if she's gonna be okay?"

She purses her lips in an apologetic smile. "If you're not family—"

"Got it." I don't look at her as I slide out of the room. I drop into one of the chairs outside the door and lean back. Close my eyes. I could sleep right here. Wait for her to wake up. I don't want to be anywhere else. I don't want to go home.

I feel someone close, too close, and I open my eyes.

"You must be Bridget?" The woman in front of me is not what I expected. Maybe I expected a miniature Minna: long, flowing goddess hair and a caftan. Just younger. Instead, she is short. Athletic. Her dark hair is pulled back in a ponytail, shot through with streaks of gray. She's wearing yoga pants with a stain on the thigh and an oversized sweatshirt. I imagine her getting a call in the middle of the night. Pulling whatever clothes she could find from the floor.

"Oh," I say. "Yeah." I stand up, because it feels like I should stand up.

"Virginia," she says. She is not friendly but not unfriendly. "And this is my daughter, Elizabeth."

A girl about my age steps out from behind her mother. She is staring at the floor.

"Hey," she says, without looking up.

"Hey," I say.

We stand there for a while, not looking at one another, exactly, strangers with a strange thing in common.

"Is she—did the doctors tell you anything?" I ask.

She rubs her eyes. "They're optimistic," she says slowly. "But she's older, you know, so these things are harder to . . ." She doesn't finish her sentence.

"Okay, well," I say. "That's good."

"Yes." Virginia nods.

I don't know what else to say. I thought maybe we would hug or cry together, or I'd tell her stories about Minna that she'd been dying to know for years. But she doesn't ask and I've learned not to tell.

"If you, ah, need to get out of here and want some good comfort food, Nina's Diner is good," I tell them. "I could bring you takeout, if you want."

"That's kind," Virginia says. "But we'll be all right."

I nod. "Yeah. Okay. Well . . . Would you call me or text or something when she wakes up?" She doesn't say no, so I give her my number and the granddaughter enters it into her mother's cell. I want to ask Virginia if Minna got my letter, if she read it, if we are okay now. Instead, I say an awkward good-bye and take the elevator down to the lobby.

When I pull into my driveway, a familiar outline is sitting on my steps. Henney looks deflated; on the verge of total collapse. Her skin is a pale gray. Her dark hair is pulled in a tight knot at the nape of her neck. Silver strands flutter around her temples. I feel a sharp, hot jolt of fear settle into my gut.

"Hi," I say carefully as I lock the truck. I linger in the yard, not too close. "What's going on, Henney? Can I help you with something?"

"He told you. I know he told you." She tries to stand up and falters. I rush to the steps and help her to standing. She's wearing a HINES T-shirt. The familiar letters swim in front of me.

"He shouldn't have told you, but he did." She leans into me, the way a child leans into her mother. I steady myself against her weight. "He loves you too much to keep anything from you, even something like this."

"I love him, too," I say carefully.

"I know you do." She looks up at me. Her eyes are wet. "I know you love him. I know you don't want to end his life, Bridget. Bridge." She peers into my eyes. "And if you report him—if you say anything to anyone—"

"That's not fair," I say. I pull away. "Don't."

"It isn't," she says forcefully. "None of this is fair. It isn't fair that I married a man who hit me, and it isn't fair Wil's father tried to kill him. It isn't fair. But I'm asking. Because I'd be dead now if it wasn't for that boy."

"I know." I take a step back. "I just—"

"Think about it," she says. Her mouth hardens into a thin line. "Think about what this would do to him. You would end him. I made a promise to him that I would protect his future, Bridge. And I'll do everything I can to keep that promise."

I'm silent. There is nothing left to say. After a while, Henney leaves me there, standing in the yard. Holding Wil's future heavy in my trembling hands.

# BRIDGE

*Summer, Senior Year*

I would dream about us . . . if I could sleep. I would dive down deep to the bottom of me and scoop up the earliest memories, the very best seconds of us, and string them together like saltwater pearls and we would go on for years. Maybe when I woke up, I would know what to do. I would know whether those memories are enough to hold us up. Push us forward. Instead, I'm lost, treading water. I can't find land.

We haven't spoken in days. Just one text from him.

*I'll wait for you to call. I fancy you, no matter what.*

I've read it a million times, because I miss him. On the morning of graduation, tucked under my stale sheets, waiting for the light, I read it again.

*I'll wait for you to call. I fancy you, no matter what.*

I type a quick response and press SEND before I can yank it back.

*I fancy you. Pick me up at 8.*

I sit up in bed and power off my phone. My skull is stuffed with sparking wires. My eyes are dry and my heart beats faster than it should. I love him. I know that. But it's all that I know, and I'm not sure it's enough. Downstairs, Mom and Micah are whispering too loudly, dropping pans, spilling orange juice. I smell burning butter and coffee. I throw on my robe and slip into the bathroom. I can't make the shower hot enough. I fill the bathroom with steam, and it opens me up. I let myself cry under the spray, and I feel closer to him.

I wrap a towel around my head and pull on the graduation dress Leigh lent me: a crisp white sheath with a white-jeweled neckline. I blow-dry my hair and straighten it. I find the fake pearls that Mom bought for my thirteenth birthday. I haven't worn earrings in years, and it takes too long to snake the posts through my ears.

I stand in front of the full-length mirror in the bathroom. I look normal (pretty, even, which should feel better). I look like a girl with a future, with a next step. But it's a lie. There is nowhere to go from here. Call the cops, tip them off, and Wil could go to prison. Keep my mouth shut, and this secret will erode us slowly. I turn away from the mirror and hurry down the stairs.

"Happy graduation to you, happy graduation to you!

265

Happy *graduuuaaaation*, dear *Briiiidget*! Happy graduation to *yooooouuuuu*!" Mom and Micah bellow from the kitchen when they hear me.

My breath catches when I see what they've done. Purple streamers wind from the front door to the kitchen faucet and back again. Someone (Mom) tied streamers to the spinning ceiling fan, which will mean a call to the landlord later. The floor is blanketed with so many balloons, there is nowhere to step. Mom blew up my senior picture into several unnecessary posters, and they're plastered on every available surface. I love the two of them, hard.

"Happy graduation, firstborn." Mom hands me a plate of Funfetti waffles. "You look beautiful, honey."

"You guys!" I set the plate on the steps and pull them both in. Micah obliges me for a full two seconds. "I can't believe you did all of this!"

"Come on." Mom grabs two more plates from the counter. "We're having breakfast in bed. Like a *sick day in quotes*."

We pile onto the pullout in the living room. Micah says, "I swear to God, if you guys tell anyone about this . . ." but I haven't seen him smile like this in months. We stuff ourselves with waffles and Mom tells us school stories that we'd forgotten years ago, like how Micah caught a lizard (Bernard) on his first day in Florida and kept it in his desk with a peanut-butter cracker and a Dixie cup of Capri Sun, until the kid next to him noticed the smell.

And then Mom gets serious around the eyes. She tells the story of my second day here. How I came home just in time for dinner, glowing with aloe and stories about a boy and his dad who made sailboats. How when she tucked me in that night, I asked if people got married on boats. She stops halfway through the story because she can't, and I can't, and even Micah coughs and says he needs to shower. He takes our plates into the kitchen and runs upstairs.

I tuck into Mom and we pull the covers up. She combs my hair with her fingers. I lean into her and close my eyes. I am happy, full, content enough to forget about Wil for a fraction of a second. But then I hear the doorbell, and I slide out from under the covers and he's standing on the other side of the door, holding flowers. Tulips.

"I fancy you," he says, kisses me.

I kiss him back. I let myself pretend that I'm an Ordinary Girl and he's an Ordinary Boy and this is an Ordinary Special Day. I hold on to the feeling for as long as I can. I want to make it last.

# WIL

*Summer, Senior Year*

WE don't speak on the way to school and I get it, but, God, I wish she would say something. It doesn't even have to be real. We could talk about the weather, about how this heat is the wet kind that sneaks down your throat and into your lungs. We could talk about what we ate for breakfast or we could guess how many last names the principal will screw up. I don't need her to say the real things: that she loves me, that she understands why I did what I did, that it will be hard, but we'll find a way. Because we are us, and that's enough. I can wait for those things. I'll wait forever.

"It's hot," I say as I snake the parking lot rows, looking for a forgotten spot. Girls in white dresses that are too short and too tight hobble toward the gym in heels. The ones who aren't naturally tan are spray-tanned (*Kylie Mitchell!* I think, and I want to tell Bridge). The guys look just as uncomfortable in khakis and shoes that aren't flip flops. I catch a glimpse of Ana in this nightgown-looking dress that's short in the front and long in the back. I can't remember us. I can't remember anything other than Bridge and me, because nothing else is important.

Bridge murmurs at the window. "I think you're gonna have to park on the street."

"Yeah." I find the closest street parking, just a block from the water, and I get this crazy idea to take her hands in mine and look into the deepest part of her and say, *Screw this. Let's just go to the beach, you and me, and swim out as far as we can.* It's a stupid thought, an embarrassing Real Me thought, the kind of thing that only happens in movies. People don't ditch their high-school graduations for the ocean. People sit quietly and smile when they get their diploma. People pretend that this is the shit that matters, that this is some kind of Big Life Moment.

Bullshit.

A Big Life Moment is standing over your drunk father with a golf club. A Big Life Moment is circling the police station six times in your truck, telling yourself to grow a pair and go inside. Tell them what really happened. Fix this.

I reach for her hand as we walk toward school, and she lets me take it. Her hand is small and cool and dry. I think that's a good sign, somehow.

"Are you, ah, doing anything after this?" I ask, looking straight ahead.

"I don't know. Minna's in the hospital. I might go see her."

"Is she gonna be okay?"

"I don't know, really," she says. "Hey, did you ever get to know

Ned Reilly?" Her hair is whipping around her face, a sunset in a million strands. My throat shrinks, and I want to tell her how sorry I am, but *sorry* isn't the word. There isn't a word for this.

"Not really. How come?"

"He's giving the valedictorian speech today and he's just, like, a nice guy. And I've been thinking about high school and about how many people I don't know and how I lost a lot of time for really stupid reasons."

I don't know if she's talking about us, and I'm too tired to ask.

The closer we get to school, the slower we walk. There are parents with giant bouquets, wearing cameras around their necks. There are kids from my class who don't look like kids today, but they're not adults, either. It reminds me of that Alice Cooper song: "I'm Eighteen." It's all about being stuck between being a boy and a man. That's exactly how I feel: stuck in the in-between, floating, waiting to land somewhere. And I won't know where until Bridge says her peace.

We stop by the classroom with A-H posted over the door and Bridge ducks in and comes out with our caps and gowns. We put them on and I feel kind of stupid, standing in front of her in a bright purple gown, but she looks at me like I shouldn't feel stupid at all. I wish this could be a normal day for us. I wish our parents were in the audience, all four of them, smiling and snapping pictures. I wish our families could go to Nina's together after the ceremony, and I wish we could go back to my house and there would be a Publix sheet cake in the refrigerator, and it would say CONGRATULATIONS, BRIDGE & WIL in blue icing, because this is real and important.

I wish.

We gather outside the gym, all of us, milling around, strange and nervous. Señora Thompson lines us up and inside the gym, the band starts playing. My whole body constricts.

I follow Bridge inside, down the shiny aisle, and onto the fake stage that sounds like it might collapse under so much potential. The principal is standing at the podium with a big plastic smile. We wind down a row of metal folding chairs, and once the whole class is on the stage, we sit.

I hear a stifled sob in the crowd, and I know it's her. My mother is a broken woman, and I don't think that will ever change. If I could rewind us, change some tiny thing in history to make her whole again, I'd do it. Even if it meant my parents never meeting. Me not existing. I'd do it.

"Today," the principal says too close to the microphone, "is the first day of the rest of your lives."

Damned if he's not half right. Today could be our first day, or it could be our last. Bridge is holding us—Real Me—in her hands, and there's no one I trust more, and still I'm scared as hell. For days now, I've had this panicked feeling moving through me, this cold adrenaline flood. It's the exact same feeling I got when Bridge and I swam too far past the breakers as kids. By the time I realized we'd gone out too far, I'd almost lost her.

Truth is, I'm scared of losing her more than I'm scared of anything else that could happen to me. I'm small, compared to the ocean, compared to the whole world. What happens to me doesn't matter, as long as Bridge loves me, still. I've told myself a million times: Whatever she decides, I'll take it like a man. Even though I want what I want so bad it burns. I want her to go to college and I want to work on the boats and I want us to be an everyday kind of happy. I think my dad would say that's too many wants, and he's probably right.

I wait. I wait while the principal talks about horizons and making an impact, and he even says something about the future being so bright, we've gotta wear shades, and some of the parents laugh and none of the kids do. I wait while Ned Reilly stammers through a speech about how we are all one, how the successes of one of us are the successes of all of us, and the struggles of one of us are the struggles of all of us. I feel a hot, quick flash of anger. Ned Reilly knows nothing.

"And now, for the distribution of the diplomas. Please stand when I call your row," says the principal.

I watch my classmates cross the stage, one by one, until it is Bridge's turn, and then mine. We flip our tassels. We toss our hats in the air like purple Frisbees. My mom and Christine and Micah are waiting in the back corner of the gym. When I hug my mom, she squeezes the air out of me. She grips my head in her hands so hard, she might crack me open. She looks at me with wild eyes, and she wants to know. I try to tell her silently, but she doesn't understand. My dad and I are the only ones who had that kind of connection.

"You kids want to go to brunch somewhere?" Christine asks. She slips her arm around my shoulders and squeezes. "Nina's, maybe?"

"Oh, ah—" I stiffen. Glance at Bridge.

"Can Wil and I have a second, you guys?" She clears her throat, and looks at everyone but me. "Just to talk?"

"We'll wait by the car," Christine says, and she loops her arm around my mother's shoulder and gives me a wink.

272

"Wil," my mom says.

"Mom," I say.

We edge out of the gym, past Leigh and her buttoned-up parents, past Ana and her nightgown dress, past Señora Thompson and the pitying smile she pitches at me every chance she gets. The courtyard is quiet and empty. Leigh's mural is neon in the sun: a cartoon version of Florida. Lime-green palm fronds and a lemon sun and foamy waters. We slide down the wall, next to each other, and stare past the parking lot.

"Do you want to go to Nina's or—" It's the only thing I can think to say.

"Wil," she says in a way that stops my heart. "I love you."

I clench my teeth until my head throbs. "He would've killed me. Both of us," I say, and I think it's the first time I've said it out loud. Those words are the most awful words I've ever spoken.

"I know," she whispers, sending tears down my cheeks. "You had no choice."

"I didn't. *I didn't.*" I can feel my whole body collapsing into itself. I need her to hold me up. I need her.

"I know," she says.

I close my eyes to stop the tears. It doesn't work. "You're going to the cops." *My mother will be alone. She'll be completely alone. She won't survive.* I dig deep, mining for anger, for the thought *how could she do this to me*, but it just isn't there.

I hear the swish of her hair as she shakes her head. "I don't know. I don't know yet."

"What do you know?"

"I know I love you. I know . . . I forgive you." She sounds surprised at her own words.

"Okay, then. Okay." Relief. I wipe tears with the heels of my hands.

"I have to think. I need time, okay?"

"Okay."

"I need more time." She kisses me, hard, her wet salt lips slipping against mine, and then she scrambles up and trips across the courtyard, her hair flying behind her. I watch her for as long as I can. I burn her image into memory: the girl with the fire hair and ice skin, the girl I won't stop loving, no matter what.

# BRIDGE

*Summer After Senior Year*

HE gives me time. I know it's killing him.

It's what I asked for, and I hate it. I feel the time away from him physically, deep inside: It's the sharp sting of stepping on a broken shell, unrelenting. The choice I have to make is impossible. If I tell, it will end him. If I don't, it will end us.

I spend my days doing other things, hoping that the answer will rise up to meet me like the tides rise to the sand. I spend hours at the hospital, combing Minna's hair or stretched out on the ugly plastic chairs outside her room or in the coffee shop on the first floor, ordering Virginia and Elizabeth lattés they didn't ask for. The nurses bend the rules for me. I stay long past visiting hours. Virginia doesn't seem to mind. We wait. Sometimes together, mostly apart.

I hold Minna's papery hand, and I tell her stories about Wil because Wil is my every thought. Wil stories are automatic. Countless blinks in a single minute. I tell Minna about the time Wil and I set up an Olympic course on the beach in the summer between fourth and fifth grades. There was a makeshift obstacle course, a one-on-one beach volleyball tournament, and medals made out of tinfoil. There were no ties, because in real life, there are no ties. We sang the national anthem and trilled on the high notes.

I cheated during the driftwood dash. Wil had won too many events in a row. So when he neared the last driftwood hurdle, I moved it. Just a little, with my toe. He fell and hit the sand hard, scraped his knee. I crouched next to him as we inspected the wound. There was sand in the cut. Salt water dripped from his hair. There wasn't a single drop of blood.

It occurred to me then that maybe Wil Hines didn't have blood in his veins like everyone else. Maybe he was made of Florida things: grains of bleached sand, sea foam, and salt. Wind and sun. Maybe he was made of the things he loved best.

But I don't think that now. I don't think we're made of the things we love best, or the things we say or don't when we think no one is listening, or the very worst things we do. I don't think we are the things that happen to us, the circumstances beyond our control. I guess I don't want to believe that I am drunken mistakes, an absentee father, or a terrible secret. I don't want to believe that Wil and I are his terrible secret, either. That it could define us for the rest of our lives.

I am sitting at Minna's bedside, reading her passages from a Pablo Neruda anthology someone left at the nurse's station ("I want / to do with you what spring does with the cherry trees")

276

when Wil brings flowers into the room. Seeing him now is like seeing him for the first time in centuries, and I'm breathless. The flowers are a deep purple that only appears on the horizon for a second before nightfall. Wil is dressed in a collared shirt and nice pants, a belt and real shoes. He's dressed for a life we don't live. Something is happening. My body knows.

"How's she doing?" He rests the flowers on her bedside, near a bunch of sagging balloons Mom and Micah brought yesterday. His brows are arched and his mouth is slightly open. His face is a constant question.

"She squeezed my hand this morning," I tell him. My eyes get full just thinking about it. "I think she knew it was me."

"That's awesome." He bends over my chair and kisses me sweetly, awkwardly on my cheekbone. His mouth, the way he rests his hands on my shoulders, the curve of his body when we sleep tucked into each other: all questions from his body to mine. Questions I haven't answered.

I nod. "The doctors told Virginia that her vitals were strong and her brain activity looks good. So I think they're hoping for a turnaround soon."

Wil pulls a chair next to me and we watch Minna. We watch the electric-green lines that chart her heartbeat.

"Want to go on a walk?" he asks. "There's a garden out back. You can almost see the water."

I pull Minna's covers around her and we take the elevator down. Outside, the air is heavy and hot, pressing me into the earth. We find the garden, a small bricked labyrinth of boxwoods and punch-colored angel-wing begonias and rain lilies. We sit on a polished teak bench with a gold plaque.

"I love you," he says.

"I love you, too." I am suddenly aware of my heaviness, of the stale sour film coating my tongue and the grainy tired settled behind my eyes. "I'm so tired, Wil."

"I know you are." His voice ripples. "Because of me."

I shake my head. Salt water leaks from the corners of my eyes.

"It wasn't your fault. What happened to you that night . . . was outside of your control." I know that more every second, feel sure of it. I lean over and my mouth finds his mouth. He is my only comfort and I choose him.

He pulls away, but we stay close. The tickle of his breath on my nose, the warmth of his near skin revives me.

"But I can't decide for you." The words escape without warning, and it's not until they are there, between us, that I realize: They're mine. "I can love you, and I do and I will. But I can't decide what to do with this. I won't make that decision for you. You have to—" My voice breaks. "That's something you can control."

He sucks all the air from the atmosphere, then exhales it.

"I know," he says. "I can't ask you to tell me what to do. And I can't ask you to hold on to this . . . this shitty secret about me." His face cracks.

"I would do it for you." I press my hand against his cheek, and he leans into it. "That's how much I love you."

"My mom told me that she came to see you. Asked you not to say anything. It's just not fair. I can't ask that of you. I would *never* ask that of you." Frantically, Wil kisses my cheeks, my nose, my mouth. His lips absorb my tears.

I fight for a breath as he reaches into his back pocket. Hands me a folded envelope. On it is a single name in his messy boy script.

*Detective Porter.*

"Wil." The tears come faster now. "Wil."

"It's everything. All of it." His hands are on me now, memorizing me, and mine do the same. I read his lines with the tips of my fingers like I may never read him again.

"You—" The what ifs swirl, a terrible tempest in my mind and body. "What if you're arrested?" I can't stand the thought of Wil without his workshop. Without the steady stroke of brushes or mallets in the dim light. Without the endless ocean. And I don't even want to think about my own life without Wil. The mere suggestion is an impossibility.

"I don't know. I don't know." He is pale.

"You can't. It wasn't your fault. It wasn't your *fault*."

"I can't ask you to live with this, Bridge. It's been hard enough just—" He gulps air. "It's been hard enough, the past few days. You have to go to college. I won't wreck that. I won't let my dad wreck that."

"Wait," I beg. "Maybe you shouldn't say anything. We know what happened. Maybe that's enough. You could come to Miami with me." I lean close and whisper it: "Come to Miami with me."

He shakes his head slowly. "If I don't say anything, I'm letting him run my life." His eyes search the horizon for water. They are gorgeous shattered glass, bright with fear and will. "I won't let him sink us like that, Bridge."

"He won't." I grab his hands, curl mine around them. "He won't."

He watches me like he used to when we were kids on the sand,

279

as if he might forget me if he looked away for a second. "I'll—I'll call you after. If I can."

He pulls me in again, for a kiss that lasts forever. Then he brushes off his khaki pants.

"I have to go now," he says.

"Don't. Don't," I beg.

"I fancy you," he says, and he pushes his hair away from his eyes, the way he used to do when working on a boat. For a second I see him there, in the watery light of the workshop. He is building something. He is the happiest when he's building something.

"I fancy you," I manage.

I watch him go. I notice his every detail: his slow gait, the lines of his neck, the late-May tinge to his skin. He is Wil Hines, no one else. He is not his father, and he is not just the boy who killed him. He is the boy who loved his mother enough to save her. He is the boy who loved me enough to forgive my thousands of sins. And I will love him through this. I watch him swim out far past the breaker until he's a dot and then the horizon swallows him and he is nothing at all. I will stay on the shore. Anchored here, always. Waiting for him to come back to me.

# ACKNOWLEDGMENTS

WRITING a novel is always a team endeavor, and that has proven to be particularly true in this case. Thank you first to the most incredible editorial duo out there: Lanie Davis and Hayley Wagreich. You have poured your hearts and souls and superbrains into this project, and I am enormously thankful for your hard work. You have been thoughtful readers and critics, tireless cheerleaders, and on-call therapists. I could not have told this story without you. The dream team at Alloy Entertainment has been there not only from the start of this book, but also from the beginning of my career, and I am so very grateful for their continued support. Sara Shandler, Josh Bank, and Les Morgenstein: thank you. There are so many wonderful souls at Harper who have helped to bring this project to life. Jen Klonsky: thank you for believing in this project. Thank you for so graciously giving Wil and Bridge the time they needed to tell their story. Thank you for your sharp editorial eye and for your humor along the way. Working with you on these past two projects has been delicious. And finally, a heartfelt thank you to the publicity and marketing masterminds at Harper: Elizabeth Ward, Julie Yeater, Sabrina Abballe, Gina Rizzo, Patty Rosati, Molly Motch, and Stephanie Macy.

To my agent, Rebecca Friedman: thank you for reading every version of this book along the way, for offering thoughtful feedback and for being there to talk it all through. You are a treasure. And last, but most certainly not least, thank you to my family. David, thank you for taking such good care of me, always. Thank you for loving (and feeding) me through this and every project, writing and otherwise. To my parents and Molly and John: thank you for your love and support. To lush, wild, beautiful Florida: thank you providing the perfect space for this story, and for being home.

# Also by Meg Haston

**paper**weight

She's got nothing
left to lose.

MEG HASTON

An Imprint of HarperCollins*Publishers*

www.epicreads.com